I Didn't Kill Abel

Devon L. Mulvihill

Published by Devon Mulvihill, 2022.

I DIDN'T KILL ABEL

First edition. November 28, 2022.

Copyright © 2022 Devon L. Mulvihill.

ISBN: 979-8215896228

Written by Devon L. Mulvihill.

For my fiance and our beautiful family

Chapter 1:
The Beginning of the Beginning

God.

The smell of rain is one you never forget if you're ever lucky enough to experience it. It can give you such comfort even in the darkest hours... Or on the other side, it could ruin a perfectly good day.

Maybe you were excited about the camping trip with your father you never talk to or maybe you dreaded the rough and uncomfortable sleep which would always end up with your back being as stiff as steel once the sun rose.

Maybe you've never experienced the joy or curse of rain, you've never heard it banging against the metal roof of the shed, you've never felt its harsh force on your face as you look up into the mud black clouds which swirled around you.

Or maybe you are one of the unlucky few who has never been able to smell rain, I never knew if that was true but I've heard some people cannot physically recognise the smell... Why is that?

Why must God give some gifts others cannot possess? Why is such an imbalance a part of life? Is the fact some cannot smell the rain a blessing or a curse? Does it depend on the person? Or... the more logical answer being... God doesn't care.

He does not burden himself with poor eyesight, broken bones or mutated genes, he simply sits upon his ivory throne and laughs at those who beg for mercy and peace. He laughs at them, and yet they pretend to not hear it.

The man heard it, he felt the clap of thunder which shook the skies and how it bellowed through the flooding streets of the town he stood in and how it sounded like his laughter.

This man stood tall as an imposing figure, his shoulder broad like a wall and his torso thick like a tree trunk. His ragged and unkempt wet black hair stuck to his skin like glue as he remained still in the torrential rain. His skin was dark and shined gently against the pale light hidden behind those mud black clouds. His eyes.. Now those were interesting, his eyes were amber and gold, his pupil fractured out into his iris like an exploding star.

His teeth were lightly stained, but for the time period was pretty well kept, the sharp and scratchy stubble on his face caught drops of water, trapping them in its intricacies.

However the two most notable features seen by most was the tattoo which lay on the side of his neck... it was that of a dagger who's handle was a snake.

And the one which all bore to see...

"God" was written on his forehead, burned into his skin as a mark.

"No wonder he drew inspiration from himself" the man thought. *"For God has no originality"*.

For yes reader, your assumption is correct.

The man finally moved, letting his tired and cold body drag him through the open air. The ground beneath his feet swirled with ankle high water the colour of the clouds, the rain was brutal, each raindrop hitting the man with as much force as water could bring.

He took several cautionary steps forward, his large form shifting and wavering with each lurch forward, his knees felt locked into themselves and unable to become loose and free like back upon his younger days, he was older than you'd think.

The street he walked across was a large slope that ran from the top of town all the way to the bottom through the very core. It was almost the lifeblood of this place, if you wanted your store to be seen it must be posted in clear view of this road.

The man found this ridiculous... he found a lot of things ridiculous but this street was definitely one of them which he thought about a lot.

Maybe it was because he walks across it every day, maybe because it reminded him of the world he lived in, or maybe he just found it really really dumb, I would say this was a metaphor for capitalism but capitalism wasn't a well defined concept at this point in time.

Even he didn't know why he hated this road, he didn't much care about the details.

The man made it across the flooded street and stepped into a golden baked light which shone into his eyes, he winced lightly before reaching out his hand pressing it against the thick wooden door before shoving.

The door swung open wide, letting in a wave of warmth which hit his soaked clothes and drenched face and hair which still stuck to his skin, nearly blocking the mark of "God" on his forehead.

He looked inside, it was a bar, several large circular tables were placed throughout the inside all capable of holding up to 20 people at once. The floor was cobblestone, small puddles built up within its cracks but most of the water had evaporated.

In the corner of the room stood a massive furnace, its steel shell glowing a gentle orange as the insides roared with piercing flames which created a barrier of warmth that the outside lacked.

Of course the outside lacked it, you may be wondering why I'm stalling, telling you such useless information about a simple bar/tavern/keep (depending on whichever time period you believe this to be).

It's because I didn't want to describe the *actual* important part of this scene laid out before you.

I didn't want to tell you that every man, woman, person and child instantly stopped speaking the moment they saw him..

I didn't want to tell you about how several men reached for their knives or other weapons...

I didn't want to tell you how the pure aura of hatred, dismay and disgust was so powerful and thick any lesser man would have thrown up their lunch, breakfast and midnight snack right then and there.

The intention of death was powerful, women cursed the man under their breath. Men told their hatred through their eyes.. The eyes of people who would hurt no one except the man. The children looked upon the man in fear and terror, some even began to cry.

And even still, the man did not frown, he barely hesitated even, he trod through the bar, letting his soaked boots splash mud coloured water onto the clean cobblestone floor as his drenched jacket, trousers and shirt leaked behind him, leaving a trail for all to follow.

He walked up to the barman and sat down, his face as neutral as ever and yet boiling under the surface was that of anger, hatred and rage...and fear.

He let none of those emotions show however, he didn't want to give the angry crowd even more reasons to hate his guts so he simply swallowed his pride and rage and looked up to the barmans face.

The barman wasn't shocked. This wasn't the first nor the last time he'd come to the old tavern named "Crooked Tooth", the barman doubted the man would ever stop coming here until it burned to the ground.

But even this familiarity of knowing this man for multiple years did nothing, his eyes read like that of hatred and disgust.

The man need not speak as the barman picked up a small glass and poured in it some liquor the colour of ash before spitting in it and handing it to the man.

The man paused, looking down at how the flem filled spit bobbed up and down in the ash coloured liquor, its smell too was foul, like that of a burning frog being stabbed into a decaying horse.

The man, clearly, did not pick up the drink, nor did he purse his lips as he definitely did not swallow the rancid liquid as it slid down his parched throat.

And now you must learn, I lie.

For he did pick it up and down it, he did swallow, he did not spit.. He took the abuse and sat there.

And you *may* already know why.

The man sat in the seat in the bar, his golden eyes looking at his mud coloured shoes as his soaked jacket continued to drip gently onto the cobblestone floor.. The burning heat shooting off of the furnace only managed to lightly dry his messy and rough black hair.

It was enough where he could push it back, but what would be the point? Why peel it off of his smooth dark skin only to reveal the marking he was given? Only to let the world, which already knew, know once more.

Why bother? Why try fighting?.. Even if he wanted to, there was no way he could.. Everyone hated him, why not let the world dictate his role?

"Because it's not true" he thought to himself.

"Because people believe a lie and treat me unfairly for it!"

His thoughts grew louder, shouting through an echoing cave even when his face was neutral and expressionless.

"Because people don't understand it's all A LIE!"

He grips the bar with his large thick hands, his eyes waver and shake lightly as moisture fills them which is quickly dried by the intense heat of the room.

"But who would believe me? Who would believe my claim?.. No.. it's not a claim its TRUTH!... Why... WHY-"

Before he could finish his thought process he could feel the sudden shocking push and force of a punch which connected against his jaw with a crunch...

The force of the blow sent him back, he slipped off of the bar stool and felt the air rush around him before the cobblestone floor came up to meet him.

He crashed into the ground as the bar stool clattered, the entire keep was now standing, aggressive and violent words were cast at him as he slowly tried to stand.

The man felt a foot on his back before suddenly being forced to slam back into the uneven floor, his face slammed against the cold rock and his mind began to spin, the world felt uneven and shaky like a lost boat in a titanic storm.

He slowly manages to push himself back off the ground to reach his feet, he hears someone shout out.

"KILLER!" it was a woman's voice, panic and fear setting into her as she screamed and shouted with penance.

The man shook his head as he slowly stood back up, he turned to the man who punched him. He was shorter, around 5'8 with lightning red hair and a softer rounder face that was red with either anger or an overabundance of alcohol.

He spoke, his voice came out like a snake's hiss, his spittle flew through the air with every second word.

"You deserve death for the crimes you've committed on us all!" He raised his fist again for another punch.

The man simply looked at him with emotionless eyes and said nothing, the drunkard lashed out another punch but this time the man caught it with ease, wrapping his large hand around the drunkard's boney knuckle.

The drunkard's eyes widen as he tries to pull back only for the man to stay strong, pulling the drunkard back in for a headbutt.

The force of the man's forehead slamming against the drunkard's nose let out a loud crack as the man felt the cartilage give way under the force.

The drunkard yelled in bloodcurdling pain and fear as he wrenched himself back and away from the man, stumbling and eventually tripping over the barstool.

He let out a shocked yelp as he came crashing to the ground with a thud, the air rushing from the drunkard's lungs and he lay there still, trying to pull back in oxygen with desperate gasps and shaky drags of air.

The entire tavern looked at the man with shock and horror, but they were all waiting for something.. Something they all assumed would happen... something they all believed to be true but was a lie... a lie told to them by the one thing they trusted the most.

He could hear them whispering about someone calling a priest.. And something snapped in the man's head that day, as he looked down at the injured but breathing drunkard, as he scanned the bar to see faces of those who expected death and those who wished for it.. As he looked at the barman who had served him nothing but ash in vodka with his flem for years on end to the point he had accepted it...

He accepted this.. Being looked at as this freak of nature, as a violent bringer of death when he was just trying to cope with the loss of his brother... he knew they just tried to do what was right.. But he knew they would NEVER believe him if he stated it... but who cares? Whether he stayed quiet in his shell, in his persona of confidence or whether he stood at a rooftop and shouted out in pride... would they believe him either way? Probably not.. But there was a chance with one.

The man took a deep breath, his eyes finally filling with emotion, his lungs filling with oxygen as he spoke without pride or fear.. He spoke words he KNEW were true... he knew he had let himself be lied to by EVERYONE... he let this happen to himself.

For his brother would never get justice if he remained quiet.

And so he spoke, with rage and sadness piercing his voice, his thick and rough words laced with emotions most never knew he even felt.

In that moment he felt like the world was watching him, even if he was sitting in a bar on a bad stormy night where only 40 or so people would even hear his words.. Let alone believe them.

But even with this truth or lie, he didn't care, he spoke true and harsh to them all.. He told them the truth.

"I didn't kill Abel"

And with that, Cain turned on his heels and walked back out of the bar, letting the seeping cold latch onto his skin, clothes and hair as the rain began to beat upon him once more.

He did not stay for the shouts of lies and heresy, he didn't wish to hurt anyone else... even though the cold echoed in his bones once more and his shoes became drenched in that mud coloured water.. He felt different.. He felt free..

Cain was framed for the murder of his brother... but Cain knew the truth.

And he was tired of people believing the word of a liar...

He was going to do more than prove his innocence.

He was going to kill the man that killed his brother.

Who is Abel's true killer you may ask? Why his name has been said before without you even knowing.. If you must know before turning the page, then might I suggest reading this chapter once more from the *beginning*?

Chapter 2:

And on the 109,575th day, Cain took an oath

Cain walked through the flooded streets, slipping in and out of sharpened corners and incredibly thin alleyways, his mind was racing with rage and hatred.

Why did he wait this long... Why did he sit there, letting the world think what was untrue.. Why did he decide to let the world use him as their scapegoat for all these years?

To blame him for all the terror that was brought onto this world.

Cain made it through the muddled town, his eyes glancing at the familiar brickwork which led him to his destination, the wind began to pick up, whipping rain into his face, they felt like dull daggers trying to pierce through his skin but only being met with defiance.

The city streets often brandished a church on every possible corner, their architecture were jagged and rough like a snapped tooth. Cain's eyes glazed past the imagery of God and his praise... he couldn't blame them for believing in the titan, but he also hated the fact they believed his lies.. That they believed a killer.

Cain eventually stopped upon the steps of a black iron door with the markings of angels burned into the metals, he lifted his heavy arm and knocked against it. The searing metallic echo rings in his ears and he winces and yet waits.

The rain continues to wear down on him as it's blown left and right by the vicious winds, that smell of rain fills Cain's nose and gives him peace.. If only for a moment, as a scratching metal soon breaks it with the door swinging open.

Cain steps through, walking into a darkened house, the ear cracking sounds of the wind quickly stop as the door is closed behind him.

He turns to the figure which opened the door for him, they stand there in a shadowy cloak, their figure hidden by the darkened room. The only light source is a distant flicker of candle light around a corner.

"Why hello Caleb" Cain said softly, his words were as coarse as gravel and as deep as the lowest note on the piano.

"What were you thinking!?" Caleb said, his voice more high pitched than Cains, reminding all who heard it of a puppy crying out for its mother.

"Many things actually" Cain said, a smirk in his voice as they both began to move towards the muted light of the candle.

"You know what I mean" Caleb said with a scowl in his voice.

Cain chuckled to himself and then became serious, letting the moment of friendly banter come to an end as he let his mind fill him with rage once more.

"...I do.." His voice deepened, a hint of hatred perpetuated throughout the darkness.

Caleb sighs and looks away, even though neither could see the other in this suffocating black.

"I've already heard that priests are being informed as we speak..." Caleb said, uncertainty and panic in his voice.

Cain remained silently, stopping just before walking around the corner, Caleb stumbled a bit before stopping with him, now bathed in the pale candle light.

"...Cain?" Caleb asked, confused about the sudden stop.

Cain didn't hear Caleb, his golden eyes twitched slightly in the darkness as he examined Caleb's body language, looking back at the light being cast by the candle and then at Caleb...

After a short pause he begins walking again, letting himself slip into the light.

"Good" Cain said quietly as he turned and walked into the main living room, the ceiling was damp and the air was thick with the smell of salt.

"Good?" Caleb followed him, tilting his head in disbelief.

"Yes. Good, Caleb. If the Church wants to come after me, then so be it" Cain said as he took off his soaked jacket and tossed it onto a nearby chair, seeping the rain into the rough fabric the moment they touched.

"Cain, I know that mark on your head makes you feel a bit big for your britches but this is a big deal!" Caleb said, pulling back his black hood to reveal his pale face and frizzy brown hair. Caleb lets himself collapse in one of the many chairs which filled the room.

"I'm tired of this... of letting people treat me like a murderer" Cain said, that anger spiking inside of him again as the words came out his mouth like they were a disease. He caught the rage before it exploded out into the room, forcing it back down his gullet.. He was used to doing that at this point.

"Yeah, I get it, you were framed.. But you're claiming GOD did this!" Caleb exclaimed, trying to get Cain to realise how ridiculous he sounded.

"Claim? So you don't believe me?" Cain said, raising a brow as he glanced at the nearby doorways and which ones were closed and not, examining and taking in his environment, even if it was supposed to be familiar and safe.

"No I do! I just think it's a bit difficult to get others to believe you when you have no evidence.." Caleb said, looking sheepishly down at the floor.

"My grandfather wrote about a death that did not occur. I didn't kill Abel, I had no reason to! And yet even in writing my grandfather makes it all about himself! In his stories I killed my brother because

I wanted his attention! How up your own ass do you have to be to not only lie about your grandchilds murder, but make it all about you anyways" Cain exclaimed, gripping the sides of his chair with such strength the fabric began to untwine and the wood began to crack.

Caleb fell silent, thinking to himself.

Cain forced that anger.. That rage.. That need for vengeance back into his chest and stomach, holding it all back as he let himself relax into the chair.

The thick smell of salt grew fainter, the only sounds he heard was the muffled thunder of rain and his own breathing.

He blinked.. Thinking back to how this all began, thinking of how long he sat there and took the abuse because he thought other people needed a lightning rod...

"Fuck that" he thought *"I'm not their fucking lightning rod anymore, I'm not letting myself be told im a killer again... not until I have done what I have to".*

"What's your plan?" Caleb said quietly, looking back up to Cain.

"...Simple." Cain said, his emotionless eyes falling upon Caleb.

"I'm going to kill god"

Caleb paused.. His eyes widened and his jaw dropped lightly, he put his hand over his mouth as his brain tried to comprehend the words that Cain spoke.

"I..you...wh-where why how who what!?" Caleb was broken it seems, Cain could almost see the steam pouring out of his ears.

Cain shrugs, saying it again like it's a normal thing.

"God killed my brother, framed me for the murder and I have yet to hear a single thing from him.. He will not admit the truth, he will not see me. I will kill my grandfather with my own bare hands, I will kill God"

Caleb opened his mouth to speak, to say words.. And yet none came to Caleb's rescue, he simply sat there trying to understand *"just how big Cain's balls are"* as the young man put it.

Cain lightly smiles, finding his reaction amusing.

He realised saying this.. Doing this.. Would leave his life in absolute ruin. So finding things entertaining is a rare resource he needs to treasure.

Eventually Caleb speaks, his words cut eachother off as his brain continues to try and process the consequences of Cain's words.

"I.. you-but.. And-we.. But-you didn't..."

Cain chuckled lightly and peeled the hair off of his skin, trying to slide it back into a less irritating position as his smile slowly fades from his face.

"..I understand that you can't join me in my journey... but it is one I must take.. It may lead to my death... It may lead to the end of all, but at this point I'm sick of it" Cain said, his voice filled with venom and dispassion.

"God will pay for what he did to my brother" Cain said, his voice rising as he stood up from the chair.

"It is my oath! That God will die by my hand!" Cain said, letting himself release the anger built up inside of his chest as he looked up to the ceiling, glaring through the stone and brick... and into the clouds, into God's domain.

Caleb blinks and looks at him as if Cain was a mad man.. As he was indeed, mad.. Or was soon going to be.

"How are you even going to try to accomplish this?" Caleb asked, slightly scared by what might become of him if he hears Cain's answer.

Cain looked down at Caleb and plainly spoke, sitting down once more.

"I work my way up, and so the person I must talk with.. Is the first man of earth, my father, Adam"

Caleb thought.. And thought.. And thought, before eventually he looked up to Cain and tilted his head.

"You're the dumbest man I've ever known" Caleb eventually said, the most serious tone in his voice.

Cain smiled at that, showing his tooth filled grin, his golden and amber eyes shined lightly against the dim light of the lone candle that illuminated the salty aired room of chairs.

"...Well.. what now?" Caleb asked, worry now written on his face.

Cain paused, thinking this through...

"I'll sleep here for tonight, then by tomorrow sunrise I'll be out of your hair and on my way"

Cain slowly stood up and stretched, Caleb stood too and remained silent for a small moment, thinking over something in his mind. Cain raised a brow, putting his hands on his hips.

"What are you thinking about?" Cain asked in a deeper tone which spooked Caleb lightly.

"I.. just thinking about the logistics of you killing god.. What would that do to us all?" Caleb worriedly looked down at the ground.

"I don't know.. But the world's only 300 years old, I assume we can figure it out" Cain said, shrugging.

"..And if it ends the world? God's death I mean.."

Cain pauses as he's taking his soaked shirt off... There's a long pause in the room between them both, Cain said nothing and Caleb understood what he meant by the silence.

"Right.. Well, you can use the usual bed.." Caleb said, turning around and making his way into one of the many locked rooms, leaving Cain alone.

Cain paused, standing alone in the vaguely lit room with only silence to accompany him.

Caleb was hiding something, Cain knew it, his eyes darted from wall to wall but sensed nothing and no one else in this house.

He wondered to himself if he should have kept his oath a secret from Caleb... *"maybe"* he thought.

"Maybe it was the first mistake of this journey... maybe the last" he thought to himself as he slowly made his bed in a small cramped side room, he slid under the rough and torn covers and turned onto his side.

His eyelids droop down as he prepares to slip into a deep sleep.

"...I'm sorry brother Abel... for hiding myself" Cain mumbled as he tossed and turned, the harsh cold biting at his skin.

"..But vengeance will be had.. As always"

And with that.. Cain fell asleep. His snores are gentle and soft...

And here is my warning to you dear reader.. If you wish for this journey to be smooth sailing, if you expect everything to end as you imagine it, with a smile and praise.

You may be mistaken, and I hope you turn back now. I am telling this story because it needs to be told.. For nothing more or less, you do not need to listen to these madenning tales.

And if you shall continue, I wish you luck, dear reader.

Chapter 3:
Our Lord, Our Maker, God we follow

Cain opens his tired eyes as he hears the pitter patter of the morning rain hit the window which laid in front of him, the golden light of the sun peaking through those now cigarette grey clouds.

Cain pauses, wondering what had brought him from such an awful slumber, as he was usually hard to wake up.

Soon he realised why, as the heavy stomps of something metallic echo with thick brass outside of the bedroom door.

His eyes widen lightly as his mind clicks several aspects into place.. And Cain only had one thing to say as his bedroom door was torn open by a man in armour, splintered wood was sent flying through the air, cascading all over him.

"...Fucking hell..."

Cain was hauled to his feet and dragged through the house by the men in shining armour, there were dozens of them all armed and prepared for him to fight back.. And yet he didn't, he simply remained limp as they dragged him through the hall and soon pulled him into the early daylight.

The gentle pitter patter of rain dances on Cain's face as he looks up into the sky, the guards around him cursed him under their breath, they all spoke venom and illness.. And even still there was a light confusion on why he had not attempted to escape.

Cain didn't let his smile through, he didn't let his anger through, he was a complete and utter shell. No emotion was seen on his face, and to those on the outside it was a disgusting mark and to him, it was control.

Before too long Cain is forced onto his knees inside of the biggest of all the churches, the architecture around him is sharp and jagged, the walls, roof and floor made of segmented stones and brick either left a shallow grey or painted a deep cobalt blue.

He lay his now dry legs on the beautiful crimson carpet which lined one side of the church to the other, the massive open space was filled with candles and curtains and tapestries of God and him creating the world.

Pews lined on each side of Cain, empty and hollow giving the church such a vacant feeling.

The silence was near deafening, the gentle breathing and rustling of the soldiers was all that filled this air. Cain remained silent, he knew why and how he came to be here, he knew what was coming next.

He slowly looked up with his golden and amber eyes, his iris an exploded star inside of them as he spotted a familiar pale face sitting in the corner...

"Oh Caleb.." Cain said out loud, his gravelly voice echoing loudly through the colosseum of fools.

Caleb didn't look up, he simply stared blankly at the ground below his feet. He murmured a word that no man or woman heard, his face was much paler than usual, guilt flooded his posture.

Cain couldn't fully blame him.. And even though he could no longer trust Caleb at least he knows it now instead of finding it out during some crucial point in the future.

Afterall, Cain was going to have to show up here anyways.

As he thought those words, a sudden blinding light fills the air and a trumpet is blown, its golden harmony bouncing off of the cold harsh stone walls of the church as Cain straightens up..

Several figures walked out from a hidden wooden door as they poured out onto the main "stage" of the church, where they performed their lies and heresy to the world for them to believe.

Cain could still remember the day they spoke about Abels passing...that woman... he could feel the rage bubbling inside of him once more.. But he decided to stay calm.

For now.

The figures were dressed primarily in black with some white highlights and a collar, they were priests, the police of this world. Their job was to make sure no one did any wrongdoing, to make sure they punish the sinners of the world.

Cain scoffed at their presence, although they weren't people to be dismissed, if they so wished they could badly injure him.

And then came another figure, this time dressed in pure white with black highlights and a hood, a smile on his face and a flash of sickening joy in his pale blue eyes.

He stands on the podium and spreads his arms wide as light begins to swirl around him and illuminate the dark, archaic church.

One of the priests speaks out, declaring the presence of the man in white.

"ALL BOW TO SAINT PETER!"

The guards did as they were commanded and slowly bowed, Cain did nothing of the sort as he simply watched the light show...

You see this world is not like yours or mine where miracles are debated and rare... miracles are the foundation of this place, and the foundation of this path that Cain must take.

"Light Miracles? Has the church been forced to resort to such tacky party tricks?" Cain thought, shaking his head.

St. Peter speaks, his voice is booming and yet soft and smooth, it felt like velvet to the ear and was almost addicting, yet Cain showed no signs of enjoyment when St. Peter spoke.

"It has come to my attention that you, Cain, are planning to perform an ultimate attempt of blasphemy!" He spoke from his chest and he spoke with might.

"If blasphemy is getting revenge for my brother, then yes" Cain sneered, the anger inside of him boiled, he'd have a hard time holding back.

St. Peter chuckled to himself.

"If you want revenge for your brother you best know how to tie a rope" he said with a snake like tone, giggling to himself.

"Great." Cain thought to himself. *"I got to deal with the weirdo".*

"For those so devout to God you sure do love kidnapping his grandchild" Cain said, a smirk on his lips as he tried to stand up... however the guard didn't waver and slammed him back to his knees, forcing a foot on his neck to keep his head down.

St. Peter's smile turned to more of a snarl.

"Don't try to pull that shit on me, just because you are descended from Adam doesn't give you privilege here" he snapped at Cain.

"I thought-" Cain begins before St. Peters snaps at him once more.

"Did you think I'd grovel at the feet of the man that killed his brother?" St. Peter glared down across the long hall into Cain's very soul.

"...I didn't kill Abel..." Cain said, holding back his rage and frustration.

"But you plan to kill GOD!?" St. Peter screeches, sounding like a bat, his pale face contorting into an over to the top grimace.

Cain smirks and chuckles.

"To kill a killer, yes, I plan to"

St. Peter glowers as he steps off the podium, a flourishing light shines behind him as he moves like he weighed of nothing, like he was lighter than a feather.

He stops right in front of Cain and reaches out to pull his face up so he can stare into his amber eyes.

"What you're planning is lunacy dear Cain, and I won't allow it" St. Peter said, his tone more of condescending than a threat.

Cain lets a more nasty smirk leak through onto his face as his eyes shimmer.

"Since when did you think you had authority over me?" Cain said through gritted teeth.

St. Peter laughs lightly before slapping Cain.

The initial hit wasn't that bad, St. Peter had soft dainty hands, the issue came after the initial contact.

A loud bang echoed through the gothic building as a sudden force whips at Cain's head, sending him flying from under the guard's boot and crashing into a pew, the force of the impact made his vision go white and for the world to spin.

"I am Saint Peters... I am the grand priest and I would suggest you understand that I am very much above you" St. Peter said in his snivelling voice as he wiped his hand clean of Cain's filth.

St. Peters begins to slowly walk back to the podium, his thin figure would make most assume him to be weak, however his control of miracles indeed placed him in his own tier.

"I can ruin your life in a moment Cain... God may have given you the mark to stop others from killing you, but torture is always an option.. And I have many Prophets at my disposal"

St. Peter smiles as he stands back up at the podium, taking his rightful place above the floored Cain.

Cain grunts and slowly shifts so he's sitting up, his head throbs in pain and his vision blurs, turning almost pink as he begins to see double.

His ear still rang from the bang.

"I'd rather.. If you didn't send the prophets after me.." Cain said, licking his lips and wincing. "I'd rather not beat the ever loving shit out of your entire army" Cain ended, smirking again.

St. Peters grabs onto the stand at the podium, the wood under his hand shattered into shards as his face turns into a monster's glare.

"I WILL TEAR YOUR LIMBS FROM YOUR BODY WHERE YOU STAND DEAR CAIN!" St. Peter shouted, a wave of power and light washes over the space.. It gives such a strong feeling of will and strength even the guards back up till they're basically outside the church.

Cain wipes his mouth and stands up, almost falling but managing to get to his feet.

"Yeah yeah.." Cain said, still adjusting himself.

St. Peter's eyes went dark as his face was consumed by a sense of hatred and rage, emotions lurched off him like sick dogs attempting to run from their bad owners.. However they stayed just out of range, their withered chains strong enough to hold them back.

Cain simply smiled, his body had no chaos within him, his emotions were kept safe and sound, no rage exploded outward, no fear overtook his legs and made him run, no greed made him beg for power.

He just smiled, he knew his worth and he knew his stance.

St. Peter takes a deep breath and slowly lets his emotions slide back inside of him, like a parasite consuming its target's tongue, Cain found the very action disgusting to watch.. Although no one else in the room could notice these things.

"You.. Cain.. are a murderer.. The first murderer of our world, you are lucky we don't keep you in a rotten cell" St. Peter hissed. "If you want to remain a free man.. Not hunted by priest and prophet.. I suggest you stop this lunacy"

Cain thinks for a moment, looking across to a nearby mural depicting Adam and Eve, Adam being of darker skin with fluffy and curly hair and Eve being of lighter skin and long red hair... Cain narrows his eyes as he spots something in the mural.. Something which gives him an idea.

He could feel that feeling again.. That lurch in his stomach which was fear and worry... if he just agreed to stop he could go back to normal- *"NORMAL!?"* he shouted in his own mind. *"Normal was everyone hating us! Normal was us letting people think we killed our brother! Normal was agony!"*

He thinks to himself for a moment, staying silent.

St. Peters taps his fingers on the podium, his eyes sharp like daggers, a shining blue hiding behind it a killer's greed.

Cain then smiled as he turned to face St. Peters, an idea solidifying in his head.

"My brother was killed by God" Cain said, pushing that wretched rat he called fear back into his stomach.

The entire room fell silent, they were in disbelief that someone would say such a thing in God's house.

St. Peter screeches, an invisible ripple quaking from him.

"HERESY! HERETIC!" St. Peter screeched, some of the priests stepped down from the stage, making their way towards Cain.

Caleb's eyes widen as his skin grows paler as he realises what he has truly done. Cain simply smiles as he watches the Priests grow closer.

"And I'm not going to stop.." Cain said, taking a step back from the priests.

"Until God is dead by my hands!"

Suddenly one of the priests lifts their hand and all the metal in the surrounding area is pulled towards him. The guards cry out as they're flung forward and their weapons are torn from them.

Cain quickly dodges the speeding spears and swords that whizz past his face with surprising speed. The second Priest summons a ball of lightning and smirks, energy crackling off of it.

Cain looks at them both and continues to talk, almost unaffected.

"And I don't care.." Cain continues.

The Priest with the metal miracle cries out, waving his hand and sending swords, daggers, spears and shrapnel flying towards Cain, his eyes widen as he focuses, his golden and amber eyes shine bright as he begins to dodge and weave in between the speeding projectiles.

His brain thought three steps ahead allowing him to bounce in between the negative spaces, allowing him to almost dance away from the attack.

The second priest however sends a ball of lightning at Cain, he tries to dodge but can't find a safe space.. He was either going to get a spear through him or a ball of lightning to the chest.. After a split second decision he dashed back, kicking off the brick ground and jumping right into the path of a spear.

It pierced through his shoulder and he grunted in pain, the ball of lightning whizzed past him and hit the wall behind him, it exploded in a wave of energy, searing a hole into the wall... it seems he made the right choice

Cain growls and ducks the metal priest's last attack before slamming into him with a tackle, the force cracks one of the priest's ribs, knocking the wind completely out of him.

He then quickly grabs both priests by the neck and with a swift pull he slams their heads together creating a thick thud sounds as they both fall to the floor unconscious.

Cain remains standing, a spear through his shoulder and blood pouring onto the floor of God's home, a wild smile on his face and his eyes sparkled.

"..if I have to burn the church to the ground first in order to achieve that goal" Cain finally finishes, slightly out of breath.

St. Peter's rage was uncontainable... and he screams, his emotions fire out of him like a misfire on a cannon, it lashes out like violent snakes.

"KILL CAIN! KILL HIM FOR HERESY!"

The priests all nodded and began to rush at Cain, their eyes focused and their miracles beginning to fill the air. The guards attempted to surround Cain but he turned on his heel and ran, slipping past some of the guards and knocking others over.

One guard grabs the spear and pulls, ripping it from his shoulder, he grunts in pain and falls.

He rolls on the ground and gets back up, the priests and guards begin chasing but he moves far quicker than they'd ever hoped to.

Cain moves fast through the still slightly flooded streets, each heavy step splashes mud coloured water high into the air, he grabs onto his shoulder to try and stop the bleeding as he whips around a corner and rushes into a thin alleyway.

The guards and priests continued to follow him, one of the priests sent out a ball of something dark which seemed to bore a hole in the nearby cobblestone wall. Cain didn't preoccupy himself with worrying about those behind him and only looked ahead. There was some sort of wall blocking the end of the alleyway.. He couldn't jump that high normally.

He kicked off the wall to his right to get some height and managed to use it to leap over the 9' tall wall with relative ease.

He flipped through the air and crashed onto the grass on the other side, its soft dewdrop covered texture brushing against his face.

He rolls to his feet and keeps running, slipping out of the backyard and rushing into the confusing and maze-like alleyways of the town, the guard and priests cursed him in God's name as they realised they had lost him...

St. Peter wouldn't be pleased...And Cain was on his way to finally set his plan into motion.. It was time for him to find his father.

Chapter 4:
Mundus Dei

Cain sits on top of a roof, a wet splurt fills the air as he takes a bite of a mouldy sandwich, the tomatoes inside pop from the force of the bite sending red juices flowing down his hand.

He had torn off a chunk of his trousers to make a makeshift bandage, it didn't do very well but it did enough for the injury on his shoulder.

The rain is light, the sky is mostly a clear blue with the sun casting its rays down onto the town. Cain just kind of sits there, not moving much, not looking around much, just stuck in his own head.

For as much as he tries being a bastion of control in his own life even he can't stop the emotions from slowly climbing to the surface...

He almost expected Caleb to betray him and yet even so... it stung.. Cain didn't have many friends in this world, hell he could make the argument he had none but now he was truly and utterly alone..

And suddenly he remembered why he didn't do this sooner.. Why he didn't stand up and fight the moment God told the world a false story... it was this reason, it was fear.. To defy God is one of the worst sins and crimes you can commit in this world.

He would lose everyone.. Everything.. In a way he felt comfort in the fact the barman gave him a special drink, no matter the pure vileness of it. He wasn't hunted... yes he got punched every now and then but that's life is it not?

Cain continued to watch the city with lazy eyes, people went to and fro, going about their days. Priests walked up and down the streets preaching from a small brown book called the bible, they were like wardens making sure their prisoners didn't stray from the path.

Cain groaned as he finished the sandwich and simply remained still. This world was focused around "miracles" as they called them, supposedly only those connected to god the most could perform these miracles.. And there were more often several levels of them.

There were commoners or lesser miracle workers.. People who researched plants and elements of the world to make amazing things such as candles, painkillers, bandages and the like.

Then there were greater miracles, either done by those in lower class "with a connection" to god or by any of "God's soldiers".

He chuckled to himself.

"Sure.. soldiers.."

In fact they were what you would describe as policemen and politicians, in a world of unequivocal truth, those in power tend to feel like they harbour more moral judgement skills than most.

There were 4 ranks of "God's soldiers"

Grand Workers, Priests, Saints, Prophets.

Grand Workers are no more than average people given a pamphlet and told to repeat the words of God again and again.

Priests are those who "have proven their love of God" they are often able to perform a miracle of some kind, whichever miracle they can use is unique to them. They're the wardens, there's a lot of them but they're not the strongest individually.

Then there's Saints *"or "Grand Priest" as that shitstain Peter puts it"* Cain thought, licking his dry lips.

Saints control all the Priests in the area.. However since the world is only 300 years old there isn't much area humanity covers yet, so only three Saints are known to be around.

However Peter is the biggest of them all.

Saints will often be able to do more powerful miracles and can perform multiple miracles.

Cain then spots someone, his body runs cold and a shiver is sent through his spine. He lightly shifts his weight so he'd be less seen by those down below.. A figure in a maroon robe carrying a stone tablet was walking by, Cain's eyes fixated on them and one word slipped from his mouth into a whisper.

"Prophets.."

Prophets don't have the political or social power that Saints do, however they are much stronger.

Prophets are few and far between, but they were handpicked by god to become prophets of specific events or abilities.

Being hand picked by god will often give you a large level of power even Saints are scared of.

Cain was no normal man, he knew that much, he was the direct descendant of Adam and had multiple small scale abilities... he was super durable, faster than the normal human and he had a few miracles of his own but he preferred not to use them.

They weren't that nice.

Even Cain knew he was nowhere near skilled or strong enough to even face a Prophet, let alone defeat one and survive.

He needed to get stronger, he needed to get better, he needed to become powerful enough to kill god with his bare hands.

This was going to be quite the task, he looked back up into the sky and thought to himself about what he saw in that church.. An idea so crazy that it just might work.

If his young memories are correct, and he is remembering the story his father told him long ago... then Cain should have a way to not only become strong enough to face any prophet that St. Peter throws his way.. But strong enough to face God and strike him down.

However to do that, he'd need to find Adam.. his father, the first man.

This wasn't going to be an easy task, at least.. Not as easy as most would assume.

Cain slowly stands up and walks to the other side of the rooftop, brushing crumbs off his exposed chest as he turns around and lets himself drop from the roof.

He lands on his feet and stumbles but keeps his balance, he looks around and quickly sneaks through a long but thin alleyway as he begins to make his way to the one place he could have any semblance of companionship or trust.

And that was a certain place called "The Snakes Burrow".

He needed this to go right, he rubs his arm and adjusts the tightness of the self made bandage as he begins to make his way to the secret bar.

He needs this to go well.. He needs to kill God... whatever it takes.

Cain walks through the hallowed streets as he finally makes his way to a steep and muddy slope which leads down under a butchers. His eyes scan the surroundings, his ears listening for even the slightest hint of movement.. He found none, a tense silence was all that awaited him.

He takes precautionary steps down the steep path, his shoes grinding against the mud lathered brick and dirt, the gentle rain still tapping against his head, almost as if it was trying to distract him.

He eventually made it to the bottom, turning to the steel door covered in markings, scratches and holes like it had been in combat itself.

On it is the sign of god scratched into the material roughly, he reaches over and knocks, letting the jealous echo of the door reverberate back at him.

Cain waits, every second ticked by as slow as a snail's crawl, his emotionless face contorted lightly as he narrowed his eyes. Again he listened and waited, the air around him shifted, wind gently picking up some attitude.

He listened closely and finally heard the faint and near silent footsteps which approached him, Cain snapped back into the moment, letting out a cold breath as the door suddenly is unlocked and swung open.

Cain lets a small polite smile shine through as he looks at the figure holding the door open, his body was covered in scars and his face was hidden by a simple white mask, his shredded tanned skin glistened in the shining orange and blue lights behind him.

"Oh.. It's you" said the figure, his voice disfigured by the mask.

Cain smiles, nodding as he slips his hands into his pockets.

"Indeed it is, I'm here to see Esther, is she in?" Cain asked politely, his gravel-like voice having a hint of honey in it.

The man looks at Cain through the slits in his mask and then back into the dark complex with gently glowing orange and blue lights. He then shrugs and moves out of the way.

"Eh, come on in, I got no orders to keep you out" the large man gestures for Cain to come inside.

Cain smiles as he slips into the dark and stingy hall, the air was thick with sweat and alcohol and the ground was sticky. The ceiling looked damp and decaying as the gentle sound of people talking was heard down the hall.

Cain looked over to the large man who pointed him to a nearby wooden door with a sign over it saying "Don't Enter".

Cain nods to the man and walks over, pushing the door open and slipping inside. Instantly the smell of weed hit his nose like a truck, it forced him to blink as a cloud of smoke drifted into his face, he looked around.

The entire room was rickety and wooden, it was made up of benches and tables, the walls were covered in faded blueprints and drawings of exotic plants.

He expected to see multiple people since the smell was so powerful and yet he only saw one.

A woman sitting on the bench opposite him looked at him with a death glare, her eyes as piercing as the spear he took this morning. She had long brown hair that ended in an orange tip and wore a torn jacket and trousers with a black stained shirt underneath, her cheeks were round but she had a chin sharp enough to cut someone.

Her skin was light tan and her eyes were a piercing ocean blue, she let a large cloud of smoke out of her mouth as it filled the air.

"Cain..." she spoke, venom in her voice and anger in her posture.

"Hey Esther" Cain said, trying to sound cheery.

She slowly stands up, the floor beneath her bent and buckled lightly causing the whole room to creak.

Cain took a shallow breath and readied himself for what might come.

Esther walks up to him and stares at him, she was much shorter than him, standing at 5'7, her eyes read of those that had seen too much and knew too much.

Cain readied his jaw to feel sore as she lifted her arm and then-

She wrapped her arms around him and tightly hugged him, Cain grunted as he felt his chest compress and the air slowly pushed from his lungs from Esther's bear hug.

She lets go and chuckles, tapping Cain on the cheek.

"You did good, finally standing up to that bastard church" she said, walking back to her bench and sitting down with a thud, pulling back out the pipe she smoked from.

"Ah, yeah" Cain looked to his right, seeing one of the blueprints had a plan to blow up the church, their symbol remained in black on the corner of the paper.. It was one of a snake wrapping around an apple.

"You finally ready to join the Snakes Burrow?" Esther asked, a smirk on her lips as she took a deep pull on the pipe.

Cain shook his head, leaning against the crooked wooden wall with a stern posture.

"I'm here to know where Adam is" he said bluntly, letting his cheerful charade fade.

Esther raises a brow, letting out a cloud of smoke which twirled around her like a planet following its sun.

"Why do you wanna know about him?" she said, leaning forward.

"I have a job to do, and I need his help to do it" Cain said, still letting his body absorb as much information about his surroundings as he can.

"A job huh? Is this why the church is after you? What shit did you get yourself into this time Cain?" she almost sighed as she spoke.

"I'm going to kill God" he said, his voice resonating with a lack of emotion. Esther pauses, choking on the smoke which poured from her lungs as her eyes widened.

"What!?" she screeched, still coughing violently.

Cain continued.

"I didn't kill Abel Esther.. God did.. I've been framed" he was dead serious... Esther had to pause.

"Look buddy, even I think that's crazy! And I'm fuckin crazy!" she coughs more, slowly letting her body calm down from such a violent reaction.

"I know what it sounds like but I'm serious, I need Adam, he's the key to becoming stronger, he's the key to beating God" Cain's eyes did not waver, Esther could tell with certainty he was being genuine.

She shakes her head in disbelief.

"You're a mad man... you'll die!"

Cain shrugged, crossing his arms.

"Then I'll die a mad man's death" he said, shrugging.

His eyes sharpened as he focused on the matter at hand.

"Where. Is. Adam?" Cain asked again, his gravelly voice sinking lower in tone than even a piano could go.

Esther pauses, thinking to herself.

"...I'm not sure that I should even tell ya, I mean that would mean it's kinda my fault you'd die by God suicide" Esther shrugs, leaning back.

Cain sighs.

"Don't you hate the church? What they stand for? The lies!" Cain barked, quickly pulling back that wretched rage which wished to spill out onto the world.. To burn it all.. But he couldn't let them be right, so he hauled it back deep inside of him.

"Yeah I hate the church, but I don't hate God! This is a philosophy debate... we at the Snakes Burrow think eating the apple was a good thing, the church disagrees" Esther takes another puff.

Cain taps the blueprint with the instructions for the church's destruction.

"This doesn't seem like a philosophical debate, Esther" Cain said, his eyes staring into Esther's very soul.

She pauses and then sighs, rubbing her eyes.

"Fine.. It's a bit more than philosophy but what you're saying is truly insane!"

"If anyone can kill God, it's his grandson" Cain said, tilting his head.

"...Maybe.. But wouldn't his son be closer to accomplishing it?" Esther asked, her face still one of slight shock and confusion.

"I know my father.. He'd never do such a thing.. But he may not oppose me directly"

Cain sighed and continued.

"Now tell me where my father is"

Esther thinks for a moment, thinking through this.

"...This is gonna cost ya" she eventually said, standing up and walking over to a nearby desk.

"How much do you need?" Cain said, rummaging through his pockets for the remaining copper he had on him.

"No, not money ya dingus, I need you to help with the Snakes Burrow" she pulled out a small black book and looked through it.

Cain saw nothing on the stained pages of the small handbook, and yet it seemed Esther was reading something fascinating.

Cain shrugs.

"What do you need me to do?"

Esther smirks and spins around, a large smile on her face, her eyes wide with a mad excitement.

"I need you to blow up a church" she said, grinning ear to ear.

Chapter 5:
Diovis

St. Peter scowled as he paced back and forth, his movements erratic and aggressive. He swiped his arms and hands around like he was shouting but no words came from his mouth. The air around him was filled with uncertainty.

Caleb sat in the corner of the large and empty room simply watching St. Peter with a pale face.. He didn't know it would go like this.. He didn't know how it would go but this was indeed not it.

He just didn't want Cain to die... he didn't want his friend to get himself lost in such a journey and get killed by God.. this is not what he wanted, it's not what Cain deserved...

St. Peter continued to pace, his voice leaked from his clenched jaw like gas escaping a punctured barrel, his tone was that of a venomous snake that let its meal get away.

"That bastard thinks he can just go around and say what he pleases.. I'll show him, I'll make an **example** out of him" he picks up a nearby potted plant and smashes its pot in his grip, letting the dirt and plant fall to the ground.

Caleb blinked, looking back up to St. Peter with a cautious gaze. St. Peter looked back at him with a glare only a mother could forgive.

"What do you have to say about this?" St. Peter snarled, walking up to Caleb with a clenched fist.

Caleb swallowed, pressing his back against the wall.

"..I...I... I didn't want this, I never wanted this! Cain is a good man that is in over his head, I came to you because I wanted you to just talk some sense into him not act like a lunatic!" Caleb barked, instantly he regretted those words which slipped from his lungs. He covered his face as his eyes widened.

St. Peter's eyes go dark as the air around them cracks and pops with strange sounds.

"You dare call me.. The grand priest.. A lunatic?" His words were cold and sour.

Caleb tries to stand up but is backed into the corner by St. Peters, even though he was skinny and pale, the very presence he brought with him and his words forced Caleb to freeze up.

Caleb stammers, trying to get words out to save him.. Yet none came.

"Say.." St. Peter began, the slimy tone to his voice rang deep in Caleb's head. "..You wished to bring Cain here for his protection.. Not because of your servitude of God? Simply for your own puny connections to the murderer!?"

Caleb tried to find an adequate response... and none came to him.

"Dear oh dear..." St. Peter shook his head before he grabbed Caleb by the wrist.

"This will simply not do" St. Peter began to drag Caleb away into another room, Caleb struggled, trying to pull away.

"No! Stop! Where are you taking me!?" Caleb pulled with all his might but even so St. Peter marched onward, dragging Caleb behind like he was but a speck.

"I'm taking you to a place where you can repent against your sins" St. Peter said, a sickening smile glinting in his pale blue eyes.

Caleb lashed out, scratching St. Peter, drawing blood...

The world seemed to stop for Caleb, his heart beat in his throat as an unearthly ringing filled his ears, blocking out any other sound.

St. Peter froze, not moving a muscle as he let his blood gently drip down onto the ground...

"It always comes down to this" St. Peter spoke, his voice cold and callice.

"I wouldn't have it any other way" he turned to Caleb, a thin lipped smile on his twisted face, his pale blue eyes filled with an unbridled emotion Caleb had never seen before...

Chapter 6:
Sunday's Dawn

The sound of ringing bells was the first thing that Cain heard, his eyes slowly fluttered open to look into the dusty room where he laid.

He could hear the gentle chatter of people outside his door and the sudden bustle of commotion from the townsfolk. Cain wondered for a mere moment what the noise was about before he remembered.

Sunday. The Lord's Day.

Cain groaned, slowly sitting up on the hard and stiff mattress, his shallow black hair a mess as he stands. He stretches, yawning lightly.

His scratchy stubble brushes against his hands as he massages his face mindlessly, he makes his way to the window and sighs as he watches droves of people make their way through the town. He only had a slight view of the main town from his window which was seemingly dug into an alleyway, but it was good enough for now.

"Such nice people..." he thought to himself, looking into the crowds of chatty people with dreary emotionless eyes *"...If only they knew their true God.."*.

Without warning a loud knock comes from his door and he reels, blinking.

Esther shouts from behind the door.

"Cain! You up yet? Hey Cain! Cain! Cain! Caaaiinnn!"

Cain sighed and rolled his eyes as he made his way over and unlocked the dusty wooden door before pulling it open, Esther stumbled lightly as she had been leaning against it.

"What do you want so early?" Cain asked grumpily, his gravelly voice lower than a piano once more.

"Weeee have some stuff to do" Esther said, smirking. She let out a cloud of smoke into Cain's face, he just closed his eyes and barely reacted.

"You're no fun" she said as she flicked the dying embers of her joint on the dusty floor, she spun around and began walking away.

Cain groaned and put on a borrowed t-shirt before following her down the hall. He glanced to his left, looking into a large room where several guys were taking turns trying to slap the other.

He looked to his right to find a room filled with women doing impressive workouts such as pull ups, push ups and some big lifting.

He didn't bother to look in the other 5 or so rooms, he just walked past them and let their shouts and cheers echo throughout the hallowed halls.

Esther then finally kicked open her door, smoke seeped from it and filled the hallway, Cain followed her lead and entered.

Inside sat two more people.

A woman with short black hair and a deadly stare, her name was Ramona if Cain recalled correctly, she was tough for her size, being able to floor Cain in a few minutes.

The other was a tall and thin man named Levi, he wasn't much of a fighter but he had the lesser miracle of mechanical knowledge. His pale face and tired eyes etched a frame of a man who was not currently in love with life.

Esther leaned on the wall and began to speak.

"We have been planning this for a while but we were missing a piece, that piece is you Cain. You're going to help plant and blow up the Church and only when that is done will I tell you Adams whereabouts" Esther giggled, smirking.

Cain looked at her with emotionless disdain, he really didn't want to do this.. It's not the churches fault God lied to them, although that St. Peter guy was weird.

"But she's caught me in her web.. I can't continue on my quest without her"

He glanced across the room to the desk she kept her black book in but never even considered trying to steal it, it would literally be useless to him.

Esther was a miracle worker, however her miracle wasn't combat based or healing based.. It was strange, yet useful to Cain in this exact moment.

"If I may ask... why are you blowing up this church?" Cain asked, raising his hand.

Esther looked at Ramona and Levi before clearing her throat.

"Let's just say we have some.. Beef with the oh divine saviour" Esther said, speaking about god like he was diseased, the words felt rotten as they left her mouth.

Ramona remained silent but clearly tensed, a piercing silent yet deadly rage flickered inside of her like a calm candle flame.

Cain quickly looked over to Levi to examine him.. But he felt almost nothing. A small smile flashed across his face, it was good that there was another of him.. Another one out there that could control it.

Cain nodded, looking back to Esther.

"Right.. So.. what will blowing up a single church do?"

Esther pauses...

"...Look, we're not all fucking crazy like you and think we can take on God, some people just gotta take out the priests of the world for our justice" Esther eventually said, pulling out another neatly rolled blunt.

Cain nodded, he understood why they were like this.. Why this place even existed.. Or at least Cain thought he understood, but whether that's true or not you must wait and see.

Cain rolled his shoulders and clicked his jaw.

"Alright, where's the explosives and which church, I'm ready"

Esther shook her head.

"We're not going to be doing it on Sunday you psycho, we want to hurt the church not kill innocents" Esther sighed.

Cain paused.

"Ah... fair.."

"We also need to make sure St. Peter is caught in the blast" Ramona spoke up, she had a raspy and sharp voice.

Cain nodded, a flicker of sick joy sparking in his mind.

"I do agree that weirdo needs to go, but if we're not doing it now then why are we all in this meeting thing?" Cain shrugs as he speaks.

Esther points to the blueprints.

"Because we don't have the explosives yet, today we're going to trade for them while the entire town is busy in prayer"

Cain nods, crossing his arms and beginning to understand, his amber and golden eyes shining in the pale orange light of the room.

"Alright, so today we get the materials and tomorrow we rig a church to blow?" Cain asked.

"Maybe.." Esther responded hesitantly.

"What's with the maybe.." Cain cautiously asked, his eyes narrowing.

"Well... we had an inside man to find out St. Peter's schedule right?" Esther shifted in place with anxiety, Ramona took a needle-like breath and Levi emotionlessly looked away.

"...Riiight?" Cain gestured for Esther to continue.

"We've lost all contact with them.. We have no idea where St. Peter is, so until we get someone new on board or we hear back from our inside man.. We're not gonna be detonating anything"

Cain paused, thinking.

"Like hell I'm waiting longer than tomorrow... I've already wasted too much time.."

"I'll be bait" Cain said without thinking first.

"What?" Esther asked, her eyes widening.

"St. Peters doesn't like me, if I get caught he's bound to come out to taunt me or even try to kill me" Cain said, putting his hands on his hips.

He wasn't wrong, he was sure that plan would work.. There'd only be one issue.

"You'd also be caught in the blast however..." Esther said, pausing as she finished the sentence.

Ramona looks over to Cain.. There was a short pause before Cain spoke.

"I'll handle it" his gravelly voice echoed in confidence.

"Are you sure about this Cain?" Ramona spoke again, her raspy and sharp voice catching Cain's attention.

Cain nodded, pocketing his hands and taking a deep breath as he wrangled the frog called fear back into his stomach.

"Yep, I've survived worse" Cain nods.

"We do the plan tomorrow, then you give me Adam's location" Cain points to Esther and she giggles.

"I knew you were bat shit insane... but sure, if you somehow manage to explode the church, kill St. Peter and stay alive? I'll tell you anything you want from the book" Esther said, holding out her hand. Cain didn't hesitate and shook her hand.

"Alright, now let's go find these explosives" Cain said, adjusting his shirt.

Cain, Esther, Ramona and Levi all walked through the crowded streets wearing light grey robes and hoods. Many others were wearing it, it was a local sign of "Respect".

"Respect... what it means is 'i'm lesser' it literally makes people celebrate being treated like animals.."

He thought back to those years of him being persistently abused by everyone around him.. Only now did he snap, he both did and didn't know why he didn't do this sooner..

It was so freeing, yet.. So scary.. His journey had barely begun and he knew one wrong move could end in his death. He might be able to survive the church's eruption if he's smart.. But if St. Peter somehow smells him out and sends a dozen or so priests or heaven forbid a Prophet.. He'd be toast.

Unless.. Maybe.. If he used his miracle.. But as I said before...

It's not very nice.

They managed to manoeuvre their way through the town, walking right past the priests set up to watch every corner on every street. They were luckily still hidden by the time the church bells rang...

Their thunderous ringing echoed into the air and reminded Cain of his younger days.. Days filled with sprite and energy, joy and belief.. Back before his parents left him and the world called him something he never was.

Killing was not something he wanted to do.. He never wanted to do it until he was framed for a murder he never committed... Even now as he walked he could feel that strange wretched drag on his stomach.

One of regret, a voice which wails *"Turn back!"* *"You mustn't kill St. Peter!"* *"It's not right!"*.. And yet Cain buried those thoughts deep in his psyche..

He didn't like letting his emotions run loose in his head..

It wasn't very nice..

So he hid them well, pushing all of his conviction in the back of his mind.

"St. Peter is basically God's human form.. So killing St. Peter is just killing a part of God, nothing more"

They watched as the entire town flocked towards the inauspicious ringing bells, the streets grew thinner and thinner, even priests broke away from their posts all to head towards a church for their praise.

Esther poked Cain and began to drag him through a back alley, they then slipped out on the other side, standing now in a large square of sand and dirt.

A man sat on top of three large black crates facing away from them, his hair was as red as fire and he wore a tight silver suit.

"There he is, now, nobody blow this for us" Esther hissed as she began to approach the man, the other three followed her not far behind.

"Heyyy Mr...." Esther begins, the man spins around and smiles, he has a welcoming round and fair skinned face.

"Oh hello there! You must be the Snake's Den! I must say I'm such a huge fan!" he spoke quite loud and explosively, to you or I dear reader we'd recognise that voice anywhere.. The voice of someone trying to sell you a product which does not work, the voice of a scam artist.

Esther seemed quite drawn to his charismatic words.

"Y-yes, yes we are.. Also thank you!"

"Yes yes yes, I hear you need three crates of tnt!?" he said, a large smile on his face as he pats the crates.

Esther nods.

"Yes, I heard you're the guy to supply us right?"

He smiles and nods, he slaps the top of the crate.

"This crate can hold so much explosive power!" His grin is wide as he speaks, his tone is charming and endearing, clearly working on Esther.

"Right so.. How much will that be?"

"45 gold or a simple price of 3 instalments of 199 silver! (tax rates do not apply)"

Esther frowns... for an example for you reader, 45 gold back then would be equivalent to 1,500 euros today.

"That's.. Quite a lot, also what was that word at the end? Tax?"

"Yes! Tax! It's a wonderful thing, don't you worry!" he said, smiling wide.

"What does Tax.. do?" Esther asked, putting her hands on her hips.

"Think of it like this, you have to pay less while getting more!" he kept smiling wide, Cain tilted his head.. This was fishy.

Cain examined the man up and down.. At first he could only see the jolly balloons of joy which floated off of him.. And then he saw it, peaking within the man's teeth was a hint of dishonesty, it grows and grows as he speaks.

Cain looks over to one of the crates and speaks, interrupting the man.

"May we see the insides of the crates?"

The man pauses, taking a breath.

"Well.. you must pay up and you get the crates in exchange!" he said nervously laughing, suddenly a massive wave of anxiety almost washes out of him but he holds it back..

Cain nods and walks over to the crate, he grabs one edge of the lid and pulls, tearing the wooden lid with ease as it splinters and bursts.

He looks down into the now open crate to reveaalll..

Dynamite? He wasn't a scammer?

"Hey buddy! That has broken our security clause and now you gotta pay extra!" he said, his anxiety vanishing and a smirk plastered on his face.

"Cain!" Esther hissed, snapping a look at him.. But Cain didn't react.

He slowly reached down and picked up one of the dynamite sticks before snapping it in half, a blackish grey material seeping out from them, he picked some and sniffs it...

Suddenly the man's face goes pale.

Cain speaks.

"..it's ground pepper"

Esther quickly picked some up of her own and sniffed it, she winced and nodded.

"It's pepper! Hey dude-"

The man had already begun running for his life as he dashed across the sandy patch hidden within the town.

"Ah shit he's getting away!" Esther shouts, but Cain picks up a nearby rock and throws it with a whipping force, his arm recoils.

It sails through the air, whizzing into a small curve before cracking against the man's head, he yelps and then falls flat onto his face.

Cain walked over to him and placed his foot on the man's back, forcing him to stay face first in the sandy dirt.

"Hey what's the b-big idea!" the man shouted, trying to scramble out from under Cain's foot.

"You tried scamming us" Cain said bluntly, his rage bubbled in him like a high pressure valve slowly getting ready to burst and yet.. He held back.. He could not let this break him.

"It was less a scam and more so a possible misunderstanding! You said TNT! You never said they had to be functional!" he cried out, trying to plead.

Esther walks over and scowls, kicking dirt into the man's face.

"So there's no explosives!?" she screeched, her jaw clenched.

"I... well, there is explosives but-" the man began but Cain dug his heel into the man's back, applying a blinding pressure which made the man yelp in pain.

"Tell us where" Cain said.

"I can't boss will kill me!" he yelped, covering his head and face.

"..Bring us to your boss" Levi said as he stepped forward, his pale face gleaming against the shining sun, his voice was harsh and callice, no emotion to his name, just air and lung.

"I don't think you'd guys would want that no offence!"

Cain sighs, digging his heel ever deeper into the scammers soft fleshy back. The scammer squeals in pain and pants.

"FINE!" he finally gives in, letting himself go limp.

"...I'll bring you to him..."

Esther keeps glaring, she puts her hands on her hips.

"Does your boss have the explosives we need?" Esther hissed, her eyes withholding a blaze of rage.

The scammer stalled, trying to think of a way out of this.

"Uuuuhhhhhhhhhhhhh wwellllllllllll- Ah!" Cain puts all of his weight onto the man, crushing him into the dirt.

"Yes.. he.. Has.. the.. Explody.." the scammer hissed as the air was ripped from his lungs, Cain instantly pulled his foot away and Esther sighed, grabbing the scammer by the collar and picking them off their feet.

"Take me to them, now" Esther hissed, her eyes flickering with that hidden rage.

The scammer groans but agrees, he leads them to the very outskirts of town where they see a small barn house which had been obviously repurposed for something.

Esther narrows her eyes as she scans the surrounding environment, eventually she clicks her fingers and points at Ramona.

"You're coming with me, Levi, Cain, you stay out here in case shit goes wrong" Esther orders, her voice brought with it a sense of power and control, she knew what she was doing.

The scammer made a pathetic whining sound as Esther dragged him down the small hill towards the barn house, Ramona silently followed behind.

Cain and Levi sat on a nearby ledge, waiting in hollow silence for the first sign of trouble...

And they waited.. And they waited.. The silence bore into Cain's skull, he was used to having the rain fill this void but the day was bright and the sky was clear.

He clears his throat, a tense wire of stress strung across it, he looks over to Levi.

He sat silent and still, his pale face showing nothing but concentration, his eyes flickering with faint feelings long bound.

Cain decided to speak, he didn't know why he did, but he opened his mouth and let his lungs and throat extrude their sounds.

He allowed the wind to pick up on his gravelly voice caused by years of abuse to it, he opened his heart like a door to let Levi enter. The sky's twisted and turned with joy and fluttering fairies.

Now reader, you may be wondering why I'm stalling, once again you seem to forget I indeed lie.

Cain didn't sound gravelly and tough, the air didn't reflect well on his voice and his nervous tone shone through as bright as the sun on such a summer's eve.

"H-hey" he paused, instantly his emotions lashing out at himself for making such a fool of himself.

He paused and grabbed the anxiety by the throat, the worry and the fear which built up in the recess of his mind, he threw it out behind his back and cleared his throat once more.

"Names Levi right?" Cain asked, his shoulders relaxing as his face returned to emotionlessness.

Levi nodded, his voice sharp as a dagger and almost a whisper.

"Yes, and I know of your name, Cain" his tone was completely neutral, no emotion infecting its crevices.

"I noticed that you were like me in a sense, someone who could quell their emotions and push them down"

Levi paused, thinking about all of this, eventually he nodded.

"I guess so" he returned his gaze to the barn house, no movement or sound was heard from them.

Cain nodded, letting himself relax a little bit more. A thought floated into his head, a question.

"..Why are you a part of the Snakes Burrow?" Cain asked simply.

Levi thinks for a moment, adjusting his grip on the blade hidden underneath his cloak as his eyes flicker towards the sky and then the ground. He shifted his weight and let out a small wheeze of air before speaking.

"..My father was taken from me too soon, his life ended by an illness unknown" his cracked and sharp tone softened, Cain saw the swirling clouds of regret fill his eyes.

"..I simply dislike God..." he said eventually, still looking ever forward towards the barn house.

Cain nodded, looking down at his cracked and scarred hands, his eyes softening with the drip of sad remembrance.

"..I know how that feels..."

Levi doesn't move his gaze, his focus remains sharp.

Cain slowly lets out a deep breath, letting his body relax, his muscles twitch and spasm lightly as he remembers back to that fateful day...

He lets out a shallow breath, trying to recalibrate his brain as he sorted through the emotions which wanted to burst out of him at any moment, suppressing them in their own little boxes and throwing away the key.

Levi suddenly speaks again.

"...I don't know if you're telling the truth.. Maybe you're just a killer wanting to blame others for his mistakes.. Maybe God did kill your brother.. I don't know and in the end it doesn't really matter.."

Levi looks at Cain, his sharpened eyes peering past Cain's hollow shell like eyes, staring into the starburst.

"..I know God can be cruel to those.. That he doesn't care who lives and who dies.. I hate how the church idolises someone who feels it fair to let my father die.. This is why I wish to heal you.."

Levi pulls out a glass vial and bites into his arm violently, crimson liquid spurts from the wound and Cain's eyes widen lightly as he leans back. Levi continues to dig into his own flesh as the blood drips into the bottle which he held up.

After a short while he pulls away from the wound and wipes his mouth clean, he places a small cork into the glass vial and hands it to Cain. Cain blinks and slowly takes the vial.

"Are you okay?" Cain asked, a hint of worry slipping past his tongue.

"Yes" Levi said, cleaning himself up. "My Miracle is that all who taste my blood are healed..."

He looks down at the ground, ashamed in himself almost, Cain narrows his eyes and gently speaks, his gravel like voice almost a comforting sound.

"...you father.. Did-" Cain began but Levi interrupted.

"I was given the gift after my father died.. Irony, is that what they call it?" Levi said gently, his eyes finally getting softer, the clouds of despair clouding his vision.

Cain paused, looking down at the blood filled vial, then back up to the sky, to the place above all man..

What kind of God would do such a cruel thing...

"...I will avenge your father-" Cain began, Levi raised his hand, stopping him.

"Don't..." Levi shook his head. "Don't get my hopes up"

Cain paused and nodded, he slipped the blood filled vial into his pocket and stared down at the farm house, his eyes slowly losing that feeling in them once more.

Suddenly movement was finally seen, Cain leaned forward, getting ready to bolt down there in case something had gone wrong...

Esther and Ramona walk out of the farmhouse carrying two large silver boxes each. Esther is grinning ear to ear and Ramona is covered in small flecks of blood.

They make their way up the small hill, Cain jumps down and takes a box for himself.

"I'm guessing it went well?" Cain said, a smirk on his dry lips.

Esther giggled.

"Yep! Four crates of explosives baby! That church is going down!" she cheered, Levi silently took one of Ramonas crates so they were all carrying one.

Cain smiled a toothy grin.

"Then let's head back and get ready for tomorrow ay?"

Esther nodded and walked past Cain.

"Yep! I think I've earned myself a blunt!"

Cain chuckles lightly, he watches as Ramona and Levi walk past him too, at how Esther jokes and laughs.. He feels something deep inside his husk shell.. Something telling him to stay..something telling him to give up on a foolish quest.. Even Caleb never made him feel this way..

He smiles as he follows them behind.

Cain, Esther, Levi and Ramona walked back through the town of Bethel, the streets were mostly empty as the churches that were pitched on every road were brimming full of people praying and saying thanks.

Different priests were stationed to give sermons and speak about all the deeds God had done for them that week, the group walked past several but tried to ignore their words.

Cain however listened, allowing his ears to pick up even on the slightest of sounds, as he walked past a smaller church he eavesdropped the priest's speech.

"And so God came down to our Saint and said 'Fear not! For the rain is here to make your crops grow twice the size!'"

The entire church erupted into applause.

They passed another church, Cain walked by the front door and his ears perked up as he listened.

"And so God appeared in front of Peter and said 'Fear not! For the rain is here to make your crops grow twice the size!'"

Once more the church erupted into laughing applause and whistling.

They moved deeper into the town before eventually stepping in front of the largest of the churches, the one that looked as jagged as a broken tooth. He could still spot dried blood drops from yesterday, he looked down at his shoulder.. It ached but was definitely healing nicely.

He heard the whining voice of Saint Peter as he exclaimed to the church.

"GOD came to me and I could feel our BEINGS bonding together! As I saw through God's eyes and I saw the TRUTH! I saw the story of the world! From the first day of light to the first murderer, Cain"

He could hear people start to boo at his name, Cain paused.. Unable to stop the magnetic pull that dragged him towards the church..

Man did he just want to bust in there and make St. Peter swallow the bible before throwing him out the window.. But he couldn't.. Not just because of that annoying little worm which tells him rights from wrongs, but because he had a job to do..

...would it be proving him right?... Cain didn't want to think about that and managed to pull himself away from the church, he made his way down the alley and into the Snakes Burrow.

He made his way through the thick smelling halls, his feet sticking to the stone that lay beneath him as he walked, he slipped into another room and placed the crate down alongside the others.

He could already hear Esther lighting up a blunt in her room, he saw Levi slip into the bathroom and he noticed Ramona leaning against the wall in a mostly empty room covered in drawings.

He walks in and looks around, the drawings seemed to be made by mostly children with some adults and teens in there too. There were a lot of them too, Cain let his eyes slowly slide to Ramona and he waved gently.

"Hey.." he said in a quieter tone, he walked up near her and leaned against the wall.

"Hey" her raspy voice croaked out past her tongue.

"...What about you? Why did you join the Snakes Burrow?" Cain asked, turning to look at her.

She paused, not answering right away.

Eventually she takes a sharp breath and speaks.

"..I see the world and its potential.. And I see how the Church is squandering it.. God doesn't care for us, he never had, he wanted to keep Adam and Eve in the garden like pets.. Like slaves.. He tried to punish them for eating an apple from the tree, and yet we are here.. Are we the punishment? If we are, we should be able to work on our own instead of praying to the man who didn't want us to exist.." she finally stopped with a shallow breath, she looked ahead and didn't move, her body writhed with worry and determination.. Cain could tell she was a powerful woman, her mind was dead set on making this world better... a small smile came to his face, he didn't know why but he felt a strange rolling feeling of.. Happiness?

He could feel it slowly growing inside his chest like a plant, its roots slowly digging into him and refusing to ever let go... but of course all plants burn with fire. Do they not?

Cain made his way across the hall and pushed open the wooden door, stepping into the smoke-filled room, his foot creaked into the wobbly floor board, the entire room creaking from his weight.

Esther looked up and chuckled as she took another deep pull of her blunt. She tapped it so the ash would fall off and land down below in between the cracks of two aged and twisted planks.

The look on her face was one of pride and mischief, Cain gently blinked as he closed the door behind him.

"Do you wish to talk about the plan once more before tonight?" Cain asked, leaning against the wall with his hands in his pockets.

"If you want" she giggled to herself and flopped over onto her side.

"Say..Cain?" she asked, taking a quick drag of the blunt.

"Yeah?" he tilted his head lightly.

"After this mission.. Instead of going off and getting yourself killed.. How about you stick around? I doubt the church will let their favourite church go kaboom without a war" she smirked.

Cain paused, thinking about it... there was a part of him which didn't want to leave, he didn't know why but he felt as if he belonged here..

"I.. Don't know.." he finally said.

"Oh come onnnnn" Esther said, standing back up, she walked over to her desk and pulled out her black book.

"What if I threw this away so you had to stay?" she giggled.

Cain's face fell slightly.. Yes he did almost feel at home here, the first time he'd been around people without getting clocked in the face but this wasn't right, he didn't feel right to leave his brother's death in vain..

"..Please don't.. I know what I have to do in this world.." Cain said gently, his eyes slowly falling to the ground.

She groaned and shook her head.

"Fineee, I'll do the book thing after the kaboom boom.."

She put the black book away in the drawer.

You see, Esther's gift was incredibly strange, yet specific.

Her ability was to create small books, however these books were not ordinary, as any person she ever met would be noted down in the book.

At all times she would be able to tell their exact position, their general mood and some information about them that updated real time.

At one point in her young life she had actually met Adam, and so was one of the few humans alive who truly knew where the first man was hiding as he had not been seen in years.

"How do you feel about that by the way?" Esther asked, looking up to Cain.

"About what?"

"About blowing up the church.. I know God killed your brother and all, or at least so you say, but you would indeed be murdering Saint Peter... so, you'd be like the 27th murderer instead of the 1st or however many there were.." she yawned lightly and looked at him, crossing her arms.

He thought about it, looking down at his scarred and permanently chipped hands.. How he'd been beaten, attacked, burnt for years after the event.. How the church deemed him a threat, how they talked about him like he was a rabid monster.. His fists clench.

"...I do what has to be done.." his voice echoed emotionless, his eyes lost that glint to them and his face became neutral.

Esther paused, wanting to fight him on this but knowing she needs him to do it for her, she shrugs and takes another puff.

"You may rest then, I'll wake you up in the dead of night and we'll plant the explosives then, afterwards you get caught by the Priests and go inside where the explody explody will happen" she sits back down on the bench.

"Right.. And are you sure about this.. War with the church?" Cain asked cautiously, his eyes narrowing.

Esther looked away, letting out a big cloud of smoke, she sighs and lets her shoulders fall.

"Yep.. I've waited too long.. It's now or never.."

Cain paused, crossing his arms.

"...They'll probably arrest you and make you public laughing stocks" Cain said as a warning.

Esther laughed and sighed.

"We're already laughing stocks, if you haven't fuckin noticed by now we aint got shit to live for... not anymore.."

Cain slowly nodded, he could feel the immense beast of despair climbing all over her, wrapping around her wrists and neck like a serpent about to strangle their meal. Her mind raced with thoughts of rage and revenge which sent cascading flames down her hair.. Although of course no one but Cain saw this.

"I hope you're successful, and if I survive.. I'll be sure to return" Cain nodded, turning to leave the room.

"Wait..." Esther said under her breath, Cain turned to face her.

"...Don't die on me okay? I'll be working on a room just for you, so when you get back you can be one of us alright? Don't just kill God and expect the world to be better, we gotta MAKE the world better" even through the grip of sadness, she smiled, a grin with determination which seeped into the air almost suffocating.

Cain chuckled and lightly smiled, that flicker of hope in his chest once more..

"That sounds nice" he said, slipping out of the door and walking down the hall to his temporary room.

As he walked he continued to grow attached to this place, he waved to Ramona and Levi as he walked past, closing the door behind him with a satisfying click... somehow, it already felt like home.

Chapter 7:
Dolorem Serpentis

The amber sky looms over the small town, the dark and shapeless clouds float through the air, slowly drifting within the seemingly weightless space that was the air.

Below them remain the shadows cast by the small and handmade buildings, the churches sharpened spires casting a darkness that resembled that of a beast's claws. The wind slowly picks up, bringing a tangerine smell to those few who were awake.

Priests walked through the amber & shadow drenched streets, their clothes rustling lightly and their breath hissing through the chilly space. Their faces were calm and collected and yet their eyes were piercing, watching, waiting for someone to show their face.

Those who were not priests remained in bed or were miners heading out for their daily round, walking along the roads covered in dirty soot soaked clothes, their hands full of toolboxes and small machines which wrapped around their arms.

Four figures remained in the harsh darkness of the sunrise, their bodies pressed against the cold, damp walls of a back alleyway. The sound of remnant rain dripping off the nearby slanted roofs being the only sound to combat their gentle breathing.

The priests walked past, not a clue in their mind about who was standing right behind them. They continued on, scanning the perimeter.

The four figures waited for the coast to be clear before one of them spoke in a low hiss so they couldn't be heard by any passerby or sleeping civilian.

"Are you sure about this?" asked a woman's hissing voice.

"..Yes.. Yes I am.." said a gravelly yet hesitant man.

"We should cause a commotion then.." a scratchy woman said, her breath as sharp as daggers.

"Or we could have him walk into the church with confidence" said an emotionless and hollow voice.

"I've got this.. I have experience in making the church mad" said the gravelly voice, its tone lower than the lowest note on a piano.

"..Fine..remember the signal, I'll light the fuse and get back to the hideout, if you survive you find us back there without being followed okay?" said the hissing woman's tone, one of the figures nodded and began to walk out of the harsh shadow, slipping into the amber baked light.

His footsteps were heavy and purposeful as he made his way through the winding roads of the cities, carefully stepping over small gardens as he made his way towards the towering church, its very form engulfed in pure black shadow with its edges brimming with amber light.

The smaller figure followed not too far behind, slipping in and out of cover as they made their way behind the church.. Slipping into a small gap and leaning down behind a long black fuse which pokes from under a mound of dirt, the smell of gunpowder still stains the area.

The man looks around, allowing himself to soak in the surroundings. The world was so quiet at this time of night, only the gentle sing song of birds and the distant march of miners dared breach the sacred sunrise.

The figure finally made it in front of the monolithic tower that they called a house of god, his amber and golden eyes scanned the bleached streets left to right as he waited for something to arrive..

Eventually he got exactly what he wished for, two priests walked around the corner, their soft and narrow faces contorting into a glower as they spotted the shadowy figure standing by the church.

They pick up their pace, making their way towards the man, the priest on the right opens his mouth and speaks, the sound breaking the silent sunrise.

"Identify yourself please" said the snivelling voice of the priest as he quickly approached, his shiny shoes squeaking with each step.

The man smiles to himself lightly and speaks with his chest, letting his signature voice boom through the air towards the priests.

"I've been trying to find you two! You know why there aren't as many priests around?" the man spoke in a gloating tone but knew what he said was true...

There were usually more priests patrolling the town, something felt off to the man, his golden and amber eyes shining against the black starburst in the heavily contrasted morning.

"What are you... Undo your hood!" the priest squeals, the other priest however didn't speak.. If anything he looked concerned, he had lightly tanned skin with short black hair and golden brown eyes, a large scar across his nose was visible.. He looked young.

The man smiled wider and slowly let his hood slip off of him making sure their eyes fell on the two marks from God.. his name marked into Cain's own skin, and the tattoo of the dagger with the handle of a snake.

The priest's eyes widen and he reaches his hand out, his miracle begins to shine through the air. It was like space itself was torn into a small shredded ball, warping light around it.

Cain noticed it instantly as the orb which bore a hole through the wall while he was escaping, he quickly ducked into the church, slipping past the large wooden doors and stepping into the large and vast gothic room.

The priest chases after him with a howling cackle, he throws the orb of black, it spins through the air and Cain throws himself to the side, landing on the soft carpet as the orb flies past him and rams through several pews, turning them to debris.

Whatever this miracle was, it was stronger than Cain expected.. And suddenly that parasite called fear was lurching up his throat.

Cain rolled back to his feet as the priest growled, his wrinkled face contouring into a snarl as he created two of the orbs. Cain's eyes widened as he jumped back, avoiding the viscous pitch from the elder priest.

Cain shouted out as he stumbled, realising he might have fucked up.

"Hey! What are you trying to do kill me!?" Cain shouted, trying to sound confident but even now that worm of fear wrapped tight around the inside of his throat and refused to let go.

The elder priest grunted and created an even bigger orb, preparing to throw it directly into Cain from near point blank, Cain's eyes widened as he looked around, trying to look for a place he could dive to or duck to avoid the incoming blast and yet he found none..

He was trapped and about to be torn to pieces, and yet even still only one thing ran through his mind.

"I bet God's laughing"

But before the elder priest could unleash the attack, a younger voice cries out as he grabs ahold of the priest's shoulder.

"STOP! Father Clementine! We must not kill!" it was the young priest, his eyes wide with fear and confusion and his voice echoing hope and mercy.

Cain narrowed his eyes lightly as he examined the boy, his body simply radiated hope, fear wrapped around his legs like iron bind and yet he still moved, his words spun around the elder man's head like stars before sinking in.

The elder priest groaned and his miracle vanished, the orb releasing a small shockwave into the surrounding area.

"He must be dealt with Son Aaron, we cannot let such a wretched man escape again" Father Clemantine scowled, his aged eyes scornfully watching upon Cain's every move.

Son Aaron thought for a moment and then walked closer to Cain, speaking softly.

"I will deal with him father, you must go get grand priest peter!"

Father Clemantine growled and turned away, quickly rushing from the building, he was fast for an older man, he slams the church doors behind him and locks them.

Cain chuckled and smirked wide, his eyes shining as he clenched his fists. He stood tall over Son Aaron, he was easy pickings.. If he wished to hurt him.. That is..

"Do you really think you can hold me?" Cain said as he grinned.

Son Aaron just blinks as he looks up to Cain, he simply shrugs.

"I don't have to hold you, I just want to talk.." Son Aaron spoke softly and with kindness, his eyes showed that too.. He meant no harm to Cain.

"..Talk?" Cain asked, crossing his arms.

"Yes" Son Aaron said, sitting down on a non damaged pew, patting the seat next to him.

"Talk with me" he smiled gently to Cain, no hatred in his tone..

Cain was not used to this, Priests weren't so kind to him usually.. He did not sit however, he simply looked at Son Aaron, no emotion in his eyes.

"I see... well.. I do not wish to speak ill of my brothers and fathers but they can be quite vindictive at times" Son Aaron said, twiddling his thumbs.

"You can say that again" Cain lifted up the shirt to reveal a large wound still not fully healed on his shoulder where the spear hit him.

Son Aaron winced, Cain could see a flurry of disgust and despair cross his face before it's swatted away. Son Aaron looks in front of him, avoiding the injury on Cain's shoulder.

"..My brothers and fathers are scared you know, they do not wish to take your claims seriously for it may affect them dearly" Son Aaron began but Cain barks.

"And so they're justified in beating me down and trying to kill me!? They're justified in treating me like an animal to be spat on and kicked because they're scared to accept they might be wrong?" Cain growled through his clenched jaw, his fists tightening.

"No! They are not justified in such actions but I.. You... There is another way.. Cain.. There is another way where we can all work together and–" Son Aarons sweet voice is interrupted by the bursting sound of a door being ripped open.

Cain's eyes quickly dance over to the front platform as a man in a white robe and black highlights walks out, his pale blue eyes shine with rage and rotting hatred as they finally meet the sight of Cain.

"Leave us be son" St. Peter spoke.

"But great priest–" Son Aaron tried to speak up but was interrupted.

St. Peter flicked his wrist and the door to the church unlocks and whips open, he points.

"Out!" his frail and pathetic voice booms across the dreary room and lightly leaks out into the butterscotch tinted streets. Son Aaron slowly stands up and walks out, making his way down the road and out of sight.

Cain turned his attention back to St. Peter as the doors slammed shut on their own, locking behind them. Cain's heart raced in his throat, his entire body shook lightly as rage and fear enveloped each other inside of him.

St. Peter shakes his head as he slowly steps down from the platform.

"Tsk Tsk Tsk.. Cain, I thought you were smarter than this" St. Peter kept shaking his head, his tone was condescending and Cain clenched his jaw..

That worm of morality wriggled into his ear and told him to run, to break down that door and dash away, to not do this.. To not make a permanent enemy of the town he so loved.. But he had to.. He needed to find Adam.. but what if he didn't? What if he had found a home in the Snake's Burrow?.. They wouldn't accept him if he failed the mission! Or..

"CAIN!" St. Peter yelled, the air became electrified as Cain felt his muscles tighten up too strong for him to move, he stumbled backwards.

"I know when you're not listening to me" he said afterwards, his voice calming down back to his frail and soft tone.

Cain took a breath his mind was racing, all he had to do was give a signal and this place would be blown sky high-

CRACK!

St. Peter slaps Cain, sending him flying across the room once more, the force shakes his very mind and sends him crashing into the ground.

Cain coughs from the blow, air leaving his lungs.. He quickly turns over so he's laying face down, grabbing at his stomach and ribs. St. Peter shakes his head. Cain squirms and pops something into his mouth.

"How pathetic you are Cain!"

St. Peter picks Cain up by the collar, his soft fingers coiling around the stretching fabric.. He smiles.. And then throws him through a pew, Cain's body recoils from the blow and his mind goes white in agony as the sharp wood pierces through his dirty black shirt and into his skin.

Cain coughs and tries to stand but St. Peter smiles kicking Cain, his foot digging into Cain's gut before the force shoots him across the floor, he skips across it like a stone across a choppy sea before he skids to a stop in the centre of the room.

His breathing was ragged and heavy, his eyes drooped as his brain throbbed inside of his constricting skull, his back ached and burned in anguish as it seared into his retinas.

St. Peter shook his head as he approached Cain, each footstep echoed inside of his skull, sending a pulse of white hot torment down his nerves.

"Tsk tsk tsk.. Cain, Cain, Cain... do you truly take me for some sort of..." St. Peter's voice slowly fades as Cain struggles to stay conscious..

His brain was screaming in fear and panic.. He should run.. No he should say the signal.. No.. he should use his miracle on St. Peter, he deserves not so nice things to happen to him..

Cain reached out and gripped onto the dirty and rough carpet, his weak fingers digging into the fabric to give him a better grip as he tried to pull himself towards the exit.

St. Peter stomps on Cain's hand, crushing his fingers under his shoes and grinding them into the ground with a sickening snap and a pop. Suddenly Cain's brain is completely overloaded, his eyes go blank as he screams out, adjusting the position of something in his mouth with his blood covered tongue.. He screams a blood curdling scream.

"NOW! DO IT NOW!" Cain's voice almost shook the building.. Or was that nothing more than the dynamite.

"What–" St. Peter was cut off as the kilos of TNT erupted, tearing the building up from its roots, a massive ball of fire and force engulfs them both as Cain bites down on something, shattering glass in his mouth and having blood spray through the air as everything is enveloped in an eruption.

The sheer force of the explosion destroyed the windows of all nearby buildings and did significant damage to some surrounding towers, debris spread across the road and homes surrounding the church, a massive blaze roared inside of the mostly destroyed church...

Smoke filled the sky, turning the gentle blue sky to one of heated coals and flame.. In the rubble, stands a single person..

Cain stands up, his shirt and trousers have been eviscerated by the blast, the ground below him is just rubble and ash, he stumbles.. But he remained unharmed. He spit the remnants of the glass bottle out as he tried to make his way out of the burning hot church.. Or.. remnants of burning hot church...

"Fuck you.. Peter..." he stumbles, trying to escape the blaze... he looks around.. People began to leave their homes and look out at the destruction.. And all they saw was Cain..

And then.. A voice spoke.. One he wished he never heard..

"Why don't you say that to my face?"

Cain's eyes widened as he spun around to see the contorted and burnt figure of St. Peter.. Slowly.. Stand.. Up.

His jaw drops and he shakes his head.

"No.. No.. You're supposed to be dead!" Cain shouted, his body suddenly filled with adrenaline.. A sense of fear filled the air.. He knew something was wrong..

The burnt husk of St. Peter looked into the sky and held out his arms, his eyes had melted deep into his charred eye sockets, his muscles had vanished and burnt, his skin hung off him like shredded paper... as his throatless voice spoke.

"OH FATHER IN HEAVEN! OH BLESS ME!"

As he wailed into the sky a golden light pierced through the clouds... Cain couldn't believe what he was seeing.. As St. Peter's body began to heal and glow a vibrant white as beautiful white clothes appeared on his regenerating body, his smile grew its teeth and his eyes reformed back to that pale blue as his blonde hair grew from his charred and shattered scalp..

St. Peter began to laugh.. People were watching now as God himself healed St. Peter, bringing him back from the brink of death.. St. Peter was not only resurrected before Cain's very eyes.. But he could sense the monumental power which St. Peter now held in his soul, a godly force which ripped through space and time..

Cain simply stood there.. His face was emotionless.. His eyes pale and faded.. His breathing is soft and shallow.. The sky swirled around them as the smoke descended into a wall which formed a ring segmenting Cain and St. Peter from anymore prying eyes..

"Did you forget who God's disciple was Cain?"

St. Peter held out his hand and two angelic blades formed from the air itself, their shining metal reflecting Cain's own face back to him.. The fire that swirled around them turned to a blinding white.

And for the first time.. Cain simply stared.. No information from his surroundings reached him, almost like a deep sleep except he was aware.. Or was he? Cain's mind and body conflicted with each other, emotions shouted and thrashed and yet Cain paid no mind to them.. He paid no mind to holding them back..

They whipped and cracked at his body as emotions pulled on him every which way.. Fear told him to run, rage told him to fight, anxiety told him to wait, greed told him to steal, hope told him to hold his ground, despair told him to give up and slit his throat...

And as St. Peters flew through the air with his shining white blades, aiming for a strike on Cain's chest... he snapped..

He decided to do something..

Something very..

Very..

Chapter 8:
Very Nasty

St. Peter rushes at Cain, his blades sing through the air like an opera's note, but suddenly Cain's body lurches, his bones snapping and breaking as he dodges the strike, St. Peter narrows his eyes as he flies past him and slides against the debris.

He quickly spins around, his pale blue eyes shining with perfect light as Cain's body reassembles itself.. His fists begin to burn and break apart like they were being cooked inside out, his skin turns to charcoal and red and orange flecks of embers leak off of him.. Floating through the air.

"..What?" St. Peter spins his blades around, the angelic energy washes over him as he grits his teeth.

"I will slay you for heresy"

St. Peter tries to dash at Cain again, using his now inhuman abilities to blitz across the air, he slashes with his twin blades aiming for Cain's neck.

Cain dodges, moving far too fast for a human, his hand shoots out, grabbing St. Peter by the face, his eyes widen in fear as he looks upon Cain's face..

His skin melts and burns, the black ash spreads up his arm and small patches of his face begin to burn too, his eyes melted into his skull. St. Peter tries to struggle but suddenly Cain's hand bursts into pure flame, something no one had seen before, it sears into St. Peter's perfect skin, leaving ash and black...

The sounds of skin melting, reader, are not so nice to hear.. And it's less nice to feel as the very flesh you call your own begins to bubble inside out as your blood vessels pop from the heat.. Is it not?

St. Peter screams in pure agony as blood drips down his face, he slashes with a blade and chops Cain's arm off completely before kicking him square in the chest and sending him flying..

Cain hits the ground and rolls, saying nothing and making no sound before slowly standing back up..

"What a foul beast.. I knew you were nothing but the snakes spawn!"

Cain didn't listen.. He simply let his rage boil and bubble out of him, bursting from his skin into pure crimson flames as his exposed tendon and blood vessels grew into sharpened and bubbling whips and string which Cain swung with force using what remained of his arm...

The blood vessels whistle through the air and crack against St. Peter, dragging their boiled and forged tips through his skin, digging into his flesh and ripping chunks from it as they're pulled across him.. Leading to him stumbling as his clothes and body are torn and cut violently, blood sprays onto the ashen covered battlefield.

St. Peter roars, his body healing as he snaps his palm against the air, a focused force of energy tears through the carbon filled air.. It strikes Cain in the chest, burrowing open his skin and bone as the wet and thick cracks echo into the crackling sky.. Only for something to reach out and grab it.. A hand forged from Cain's own heart as it crushes the miracle in its grasp, his ribs shatter and reform into small thistles of fibre which fill the air into an almost white gas.

St. Peter's eyes widen as he tries to leap into the air, wings bursting through his back but it was already too late.. The thistles stuck into his spine and began to reform, creating a cage in the shape of Cain's rib cage around his arms and wings, forcing him to fall back down to earth with a crash and crunch as the debris is sent skidding.

"ENOUGH YOU FOUL BEAST! YOU FORSAKEN THE VERY EARTH THAT OUR CREATOR HAS GIVEN YOU!"
St. Peter screams out, his eyes widening in fear as he breaks and shatters the rib cage around him, he launches at Cain, holding out his hand..

They collide, St. Peter places his hand on Cain's face and screams, holy magic flowing through him and blasting against his burning flesh.. While Cain quickly reacts, grabbing St. Peter's face with his other arm, his skin black and bubbling as if lava was trying to spill from his cells.. But no.. no lava.. Just..

Anger.

Anger spills from Cain's husk, enveloping St. Peter's head in a crimson flame of agony and blood as they feel their skin begin to bubble and burn.. St. Peter's face turning as black as ash as his nerves are incinerated.. Cain's face turns to a bubbling mess of liquid and bone as the holy magic attempts to pry out his unholy miracle.. And yet even as the rage is pulled and tugged through Cain's own body..

St. Peter falls back, the pain too much for him to bear as he lashes out a kick, it strikes Cain in the gut and sends him flying across the thick smokey air. He smashes through the ring of smoke and vanishes.. His presence is no longer even present..

St. Peter gasps as holy energy fills his body and heals him.. But his breathing remains ragged and fearful.. Any man or monster would be shaken by the unholy horrors they witnessed.. Their wings fell from their back and vanished as the smoke ring and white fire flickered into nothing..

The entire town was now outside the circle.. Waiting.. Watching..
And even so.. Even through the pain and fear...
St. Peter laughed..
Even if Cain was not dead..
St. Peter laughed..

As he raised the burnt and charred arm of Cain above his head for all to see.. As he spoke his holy words..

"THIS IS WAR!"

The echoing cries of happiness and joy fill the air.. As a figure, missing his arm stumbles down a dark path, falling down to their knees as blood runs down their side..

The figure coughed, throwing up what little food they had in their system as the pain overloaded them..

Suddenly three other figures grabbed them, pulling him inside of the warm and cosy Snake's burrow.. Their smiles put him at ease as they heal him and get him ready for tomorrow..St. Peter died of a random heart attack.. As everything turned out well..

But oh dear reader..

You must know I lie...

Because no one reached out to Cain as he stumbled into the Snake's Burrow.. His mind was too foggy to realise the door was already open.. The pain and blood loss took too much from him to realise that he didn't step into the sticky substance that lines the hall.. But splashed in cold crimson..

He didn't notice the body lying in the corner with their throat slit.. Nor did he realise no sound or chatter came from any of the rooms.. He stumbled, tripping over something.. He fell face first into a harsh cold yet viscous liquid, flecks fell onto his tongue and he tried to spit it out...

Near instantly he felt the wound on his arm close to a stump.. He felt his brain return to normal.. He felt his breathing get deeper... he felt his heart pound and his head spin as he looked into the cold.. Dead eyes.. Of someone he may have called a friend..

He simply froze.. As he looked around, realising he was drenched in blood.. Looking down he saw the decapitated head of Levi.. his pale skin ever paler.. His sharp eyes now soft and motionless..

Cain said.. Nothing.. Did.. nothing..

He looked into the other room, to see the still legs of Ramona.. He stumbled to his feet but fell, crashing through the wooden door that was split in two.. And looking in horror.. At the still girl.. Blood drenching her.. Her stomach torn open.. Her eyes dull and aimless.. A black book in her hand..

Cain.. felt nothing.. Not in the usual sense of him repressing his nasty emotions.. No.. his sense of touch had left him, only replaced by the gentle static which echoed in his flesh sack he called a body.. He picked up the black book, his grip too weak to hold it and yet he persisted..

Written in blood were the last words Esther ever wrote...

"I'm sorry if I don't make it out.. The least I can do is fulfil my promise.. Adam resides on the north side of the blue mountain in a farmland with three red roses on the front gate.. Goodbye Cain, I hope you told me the truth.."

Cain fell to his knees.. He had got what he needed.. What he wanted.

And yet he felt more hollow than before.. His eyes glossed over as his body shut down, unable to move.. Or even breathe..

He knew it was strange that Priests had been missing.. He should have something.. Done something.. And yet he sits in the pool of cold blood.

No thoughts..

No feelings..

If that were true, he didn't need to scream..

He didn't need to..

But did he?

That's not my question to answer.

Chapter 9:
A Life Called Praeteritum

The sun shone beautifully through the pure blue sky, its warm glow beamed against the happy smile of a boy as he marched through the gleaming green grass, his amber eyes wide with excitement.

He was wearing a dirty white shirt with some brown trousers tucked into themselves to make some shorts, his shoes had more holes than not, but he didn't care, he rushed down the hill, his eyes gleaming with joy as he laughed.

Down the hill his younger brother ran from him, his hair was a curly red, he had light pale skin and bright pink eyes. He wore a black shirt that was covered in tears and cuts, his trousers were more like rags by this point, he didn't even wear shoes as he slid down through the brambles.

"Imma get ya!" shouted the elder brother, giggling.

"Nuh Uh!" the younger brother shouted back, they made their way across a small dip in the landscape which funnels down to a river.

The elder brother begins to speed up, his eyes sharpening as his slightly longer legs allow him to begin to catch up. The younger brother whips his head around and grins, he continues to head right into the river.

The elder brother stumbles, his foot getting caught on a rogue tree root but he didn't give up, he kept running no matter what.

The younger brother stops at the river's edge, it's cold calice water slowly flowing downstream to the nearby camp. He glances at the width of the river, he plants his feet into the pebbles and his smile grows wider.

"Give up! I've cornered you!" the elder brother said, slowing down as he approached his brother from behind, panting.

The younger brother looked over to him with a shine in his eyes. The elder one pauses..

"You can't make that jump!"

And yet the younger took that as a challenge, he leaped through the air, kicking off the pebbles and reached out as his body outstretched to the brighter grass which laid on the other side of the icy cold river.

The elders' eyes widened as.. He landed it, stumbling but quickly standing back up with triumph in his face.

"I.. How the-"

"Catch me if you can Cain!" the brother said, blowing a raspberry as he turned on his heel and rushed over the horizon.

"Abeeeel!" Cain cried out, a smile on his face and some worry in his eyes. He had to find a way around the river, there's no way he'd be able to make that jump.. Even if the river wouldn't sweep him away, the cold wasn't something he really wanted to deal with.

It took Cain over 20 minutes for him to find the right place to pass by the river; he had managed to find a fallen tree which acted as a substitute bridge. The slimy moss which had covered the trunk was hard to get a grip on but Cain moved slowly and with reason, not taking any extra risk.

He made it to the other side and jumped off into the slightly soaked leaves before dashing through the woods, looking around to see where Abel must have gone.

The sun glints through the thickly wooded trees, his eyes light up as he looks into the rays which leak through the treetops.

He looks away, making a cheeky face before speaking to the air in front of him.

"Oh Grandpa? Could I have a hint?" Cain smirked and waited.

There was a long pause before suddenly the trees all rustled from a sudden wind. They all bent and pointed towards a certain point deep in the woods.

"Gotcha. Thanks gramps!" Cain smiles and waves to the sky as he runs through the woods, leaping over fallen trees and stumbling past some brambles and stinging nettles.

Eventually he makes it to the edge of a clearing, in the middle stands Abel.. his back turned to Cain, not moving..

"..Abel! I found ya! Don't you run from me!" Cain shouted out as he ran into the clearing, his eyes narrowing.

And yet Abel didn't move...

Cain slowed down, why wasn't he moving? Cain walked in front of Abel and paused..

Abels face was pale, his eyes were dim.. Unmoving..

A nasty.. Nasty image fills Cain's head.. But.. a memory? A memory of a life he never lived? Or at least hasn't lived yet?

"You almost caught me haha!" Abel suddenly blurted out before dashing out of the clearing, Cain was taken aback before he slowly forgot about it.. If you were to tell him about Abel at that moment, he wouldn't know what you were talking about.

They chased each other around for hours and hours, Cain continued to stumble and fall over his own feet as he struggled to catch Abel, he was just too quick and agile, he took risks too.. Jumps Cain would never even think of doing, climbing up dead trees which could fall over at any moment.

After a while the beautiful sun slowly began to sink below the mountains, baking the sky into a calming amber which wrapped around them all like a comforting hug.

Cain and Abel sat on top of their roof, watching the sun set with shining eyes.

Abel burped and Cain giggled, they fell silent as they let the gentle sounds of nature wash over them.

Abel laid back on the roof and looked up into the sky, his eyes shining gently.

"Cain..?" he asked gently, like he was trying to not be heard.

"Yeah Abel?" Cain turned to him and smiled.

"Why do you think some people have miracles.. And others don't?" Abel asked, his eyes narrowing.

"Hmm.. I don't know" Cain scratched his head.

"We're all God's children are we not? So why are some given better than others?" Abel keeps looking straight up into the sky, his shining pink eyes reflecting the last remaining amber of the sunset.

Cain shrugs, sticking his tongue out.

"I don't know, but God knows what he's doing! I bet there's a great explanation!" Cain said, hope in his eyes and a smile on his face.

Abel chuckled and sat up.

"Yeah, I bet you're right"

They continued to watch as shadows enveloped the once peaceful sky.. Coating it in an inky black which threatens to reach out and grab you at any moment, they quickly make their way back inside their house.

Abel looked out the window before his father and mother tucked him to bed, saying goodnight.

Cain looked over to Abel, he could feel it.. A sense of wonder and uncertainty.. Like a curious lizard trying to make its way out of Abels brain.

As the lamp went out and the two were drenched in that same inky black that the outside world saw.. Cain spoke.

"..you have a lizard in your eye"

"What?" Abel asked, confused.

"...Nothing" Cain turns over and falls asleep.

Abel shrugs and slips into sleep too, their gentle breathing only heard by that inky black.

Abel stood up, he was now 14, he wore a tight fitting black shirt and had styled his red curly hair back into a shorter style, his baggy brown trousers remained torn and shredded. He made his way to the front door, a glint in his pink eyes.

"Abel dear, come eat breakfast with your family first" Eve said gently, her voice was as soft as snow and as soft as velvet.

Abel pauses and groans, looking down at the floor.

"I have stuff to do maaaaaa" he said, irritated.

Adam spoke, his calm words and gentle breath filled the air with comfort and care.

"Please listen to your mother, she made plums for breakfast!" he said, smiling kindly.

Cain sat in mostly silence, slowly eating his plums, he looked a little shaggier now, he had the hints of stubble on his chin and was just over 17. He wore some beige shirts and white trousers.

Abel sighed and decided to accept, he sat down and began to eat the plums from his plate, they were quite tasty, their juices filling Abels mouth forcing him to swallow more than he'd want to.

Cain finished his plate and stretched.

"Thank you mother, I shall be heading to my room now" Cain said, burping.

"Nah you're coming with me!" Abel said as he leapt to his feet, grabbing Cain by his collar and pulling him along.

"Eep!" Cain exclaimed and tried to pull away from his brother's grasp but couldn't, he was pulled through the door.

"Keep your brother safe Cain!" Called Eve before leaning back into her chair with a sigh.

"Kids these days, amiright?" Adam said with a chuckle.

"Oh stop it Adam hehe, I mean we were kids one day too" Eve said, smiling to herself.

Adam paused, thinking back through the hundreds of years they had existed.

"...Nope, we actually never were children" Adam said, a small tone of sadness in his voice.

"Oh.. yeah.." Eve said, her shoulders sinking.

Adam pats her head and hugs her.

"It's okay, how about we go to bed and do some knitting"

"Yay knitting!" Eve shouted before they both chuckled.

They indeed do some knitting, where do you think most of Cain and Abels clothes came from?

No sex in my holy book I say.

Two figures dashed through the woods, their shapes blitzing from tree to tree, one shape was clearly better at this than the other.

Cain ran straight into a half fallen tree, grunting as he fell to the ground with a thud, leaves kicked up into the air from the fall. Abel chuckled as he appeared above Cain, offering him a hand.

Cain groans and takes his hand, he gets pulled up and rubs his head.

"Why do you even wanna do this shit?" Cain grumbles as he slowly heals, Abel chuckles and backflips through the air, landing on a branch of a nearby tree.

"Don't you see this world and just wanna.. Run!? Explore everything, find the answer to everything!" Abel exclaimed as he leapt from one tree to another, his eyes sparkling with wonder.

"Eh.. not really, I got enough stuff to deal with myself" Cain rubbed his neck and slowly followed Abel as he launched through the woods.

Abel skids to a halt into a pile of leaves, chuckling to himself.

"Come on! When are you gonna get out of this boring slump ya got?" Abel jumps up to a branch and wraps his legs around it so he can hang upside down.

Cain walks past him, pushing him away by his face.

"I don't know how it works, but I'm pretty sure that's not how it works" Cain grumbles to himself.

Abel flips back to his feet and bounces as he walks besides Cain, they move through the crowded forest, the sun glints through the treetops again, shining right into Cain's eyes.

He looks around at the forest, he sees a fox in the distance going about its day.

He trods through dry leaves which snap and crunch beneath his feet every step of the way.

Abel is bouncing off tree to tree, unable to stay still.

"Let's do something cool!" Abel says, smiling wide.

"No thanks.." Cain grunts, his butterscotch voice as low as a flute can go.

"Awwww but Caaaaiiiinnnnnnnnnnnn" Abel draws out his words in that annoying way again, Cain grunts.

"Fine, you do something.. I'll just watch.." he eventually says, adjusting his shirt.

"Yay!" Abel instantly begins to run full speed to the left, dashing deeper and deeper into the forest, Cain reluctantly follows him.

Eventually he pushes through a large set of bushes to find Abel standing at the edge of a large ravine which seems to slowly cascade down into oblivion.

"...Oh hell no" Cain said plainly as he grabbed Abels shoulder and pulled him back.

"Cainnnnnnn! I'll be fine! This is gonna be fun!" Abel bounces up and down.

"No, it's.. Well I don't know the exact words for it but self death is not good that's all I know" Cain shrugs and keeps a firm grip on Abels shoulder.

"Just one jumppppppp after that I won't bother you ever again!"

Cain looked at Abel, then back down at the darkness which the ravine dips into.

"Nah, I can handle your annoying ass" Cain shrugged.

"If you don't let me I'll tell mom and dad about the girl you kiissseeedddddd" Abel said teasingly, a cheeky grin on his face.

Cain paused, thinking about how they may react..

Eve: *"How could you do this to our family!?"*

Adam: *"no son of mine will be kissing women! Only men!"*

Eve: *"(wailing noises)"*

That's one way it could or maybe it goes something like..

Eve: *"I'm so proud of my baby"*

Adam: *"yes son, we're proud of you and we need to meet this girl for a meal of nothing but fruits and seeds as our tradition"*

Eve: *"What tradition?"*

Adam: *"the one I made up just now"*

Yep. Cain didn't want either of those things to happen, he looked back at Abel and sighed.

"Fine." Cain took a step back and let go of Abels shoulder.

Abel chuckled and prepared himself, he did a few stretches before leaning off the ledge of the ravine, he took a deep breath before he leaped through the air.

Cain peaked over the ledge to see Abel fall through the air at speeds, he crashes into the other side of the ravine and then slips.. His foot refuses to give grip on the moss as he's sent stumbling and falling down the ravine.

Cain goes cold as he could feel the pure fear shooting off of Abel as he reaches out for something to grab him..

He fell into the blackened abyss below, Cain shouted out and rushed, sliding down the ravine on his back, his hand gripping into the moss to try and control his descending speed.

He quickly reached the ledge where all light seemed to stop and shouted.

"ABEL!" Cain shouted out, his eyes widening.

There was no response..

Cain quickly looked up into the sky and shouted out.

"GOD! Help me get down there and bring Abel out!" he shouted up into the heavens for help...

And yet nothing happened..

"GOD!? GRANDPA!?"

No one came.. Cain's mind began to panic, unsure of how to feel, his body began to shudder and shiver as his emotions fight against each other to rip and pull at his skin, he felt his insides twist and burn.

He begins to pant and shakily breathe...

"Abel! Abel! Do you hear me!?" Cain snaps his eyes back to the sky and shouts.

"God! DO SOMETHING!"

Again.. Silence..

And something clicked in his mind, he spun on his heels and dove into the darkness, his body fighting against itself as the emotions tore at each other like rabid dogs..

And so there was silence... such piercing silence as the trees stopped their whistling rustle and listened..

Something flapped.. Something rotten... as something pulled Abel out of the ravine, his head had a light injury on the back, he was unconscious..

And God did nothing...

Nothing but watch..

As Cain hugged Abel tight, tears flowing down his face..

Chapter 10:
This is War, Ecclesia

Black.

That's all Cain saw for a moment, a pure pitch darkness.. One that reminded him of that inky black which would listen to his sleeping breaths, its eyes never seen and yet always there.

He struggled against the feeling of restraint, like his muscles refused to listen to him. He pulled and wrenched at his own body, his own muscles fighting each other to move.. To open his eyes.

He heard a familiar voice, one which cut through the inky black like a razor through skin. His eyes snap open as his tired and broken body aches in retaliation.

"Hey, don't move, just rest" said a young voice, hope simply spilled into the air with every word he spoke.

Cain found himself half sitting up with his shirt off and covered in bandages with some strange smelling liquid on his cuts and bruises. He looks over to see Son Aaron sitting in a chair right next to him, he had his casual clothes on and yet retained that collar.. The black and white burn into Cain's mind.

There's a certain silence in the room as Cain's eyes widen and his pupils sharpen into blades as he looks at Son Aaron, suddenly his weak body is filled with an unbridled emotion he couldn't identify.. It bubbled and boiled at the surface of his flesh, his skin began to ache and stretch as it attempted to contain the force...

The silence was like one of a predator about to strike down a prey.. Son Aaron's eyes widened lightly as he noticed Cain's flesh bend and buckle under the extreme weight of the emotions..

Son Aaron spoke, his mouth moved and the air vibrated.. It reached Cain's ears and yet he never heard it.. His mind simply repeated one phrase..

"Kill. Kill. Kill. Kill. Kill. Kill" he must kill him, he was one of them.. One of those who- images flashes through his mind of blood and bone, something threatened to burst to the surface when-

"Calm" Son Aaron said, his voice soft and peaceful, suddenly the emotions vanished.. Cain felt.. Hollow, his body instantly slumped as it wasn't strong enough to hold him upright.

He collapsed back into the soft couch which bent under his weight, he growled.. His weakened mind tried to lash out but.. Couldn't? His emotions weren't writhing beasts threatening to spill, they were nothing but breezes in his own mind..

"What.. are.." Cain began, it was painful to speak though and he shut up, slowly going limp.

"It's my miracle.." Son Aaron said, pulling back, his hand slowly glowed gold. There was a hint of regret in his tone as he spoke, his light golden brown eyes soft and relaxed.

Son Aaron was wearing a dirty white button up shirt and some black trousers which were tucked into shorts. He noticed Cain wince as he swallowed and stood up.

"I'll go get you some water!" he said, his eyes lighting up and a small kind smile appearing on his face.

He quickly rushed out of the room, heading down a nearby hall to get some.

Cain finally looked around the room.. It was about 7 metres long and 6 or so across, the walls were painted a pure white and the ceiling had this interesting gold pattern woven into the paint.

He lay on a soft red couch, also in the room lay several chairs, one big comfy looking chair, a long table in the corner with some first aid materials on it.

And finally a small stool where Son Aaron had been sitting before.

Cain groaned, wincing his eyes, his body was broken and raw.. He could barely feel his legs and hands, the emotions inside of him began to grow power but were still far too weak to burst from him.

His face retained his usual emotionlessness.. But this time he couldn't hold it, he could feel his breathing get shallow and his eyes moist.

The images.. The thoughts.. The sounds.. It was too much for him and his facade broke, he gritted his teeth and tears flowed down his face.. Getting trapped in the intricacies of his stubble as they flowed down to his jaw and cheek.

He grunts as he slowly grips the side of the sofa, he tries everything in his power to sit up but the agony which throbbed in his chest was too much and he fell limp again panting, sweat began to bead upon his forehead.

Son Aaron came back into the room carrying a large jug of water, he sat down and quickly took out a smaller glass to pour some out. He hands a glass to Cain for him to drink, Cain slowly reaches for it.. Wrapping his bruised fingers around it he slowly began to sip.

The cold water slipped past his parched and ashy lips as they fell onto his tongue, coating it in a cool moisture which sent shivers through him, it slid to the back of his throat, drenching his uvula in its sparkling perfection.

He swallowed, his throat forcing it down him, it completely soaked his oesophagus and hydrated him.

He reached out the glass for some more, Son Aaron quickly poured some more and Cain chugged it, forcing it down his throat, he asked for another and swallowed that too.

He suddenly began to sit up, the water flowed throughout his body, slowly calming his burning and tense muscles as a coolness washed from him..

He gasped after finishing his last drink and bent forward, resting his elbows on his knees. Son Aaron smiled at him.

"Do you feel better-" Son Aaron began but suddenly he dodged Cain's sloppy punch.

"Die.. Die... Die.." Cain repeated in a hushed and sandpaper tone under his breath.

"Cain, please.. I don't want to hurt you"

Son Aaron backed up, his eyes narrowing as he dodged a weak tackle from Cain, he stumbled to his feet and caught himself before he fell..

"...Kill.. Kill.. Kill.." the emotions begin to build up in Cain again, trying to pull at his skin and push out of his mouth..

Son Aaron quickly placed his hand on Cain's shoulder and spoke gently.

"Calm.." he said gently and Cain could feel his emotions vanish like a candle blown out by a gentle whistle.

He felt hollow.. Empty.. Like his skeleton had been taken from him.

Cain crashed into the ground, falling like a great oak with a crash and crunch.

"Oh Jeez! Sorry there!" Son Aaron reached out to help him up but Cain lashed out, snarling.

"What do you think you're doing!?" he snapped, his eyes wild.

"I'm trying to help.." Son Aaron said gently, pulling his hand back so it doesn't get bitten off.

Cain grunts as he forces his muscles to work together and forces him back to his feet, he wavers, his mind not ready.. But his determination was.

"You're one of them" Cain snarled.

"Them?" Son Aaron asked, genuine concern in his voice.. Cain cracks, he begins to laugh.. A pale crooked laugh.

"Haha..hah.. Hahaha.. You don't know?" Cain wheezed as his body went limp once more, slamming into the wall.

"..Know what?" he tilted his head, not approaching Cain this time.

"..Your.. kind? Your.. people?.. I.. Priests.. They slaughtered my.. The Snake's Burrow" Cain wheezed out, gripping onto the side of the doorframe.

"You mean the terrorists?"

"THEY WEREN'T- they.. Just..." Cain groaned, his balance went off and he almost fell over.

"...they kinda blew up a church.. I think that counts as terrorism" Son Aaron said, shrugging anxiously.

"...fuck.." Cain groaned and stumbled forward, using the walls to help prop him up. "..yeah.. I guess you're right.."

Cain sighs, chuckling to himself.. The emotions boil once more, threatening to spill from his flesh and yet.. He slips them down deep into his chest as he takes another confident step.

He was getting used to this now, his weight distribution was different but he didn't care. Cain's eyes light up with a flare of rage and hatred as he marches towards the front door, Son Aaron steps out into the hall behind him and shouts out.

"Wait, Cain! You're in no condition to leave!" He called out, trying to pull Cain back but he kept going, ignoring Son Aarons attempts.

"..They.. killed.. Them.. hahahahahaha.. Hahaha.. HAHA.. they call me the murderer and treat me like shit!? FUCK YOU SAINT PETER!"

Cain screams, his face contorts to one of madness, his eyes flicker as he rip opens the front door and slams it into his skull.

"FUCK YOU AND YOUR HIPOCRITIC-" Cain continues to slam the door into his face, his skin splits and crimson spills.

"CAIN STOP!" Son Aaron shouts out, trying to stop Cain from hurting himself.

"-MURDEROUS, PREACHY FUCKING ASS-" he crunches his skull into the door, spraying his vile liquid onto the clean floor.

"-THIS. IS. **WAR!**" Cain screams, his body contorting and changing into something.. Something very.. Very.. na-

Son Aaron touches him, his hand glows golden.

Cain falls limp, his body collapsing out cold on the harsh stone floor, Son Aaron sighs and picks him up, barely being able to lift his body weight as he grunts and gasps while dragging him back to the couch.

Several hours had passed before Cain slowly began to wake up, the gentle clatter of pots and pans echoing into his ears and forcing his eyes to snap open.

He looked around, it was dark now.. Night. The inky black threatened to slip through the windows but was kept at bay by the candlelight which filled the room with its warm flicker.

Cain groaned, his body ached and throbbed but he was able to move, he slowly shifted his body so he's sitting up before noticing something besides him. He turns his head and sees a bowl with some rice, carrots and egg. It was still warm, steam slowly rose from the meal and slipped into his nose.

The smell was heavenly.

He looked around, seeing no sign of Son Aaron before slowly taking the nearby fork and grabbing a bite, as soon as it slipped into his mouth he stopped. The taste exploded in his mind, a flurry of spices and savoury tastes he'd never experienced before, his eyes widened and he began to chow down all of it.

As he scraped out the last bits of rice from the sides of the bowl he heard a set of light footsteps. He pauses, placing the bowl down and narrowing his eyes, a gentle pulse of emotion gurgled deep inside of him, his eyes were cold and emotionless as he watched the doorway.

Son Aaron walked into the room, he paused and smiled.

"You're awake!" he said, a warmth washed over the room from his voice alone.

Cain remained tense and stressed, his sore muscles screaming at him to stop and relax and yet he stood. His figure is that of an apex predator.

Son Aaron blinks and rubs his neck.

"Hehe, I hope you liked the dinner I made of you-" he was interrupted by Cain's shout.

"Bastard!"

Cain lashed out, trying to punch Son Aaron across the jaw but he blocked, his golden touch stopping Cain where he stood.

"...." Cain remained silent, his breathing was shallow and shaky.

Son Aaron sighed and tried a comforting smile.

"I really don't want to hurt you.."

"...I'm leaving" Cain said as he slowly walked past Son Aaron.

"You're in no shape-"

"Don't want to hear it" Cain waved him away and reached the door.

"Look! You don't just get to run away!" Son Aaron barked, finally getting ticked off.

"I can do what I please" Cain scoffed as he reached for the door handle.

"You fucking blew up Saint Peter's church! You tried to kill him and you're not even wondering why I'm STILL trying to help you!?" Son Aaron tensed his arms so they shook.

Cain paused, his eyes shining gently.. He slowly turns to Son Aaron.

"Why are you trying to 'help' me then?"

Son Aaron let out a breath and let his shoulder sag.

"Because unlike you, I trust in God's plan.. I know he made us meet for some reason, and I think I can save you"

Cain burst out laughing, he put his hand to his head and doubled over.

"Hahaha, save me? Save me from what!? Save me from killing those who have hurt others? From avenging my brother? From avenging Snake's Burrow?"

His eyes were wild as he stared deep into Son Aarons soul, the feeling of the air was tense.. Dark tendrils of seeping hatred slowly spun through the air, heading straight towards Son Aaron.

"You just don't get it.. There is a purpose for everything! Even in our darkest moments it is our trust and belief in God which leads to everything leading to happiness" Son Aaron said, placing a hand on his chest.

"..You don't know God.. you don't know his thoughts or his feelings.. And if everything is a part of a plan.. What God would send your priests to slaughter my friends? Kill them without mercy?" Cain hissed through his clenched jaw as he stood tall over Son Aaron.

"You must be mistaken, they wouldn't do that" Son Aaron shakes his head.

"I'll show you" Cain tilts his head upwards, looking down at Son Aaron.. He pauses and thinks before nodding.

"Fine, show me proof of this event and i'll reconsider"

Cain took a deep breath and spun on his heel, he reached out for the handle as the inky black swirls around them..

Cain and Son Aaron now stood in the middle of a thin alleyway in the middle of the night, the pitch black darkness surrounded them with inky reassurance.

They stood in front of an old iron door, Cain wasted no time and kicked it, the lock snapped on the inside and it swung open with an old creak.

Son Aaron held up a lantern, turning it on.. Its warmth bakes the surrounding area and pushes back the blackness which tries to envelope them.

As they step inside Cain furrows his brow.. The floor beneath them is clean, no dried blood remains pasted against the stone floor.

"Where did this happen?" Son Aaron asked gently, looking around.

"...It was here.. It was right here.." Cain mumbled under his breath..

"I see no sign of murder or violence.." Son Aaron said, moving forward.

Cain quickly slipped into Esther's old room and- empty.. It was all empty..even the creaky floorboards were gone, replaced with the dusty stone beneath them.

No blood soaked into the walls or floors, Cain dashed between room to room desperately searching for any sign of blood or violence but found nothing..

"..Maybe you hallucinated it? I hear smoke is very bad for your brain-"

Cain grabs Son Aaron by the throat and pins him to the wall with a thud.

"You did this, didn't you? You set me up, You're trying to make me believe this didn't happen! You fucking spy!" Cain snarled, his teeth clenched and his eyes that of a vicious animal.

"Please.. Cain..." Son Aaron struggles, dropping the lantern.. It shatters on the ground and they both hear voices.

"Hello? Who's there?"

Cain instantly lets go of Son Aaron and slips into a nearby room, pinning his back to the wall and holding his breath.

Son Aaron coughs and looks up, four priests walk into view.

"Who goes there?" they shine a lantern into the claustrophobic hall, Son Aaron waves to them, still coughing.

"Son Aaron?" One of them said, shocked.

"What's happened to you?"

"Oh I just dropped my lantern and the.. Fumes made me cough" he winced and tried to smile.

"Oh.. well this place is off limits to Priests" said another, her voice thick and sturdy.

"I-I knew that, just saw the door was broken so I came in to investigate" Son Aaron said, slowly getting his breathing back under control.

Cain's eyes narrowed, he slowly etched closer to the open door, his emotions beginning to flare up.. Rage buckles and pushes on his bones and ribs.. He could kill them all.. Right here, right now.

His body could contort.. And he could do very not nice things..

His mind was slowly getting dizzy, the images of the Snake's Burrow massacre flashed in his mind.. His body began to shake and his breathing hissed out of him like gas.

"Oh right.. Well you need to be careful Son Aaron"

"Oh?" he asked, rubbing his throat.

"Saint Peter has given out an order for all Priests to travel in groups of at least four.. Cain is on the loose and dangerous, did you not hear about this?" said the female voice again, her tone was serious.

"Oh.. I guess not.. Hehe I'm sure I can handle myself though so don't worry" he said anxiously.

"Maybe, but you're not the one to go through with the rest of the order"

Son Aaron narrows his eyes.

"What's the rest of the order?" he asked cautiously.

"The Church is at war. We kill Cain on sight, an order from God himself"

Son Aarons eyes widen as Cain takes a dagger sharp breath.

Chapter 11:
Falsus Angelus

A man danced back and forth throughout the empty and vast room, the cracked marble floor and tired granite ceiling bend and warp with each step he takes.

He spins on his heel and lifts up his leg, posing like a ballerina as he dances to a song invisible to all.

He spins and pirouettes and lands on one foot, he looks up into the open skylight and speaks through the inky black.

His pale face and shining blue eyes a perfect canvas for emotion and art.

"Oh God, Oh God, I thank thee for gifting me such bright light and wonder as your Gospel!" St. Peter smiled into the ever watching ink.

"I shall make you proud oh father oh mine oh may I have your blessing to be your child!?" his voice spoke soft and yet his throat spoke loudly, it echoed across the empty room.

He listens to words none hear.. On a pedestal of which no one will ever see, and he smiles and dances.

"Oh great God of mine, how much you have given me in gift and chance.. For it is my wish to serve you! And to kill Cain is my chance!"

He dances through the air, leaping high and using his wings to slowly descend like a fairy touching the ground.

His smile was thin lipped and unreasonable, his eyes sparkled like diamonds stuck in tar.

"I have always believed in your power oh father great! I cannot believe your child would betray you like this! First he kills your spawn and now he tries to kill your last remaining child, me~" he posed, sweeping his ivory white hair behind his ears.

The wind blows and rustles as the inky black shifts and changes.

"I understand father! I know what I must do! My priests are puny compared to me and you! Our connection is power and bliss immense!" he laughs as he bows backwards, simply staying floating against all gravity, his angelic wings spreading wide.

"Oh to be a world born angel, how euphoric!" he clutches onto his own arms, caressing his smooth skin.

The inky black shifts once more and the moon rings to but one figure who could hear.

"Yes, I apologise for my great misdeeds oh father great! I shall accomplish your task not a minute late!"

He continues to dance, his smile inhumanly wide as his closed eyes glow and gleam, his graceful body careens through the air as euphoria envelops him whole.

But oh reader, did you realise that I still lie?

For yes what I told you did happen, but what I failed to correct was that he was not alone in that vast room..

For Caleb was strung up into the air in needle sharp thread which sank into his skin and made him bleed into a brass bowl, his constant and slow dripping echoed as a backdrop to St. Peter's music.

Caleb's eyes were filled with tears of pain and hollow, as his very body bled.. It bled for god..

And it bled for the false angel who drank it.

Chapter 12:
Dead Drop Coordinates

Two figures walked across the wild and untamed lands, one of them slipped over the tree roots with ease while the other continued to stumble and had trouble keeping up.

The sky was slowly being baked in a light purple as the gentle echo of the sun rose, shining the palest light on them.

One had dark and smooth skin, a mark of "GOD" which burned into his forehead, a tattoo of a dagger with a snake handle on his neck and some stumble on his face. He wore nothing but bandages and trousers, he didn't mind the cold, the mosquitos avoiding him.

The one which stumbled behind him was sweating profusely, his shirt was now damp and his feet ached and screamed at him from how many times he'd accidentally slammed them into tree roots. He continued to swat the mosquitoes away.

"Please.. I know you're God's creature.. But please leave me alone" he panted, the pale light shining on his light brown skin, his golden brown eyes shining with hope even in the palest lights.

Cain continued to move forward, his footsteps crushing anything which so happened to be below his step, his eyes were emotionless, his body slowly healing.. Even though his muscles screamed in agony.. He kept walking.

They had been walking all night, Bethel was nothing but a distant speck within the large greenery of the forests. They were making their way up a large mountain now, every step became steeper and steeper.

"Cain.. can we.. please.. Rest..." Son Aaron gasped, his legs were numb and he barely was able to drag himself up the hill anymore, the mosquitoes continued to divebomb him.

"You shouldn't even be following me" Cain said in a low tone, his eyes stuck ever forward, making his way higher and higher.

"You.. need.. Help.. guidance.." Son Aaron collapsed to his knees but he managed to pull himself up with a gasp, he was basically dead at this point.

"You heard God, it's an order to kill me on sight, so go on.. Try it" Cain didn't even look behind him as he said it, emotions flowed off him like steam, each one a slightly different tint.

"That's.. Not.. it.. There must be some misunderstanding! If we just let you and Saint Peter talk it out-" he collapses again, coughing.

Cain continues to move, his burning legs only motivating him to go further, his eyes scan the oncoming environment, they are about to enter a small forest.

"Talk with him?.. Not gonna happen" Cain said plainly as he jumped up to a nearby tree root, balancing.

"Please, this doesn't have to be a war or anything-" he collapses again, pulling himself up to his numb and screaming legs.

Cain shakes his head as he weaves around trees.

"Your view on the world is very.. Very flawed" Cain's ears pricked up.. Something was coming, although he couldn't fully sense it as his body was not in peak shape.

"No.. I'm optimistic!" Son Aaron said with a gasp as he landed on a tree stump.

"Exactly, Flawed" Cain grabbed a few branches which were in his way and tore at them, ripping them in twain with a satisfying crunch and snap before throwing them behind him and moving forward.

"No.. I..." Son Aaron just goes limp, unable to fully catch his breath he just lays there and tries to rest.

As Cain moves through the woods he looks around him.. At how the leaves crunch beneath his torn and muddy shoes.. How the gentle sounds of bird song could be heard echoing within the shards of green that is the woods.

He sniffs the air, it smells of old rain, he smiles lightly.. He just can't help it, that smell has always helped him.

He continues moving forward with more vigour, his legs hurting less and less as the air around him becomes thicker with moisture and the smell of old rain, the trees still dripping wet from whenever the clouds passed by.

His smile grew and grew.. It almost let him forget about everything and just.. Exist.

Exist within the moment, think about nothing but the present, not caring about the past or worried about the future.

But of course that did not last for long, as an ear splitting crack sound was heard as the creaking trees all began to bend and buckle..

Completely healthy trees all began to fall on him, Cain's eyes snapped open and he didn't miss a mark. He launched himself through the woods, ducking under and jumping over fallen or falling trees.

Eventually he rolls into a small little burrow in the side of the hills, the trees crash against the ground with a massive might sending dust flying into the air.

Cain groans, slowly making his way back out of the burrow and looking around.. What a nice forest.. Now gone.

Son Aaron stumbles close again, gasping in panic and exhaustion.

"What just happened!?"

Cain answered plainly as he pocketed his hands.

"God tried to kill me, simple as"

Son Aaron goes silent, his jaw opens slightly as he thinks.. Cain simply turns on his heel and makes his way higher and higher through the mountain.

He remembers the old days.. When he and Abel used to come up this way..

He saw two figures in the distance.. And he smiled.. One leapt from tree to tree.. The other stumbled behind, trying to keep up.

"What are ya lookin at?" Son Aaron turned to look where Cain was staring.. He saw nothing but a distant wood which leads into a river.

"Nothing. Mind your own business" Cain scoffed, going back to staring ahead his golden and amber eyes shine.

They make their way through a patch of tall grass, Cain crushing the grass in front of him with each step while Son Aaron actually got a bit lost, drifting away from Cain.

Cain blinks, not thinking about it much before he sees something move just out the corner of his eyes, a shape shifting through the grass.

The shape was small, not bigger than a small cat.. His eyes widen as he jumps into the air avoiding the snake as it tries to bite his ankle.

He quickly grabbed it by the neck and threw it, sending its little noodle body spiralling out of view and landing outside the tall grass with a thud.

"..Another try.. So this is how it's gonna be huh?" Cain said, looking up at the gentle blue clouds which gleamed in the pre-dawn.

Cain sighed, he continued his way until he pushed past all the tall grass, he was getting closer to the peak now.. Son Aaron calls out, clearly lost.

"Hello? Cain? How big is this field?"

Cain smirked with a toothful grin and shouted back.

"Oh yeah it's suuuuper big, just keep going!" Cain snickered to himself and carried on.

"Okay!" Son Aaron continued walking around in semi circles.

Cain slowly made his way towards the peak, now having to climb over large boulders which seemed to pierce from the ground, he leapt from one to the other as the path got incredibly steep.

He treated the stones as platforms as he begins to make his journey to the top, he leaps onto the second to last stone and- it shifts, breaking away from the earth it dislodges.

It sends both itself and Cain into a freefall, his eyes widen and his jaw clenches.

He quickly lashes out, stabbing the ear with his hand and digging his fingers into it so he has a good grip, the dirt bursts from the hole he's made, some of it floats into his mouth and he spits.

He pulls himself back to his feet and climbs onto the nearest stone.. It slips, pulling itself from the cliff face as it descends, rolling all the way down the hill.

"Fuckin hell.."

He braces himself and punches the dirt in front of him, it explodes into a small hole where he can place his foot, he climbs up, using punches and kicks to dig his own platforms into the side of the rocky and crumbling cliff.

He grips the grass on the top and hauls himself up, rolling over and getting to his feet with a quick kick. He lets out a deep sigh and takes a breath.

"That was cool!"

Cain's eyes snap open again and he sees a panting Son Aaron laying on the grass in front of him.

"How the hell did you get here..." he growls.

"Oh I found like.. A path that just leads up here" Son Aaron points to a nearby path which wraps around the mountain to the peak.

Cain takes a deep breath and sighs.

"Of course you did.."

He looks out over the surrounding landscapes, the sun was just beginning to rise now, its orange brilliance glowing against Cain's dark and smooth skin.

The sky changes to an amber fading into a shallow blue, the clouds were a pale blue with harsh orange highlights.. They swirled through the air peacefully.

"..Why are we even up here?" Son Aaron asked, looking around at the fantastical view.. How they saw caverns and crevices flowing through tall mountains and peaks, how Bethel just seemed like a small speck now..

Cain said nothing, the instructions still clear in his mind

"Adam resides on the north side of the blue mountain in a farmland with three red roses on the front gate.. Goodbye Cain, I hope you told me the truth.."

Rage bubbles and boils under his skin, small pieces of him burned and turned to charred ash.

He pauses... his eyes lighting up as he notices it, in the distance, hidden between two smaller hills, a large green and lush garden surrounded by farmland.. A beautiful cottage sits in the middle of it all with three small red roses..

Son Aaron looks up to Cain, he furrows his brows in wonder.. He hears Cain say something under his breath.. Something which brings silence to the mountaintop..

"Father.."

Chapter 13:
Oblitus Somnia

The sound of rushing footsteps echoed through the hallowed wood as deep laughter followed.

Something blitzed between the trees, a boy.. No.. a young man in a torn and tight black shirt with red curly hair and some crimson stubble jumping from tree to tree.

"CAAAIIINNNN!" Abel shouts, bursting from the treeline and flying through the air, he lands against the grass and slides.

Cain looks up suddenly, his black hair falling in front of his eyes, he puffs it out the way. He's working on building some sort of house, he has a saw in his mouth, he takes it out and waves.

"Ay Abel!" Cain's eyes sparkled and he smiled wide.

Abel chuckled and quickly made his way over to Cain, he looked much older now, around early 20's. Cain was a little older, his stubble starting to follow grow in.

"What's all this then?" Abel said, placing his hands on his hips and shifting his weight to his right foot.

"I asked Grandpa for the gift of building, and I got a bunch of tools!" Cain said, pointing to the pile of tools on the floor.

Abel nodded, pursing his lips.

"Neat, you still callin him grandpa?" Abel laughs, pointing some finger guns at Cain.

Cain's smile turns to a grumpy frown.

"Yeah? So what!? He is my Grandpa!" Cain crossed his arms.

Abel shrugged.

"I dunno, you're just kinda related to him by proxy" he chuckled.

Cain pointed at Abel.

"We both know we have miracles other people don't! That's proof we're related!"

Abel chuckles and flashes his cocky yet endearing smile.

"Seems like your 'God' complex is talkin hahahaha"

Cain pouts and sits down in a grump.

"Aw come on Cain, I'm just messing with ya need any help building this house?" Abel gestured to the somewhat built foundation, Cain nodded.

"Yeah.. I definitely need help with this, thanks"

Abel wraps his arm around Cain.

"Ay what else are brothers for ya know?"

Cain and Abel worked for hours on the building, slowly constructing a solid foundation and then marking out the different rooms. Cain kept messing up the measurements but Abel managed to help him by telling him his bathroom probably shouldn't be bigger than the kitchen and bedroom combined.

After over 7 hours of work the two men collapse, completely exhausted.

"That.. was.. Tough.." Abel said, chuckling.

"Yeah.." Cain wiped the sweat from his forehead, his smooth dark skin glistening.

Abel blinked, looking up into the clear blue sky.. Not a cloud in sight, he seemed to stare at something beyond the great blue, something Cain couldn't quite see.

"What's your dream.. Cain?" Abel asked, looking over to him.

"My dream? Well I had one a few days ago where I was a tree and-"

"No no.. I mean.. What do you want to do in 20.. 30.. 50 years time?" Abel asked, looking back up into the infinite blue.

"Oh.. Huh.. well.. I wanna make people feel welcome in this world.. I want to make people safe" Cain nods.

"I also wanna meet Grandpa one day.. Up there in the clouds, I've only seen him a few times.."

Abel remains silent, not responding.. Just staring.

"Uh, you?" Cain asked.

"Oh me?.. I want to explore the world! I want to know every type of bug, plant, tree, animal, cloud, rock, water.. Everything.." Abel said, inspiration and determination in his eyes.

"Pff, you're silly there's no such thing as different types of water" Cain giggled.

"There is! I swear I found this big big big lake as far as the eye can see! And the water tasted of salt!"

"How would there be salt in a lake? I don't see the logic"

"Ah whatever" Abel waved it off and went back to staring.

"...Would you leave us? The Village? Me?" Cain asked carefully.

Abel paused.. Thinking..

Then he nodded, determination still strong.

"Yep. I'd travel the world!" Abel jumps up to his feet and puts his hands on his hips.

"I'll document everything! That way we don't have to rely on God for everything and we can do stuff ourselves!" he said, his eyes shining.

"Woah, I mean.. God's pretty cool though, he knows everything already so.. Why bother? Hehe" Cain said, sitting up.

Abel's face fell as he looked down at Cain, his eyes flickering lightly.. Cain could feel the cold chains of disappointing wrap around Abel's wrists.

"...I thought you'd get it.. Eh.. it's fine.. See ya later Cain" Abel waved as he began to walk away.

"Oh.. um.. See ya later Abel!" Cain waved.

"..Sure thing bro!" Abel said back, pocketing his hands and walking into the woods.. Out of sight..

"I should have seen it sooner.. He wanted to run around the world twice over.. I was content with staying and building a happy family..."

"..our drifting apart got worse when the unthinkable happened.."

Cain and Abel stand in a room filled to the brim with people, they're all watching a kid on a clean white bed.. His eyes half closed.. His breathing ragged.. His leg covered in cloth, they could see the infection had spread up his whole body..

"..the first person to ever die in this world.. Was a child.."

His last breath was taken.. And he went limp..

The room was filled with wails and sobs, people didn't understand.. Cain had tears flooding down his face, when he turned to Abel.. he froze..

Abel had nothing on his face.. No emotion.. No sadness, just dark bags under his pale pink eyes.

Abel didn't shed a single tear that day..

"What Irony"

For Cain chased Abel up the hill.. As Abel walked home..

Cain tripped over tree roots and fell into rivers, panting and gasping for air.. As Abel said nothing, and moved with purpose.

"I'm sorry it took so long for me to understand..."

As Cain tried to follow Abel he slipped, the moss giving him no grip as he skidded down a hill, being sent over the ledge into a ravine.. Deep and steep, leading back there.. The darkness.. From all those years ago.

I guess it was his turn now.. He thought to himself as he tumbled towards his possible death..

As Cain began to fall into the darkness.. He felt weightless, he felt the air rush past him, he reached out.. Almost expecting God to take his hand..

And yet..

It was Abel's pale hand which grabbed him, his concerned face was not one of fear but of thinking.. He dug his heels into the rock, finding its imperfections and using them to hook his heel into so he could pull at Cain, lifting him up out of the darkness..

Cain's eyes widened.. As Abel quickly pushed him into a safe spot.

Sweat poured down his face, and yet even so.. He seemed not happy nor angry.. Nor sad nor scared.. He was simply thinking.

"I didn't do enough.. Oh brother of mine.. I failed you.."

Crimson.. Motionless.. The images flashed through Cain's mind..memories he was yet to have..

But oh well.. That's a story for another time.

Chapter 14:
It's Been A While

Cain walked through the beautiful green garden, each step he took crunches into the solace covered dirt, the air itself smelled like home.. Even if the house he once knew was long gone.

Son Aaron stayed at a distance, watching with wide eyes as Cain makes his way up to the cottage, his eyes narrowing.

He reaches the front door and looks down at the three roses..one of them is wilting..

Cain looked back up to the round light mahogany door, he paused.. His emotionless face almost cracks for a moment a massive torrent of memories flooded back into him.. He reaches out to knock when-

The door slowly opens, Cain's eyes widen and he steps back. Behind the door is a small and cosy living room with a fireplace and some flowers in cute little clay pots.

A man stands in the doorway, his skin is dark, he has curly brown hair and perfect apple green eyes.

He wore a white button up shirt and some black trousers.

They both pause.. The air is dead silent, not even a bird threatens to break the peace.. Cain looked upon his father.. And Adam looked upon his son..

"Leave" Adam said, his tone as calm as the ocean waters.

The sky above them slowly begins to warp, wind blows past them as a storm arrives..

"Dad-" Cain begins.

"Leave, now" Adam slams the door shut, the sheer force of it sends Cain stumbling.. He pauses, his body filled with conflicting emotions.. He buries them all and walks up to the door.

He begins to knock aggressively.

"Dad! Open up!" Cain shouts, the door swings open and-

Adam is pointing a revolver at Cain's head, his apple green eyes are sharper than any blade known to man. Cain pauses.

"..What is that?" Cain asked cautiously.

"It's called a gun, a revolver specifically, you can just call it what the locals do. 'A death stick', it takes me clicking one little trigger and your brains are gonna be my new pathway paint" Adam snarls.

Cain pauses and swallows, slowly calming himself down.

"..Dad.. I didn't kill Abel.." Cain spoke with confidence, Adam glanced at the tattoo on the side of his neck and then at the mark of "GOD" burned into his forehead.

"...Don't you think I know that?" Adam hissed, he shifts the revolver in his grip.

"...What?" Cain's eyes widened.

"...I know what happened that day... so does Eve.." Adam said, slowly lowering the revolver..

"But.. why didn't you-" Cain began but Adam barked out, his eyes glowing.

"WHAT DO YOU THINK WOULD HAVE HAPPENED CAIN!? IF WE FOUGHT BACK!? YOU THINK WE'D BE ABLE TO SURVIVE THAT!?" Adam's words were light and shook the air lightly, Cain froze, he didn't say anything..

"WE WOULD HAVE DIED CAIN! EVE WOULD HAVE- I WOULD- You... You would have been taken with him too.. It's fucking God.." Adam lowers the revolver.

"...Dad...I'm going to kill God" Cain said plainly, his breathing was stable, the fear and anxiety and regret which swirled inside of him was forced deep down.

"You're not only insane but you're endangering the world.. Your family.." Adam said gently.

"The family which left me!? The family that never defended me and called me a murderer even though you APPARENTLY KNEW!?" suddenly rage boiled inside of Cain, his skin began to burn and char...

Adam nods, looking at the ground below him with his shining apple green eyes.

"You stand.. NO.. chance.." Adam looked up into the sky, a glare in his eyes.

"I want that bastard dead just as much as you do Cain.. but it's too dangerous.. I know what he's like.. I know the damage he can cause" Adam shook his head.

Cain blinks, a solemn expression across his face.. He lets his shoulders relax lightly.

"...I have an idea... of how I can kill him.." Cain said, his plan slowly clicking into place..

Adam looked up, he narrowed his eyes.

"..What are you saying?" he asked cautiously.

"The apples, dad, the apples" Cain said, letting his eyes darken.

Adam pauses, thinking to himself.

""Would it work dad?" Cain asked, a slight hint of desperation in his tone.

"....." Adam says nothing, his apple green eyes drift off into the corner of the room.

Cain tensed up, if the apples weren't possible... or if he'd misremembered something.. This could mark the end of his journey.

"Dad! Please, remember the story you told me? You took more Apples from the tree and spread them around, please tell me you were telling the truth! Tell me where they are, I can do this!" Cain shouted, stepping closer.

Adam sighed, his eyes having a veil of sad comprehension on his face.

"Yes.. It would work" Adam said quietly.

"Yes! Then I can do this dad! I can kill God!" Cain's eyes lit up with bloodthirsty desperation.

Adam looked into his son's eyes before glancing back at the floor.

"It's not that simple son.." he rubbed his arm.

"Dad, please..."

Their eyes met, a pure apple green staring into a starburst surrounded by amber gold. Adam took a sharp inhale and began to speak in a more subtle and saddened tone.

"The Apples are born from God.. brought into this world with knowledge and power of the most extremes.. All of humanity exists off this one apple alone, their knowledge, their existence is perpetuated through this apple.. Upon consumption of another.. You won't be human anymore Cain, you'll be above us all.. A different breed, you'll sense and see things no other human could ever attempt" Adam finished, letting out a sigh.

"...What's the issue then?" Cain said, he didn't care if he was different.. He needed God dead.

"You're my kid.. Meaning your body is used to the ability of one apple.. Taking another will effect your mental state greatly"

Cain thought about it for just a second, that's all he needed after all, his mind and body swirled into complex and conflicting emotions but he spoke with certainty.

"I will kill God" Cain said, a small smile on his face.

"And I don't care what I have to go through to do it"

Adam nods.. Then he punches Cain, his knuckles cracked against his cheek as Cain sees the world whip around him.. The ground shot out from beneath his feet and his body spun. He crashed into the pathway with a thud.

He groaned as he slowly managed to get up to his feet, his eyes still spinning.

"What was that.. For.." Cain began, only interrupted by a metallic thud.

He looks down to see the revolver by his feet, he glances back up to Adam.

His back is turned to Cain, his eyes glow gently.

"Cain.. If you go through with this.. If you take those apples and you go up there and fight or even kill him.. Don't come back here.. I will kill you myself" his voice was serious, his tone sent a chill down Cain's spine.

"Dad-"

"Adam!.. Call me.. Adam.." he sighed, his eyes growing dimmer.

"..The first apple you need to seek is held within a glass case in a hidden church underneath Bethel, take this gun, and if you fail..."

His apple green eyes pierced through Cain like spears..

"Shoot yourself, because death will be better than what I do to you"

Adam slams the door behind him, locking it with a strange glow.

Cain simply stood there, a shocked expression on his face.. The sky began to cloud over as the first drops of rain hit his face, slowly etching down his cheeks and chin, eventually getting trapped in his stubble.

He nodded and picked up the gun, he didn't know how to use it properly and simply placed it in his back pocket.. He turned to walk away as the rain started to come down harder and faster.

In the distance he saw a beautiful woman with light skin and long red hair..

His mother said not a word to him as she watched him leave.. His head lowered, a gun in his pocket.. And yet, a new goal.. No, not a new goal.. The goal he always had.

But now he knew how to do it

How to kill God.

Son Aaron tried to speak to him, but he walked past him with empty eyes, the emotions that thrashed inside of him were both viscous and calming.. He felt so much better..

As the smell of rain fills the air.

Adam looked out the window with a glance.. He mumbled to himself.

"Let's hope the old man knows what he's doing.."

Chapter 15:
Cain Moriendum Est

Within a darkened room sings the hymns of those that bleed for God.

Their maroon robes cover their faces and bodies, each carrying a stone tablet the size of their head.

The deep and vibrating sounds which echoed through the cobblestone halls would put a chill down the devil's spine.

And in front of them all stands a man.. Nay.. a vessel of god, his skin as pale as paper, his long white hair flowing down his back as his piercing blue eyes shine even in the darkest of nights.

He held himself as his robes flowed and whipped in the wind, his eyes reflecting the perfect moonlight.

"PROPHETS! I SEE IT! I SEE IT NOW!!" St. Peter screams, his voice as light as a feather and yet as heavy as the hands of God.

He points to one of the nearby prophets and they slowly pull down their hood, revealing their pink hair and darker skin.. Her eyes shine bright as she summons a crystal ball, letting the moonlight fill it to the brim with dust of an unknown origin.

She whispers into the orb as the dust begins to sway back and forth, the hymns continue to shake the very ground they stand within.

"OH PROPHET OPHERIA! LEND ME YOUR EYES!" St. Peter yells, his arms outstretched towards the distorted moon.

She takes a breath and her eyes begin to glow.. Opheria, Prophet of Time.. she watches the entire earth move and shift through time, she watches men rise and fall, she watches suns set and birth.. She looks at the figure known as Cain as he marches into Bethel, Priest by his side.. Her eyes shine bright as she looks into the future..

She gasps and falls upon the ground, covering her head and screaming in abject agony as the hymns begin to surround her in a dirty mist.

"TELL ME OPHERIA!!" St. Peter roared, his skin began to be enveloped in the moon's cold touch.

She opens her mouth to speak as a wretched purple energy flows from her.

"CAIN WILL TRY TO TAKE THE APPLE FROM THE UNDERCHURCH, HE WILL CONSUME IT AND BURN THE EARTH!" she screeched, the hymns continued to flow.

"This is not good" St. Peter said, feeling the cold and gentle touch of the moon's hand.

"CAIN MUST DIE!" he chanted to the room.

"CAIN MUST DIE!" they responded.

"CAIN MUST DIE!" Opheria screeched, her body contorting and twisting.

"CAIN MUST DIE!!"

Chapter 16:
Goodbye Peace

Cain slowly made his way into town, the sun had risen on a new day and his eyes were tired, his body twitched as his mind drifted into thoughts. Son Aaron wasn't far behind, he had fallen asleep in a bush for a few hours but was catching up fast.

Cain was lucky enough to sleep walk for a few minutes, but he knew he had no time to waste, God knew of his plan and no doubt something would stand in his way. And so he debated all night, to attack the church which he didn't know existed as soon as possible.. Smart.. Or dumb..

A straightforward and early attack gives the enemy less time to prepare, he was ready for a war.. He didn't like the thought of killing other people, but his body was too tired to reject the thoughts of tearing every priest limb from limb.

However, he would be tired and therefore weaker.. Plus he doesn't even know how to access this church or where the apple is kept.

The second option is to find a safehouse and rest, this would give him a better chance at surviving combat but would give the church at least 6 hours extra to prepare..not only that they could catch him off guard, Son Aaron could find him and betray him.

It was a risky play, he could hang back, try to stay hidden.. Learn of the location and then make a plan..

But Cain wasn't exactly one for plans, he wasn't exactly one for waiting either.. But did they know this? Could they expect a first attack? That means defences would be at an all time high and his level of energy and power be at an all time low..

So maybe waiting WOULD be the best option, I mean after all if he waits long enough their guard should slip up, leading to a perfect strike, he gets the apple and gets out.

Cain didn't have to ponder about his plan of action for too long as he saw two figures in the distance.. Both wearing maroon robes, his eyes widened and he quickly jumped into cover.

He pushed open a random door and slipped inside, hiding as the figures walked past.. Each carried their own stone..

Prophets.. If he came across one, he'd most likely die..

He remembered back to the fight with St. Peter.. How his mind went blank and he let his emotions take over, he remembered his arm being cut off.. But it was back now? Cain blinked and thought about it.. For he forgot when it returned.. He remembered it being healed into a stump when he-

Cain stopped thinking about that, his mind shouting and screaming at him to stop as adrenaline rushed through him.. He began to shake lightly as he clenched his jaw.. The rage came back, he could feel his back begin to burn and bubble but he pushed it down.

Forcing the beast back into its stupid little cage.. He lets out a pained sigh and relaxes, the prophets have moved away.

He suddenly hears footsteps coming closer, he quickly stands up and tries to leave but a figure walks into the room.

They pause.. Cain pauses, realising he'd probably been recognised, he turned his head to see who had caught him..

Ah yes.

Of course..

Father Clemantine snarled as his miracle began to spark, his eyes widened as he pointed at Cain.

"YOU! YOU! YOU!" Father Clemantine screeched, he threw a black orb which tore a hole in his own house, Cain ducked out the doorway and began to sprint.

Father Clemantine quickly rushed out after him, hurtling balls of matter destroying material, they bore holes into the ground and nearby houses as Cain zig zagged across the street as fast as he could before diving around a corner.

Father Celmantine followed, the orbs sparked a black energy as he screeched, Cain managed to slip into a smaller alley and leap over a small wall.

Soon after an orb went flying through it, erasing anything in its wake. Cain hit the ground and rolled, his body screamed at him to move faster, yet his muscles locked up on him and he tripped falling face first into the muddy and sharp cobblestone.

The man carved a hole big enough for him to slip through and he cackled.

"I fucking got you now you terrorist serial killer!" he howled, a large smile on his face.

"Fuck off you old twat.." Cain stumbled to his feet, the man summoned another orb.

"Don't you move sunshine, I'll tear you in half!" he cackled, his crooked old voice like nails on a chalkboard to Cain's ears.

Cain let out a deep breath, his mind scrambled for something to do or say.. He couldn't die like this.. He just fucking got back, he was NOT gonna die like this.

"I've been given express orders to kill you Cain, but I think I'd rather if you BOW!" Father Celmantine throws the orb, it spins through the air and Cain manages to jump out the way.

He goes to say something but another whizzes through the air and hits his knee..

Slicing right through it and erasing the connection between his thigh and calf... his eyes widen with fear as he sees his own leg fall limp, blood spilling out..

He stumbled, the pain took a short while to register, when it did he tensed up and fell, collapsing to the floor.

He looked up into the air with fear enveloping him.. His body twitched and his muscles pulled.. Father Clemantine threw another orb, severing his other leg in two, Cain held back a blood curdling scream.. As it began to rain..

Father Clemantine chuckled as he sauntered towards Cain, a nasty grin on his face.

"What are you gonna do now monster?"

Father Clemantine kicked Cain in the jaw, forcing him to roll.. He coughed blood and curled up, his legs slowly stopped bleeding.. The rain came down harder..

"You gonna try and kill me? With no legs!? HAHA!" Father Clemantine stomps on Cain's chest, cracking his ribs.

Cain winces, his brain too blinded and dizzy to even make him scream, he just grunted and lay there as the pain covered his body, turning him almost numb..

"What you're not gonna answer me huh? You're gonna just ignore me!?" Father Clemantine kicks Cain again, he barely reacts, just lays there twitching.

The rain suddenly begins to piss it down, the raindrops begin to drill into Cain and Father Clemantine, he shakes his head.

"I best leave your head for proof" he chuckles and summons one final orb, he positions himself so he can throw it through Cain's neck and chest.

He raises his arm.

"Any last words?"

Cain opened his mouth to speak and something landed in his mouth.. Rain.. water.. The moment it touched his tongue a cold chill was sent down his spine and his mind became clear.

The pain seemingly faded and his muscles calmed.. Another drop.. Another.. Another..

With each drop of water his body seemed to be.. Healing? How had he never noticed this before.. Something clicked in his mind.. And everything made sense..

He pulled himself out the way last minute, the orb flew through the ground and ate out a circular chunk, he opened his mouth wide and caught as much water as he could.

The smell of rain filled his nose and his eyes lit up, he slowly pushed off the ground and stood up, his legs regrown, fresh.. Weaker than before but there.. Allowing him to stand back up and laugh.

"HAHA! Did you really think it would be that easy old man?" Cain said, a snarl in his voice as his eyes gloss over with anger and new found confidence..

He stuck his tongue out and with each drop of rainwater he took a more confident step, his fresh bones hardened, his muscles cooled and relaxed, they stopped fighting against each other.. Blood flowed easier through his body, his heart beat more efficiently.

The old man snarled and summoned another orb, he launched it at Cain and he dodged to the side, he quickly pulled his hands back and clapped.. He let loose, a flash of fury and fear filled his arms and the shockwave shook the local area.

Father Clemantine stumbled back from the shock, trying to stay standing.

Cain's arms and hands were broken, but he looked up into the sky and drank the rainwater.. As it dripped into his mouth he felt a surge of rejuvenation.. His arms and hands healed and he smiled.

He launched forward, punching the old man in the gut; the sheer force of it broke Father Clemantine's ribs and Cain's hand. As

Father Clemantine fell back, coughing.. Cain drank the rain and felt his hand snap back into place.

"What was that about last words?" Cain hissed, his eyes wide with rage and pride as he stepped on Father Clemantine's shattered ribs. He let out a blood curdling cry into the raining sky.

Cain let rage fill his arms as his body began to boil inside out, his hand turned to charred ash as his skin shed off into embers which floated through the sky.

He slowly lowered down, his smile wide and wild as he lowered his hand to burn Father Clemantine alive, he tried to resist but.. It fails..

Cain placed his hand on Father Clemantine's face and watched as it began to burn and sear his skin, he screamed in pain and as Cain was about to ignite him on fire and melt his brain-

"Calm!" a familiar voice spoke, placing his hand on Cain's shoulder.

Cain blinked, his emotions vanished and he screamed in agony as he lept back, his hand was burned from the inside out.. His muscle basically soup, without his miracle it began to crumble apart... he quickly tried to drink the rainwater but it wasn't working..

Son Aaron looked at him with scared and panicked eyes before rushing to Father Celmantine's side. As his golden touch left Cain his gift slowly returned.. Tears flowed down his face from the agony as the rain barely managed to quell it.

He stumbled, falling to his knees.. Agony painted across his face.. Slowly the gift returned enough for the rain to heal him.. His hand began to regrow skin, bone and muscle tissue.

He fell limp as the pain vanished, he panted.

"What is wrong with you!?" Son Aaron screeched, tears welling up in his eyes.

"..he was going.. To kill me." Cain hissed, slowly getting back to his feet- Son Aaron pushed him.

"Liar!" he shouted, his voice cracking from the overwhelming emotions, Cain glanced at him.. Even with his weakened gift he could see the confusion and sadness leaking from him.

"Liar!!" he screams again and tries to punch Cain, he blocks and sloppily connects a right hook, it connects and there's a cracking thud as the force sends Son Aaron stumbling; blood pouring from his nose.

"I don't lie" he grumbled as he adjusted his stance, his body drained but the rain water slowly gave him back energy.

Son Aaron remained quiet, hiding his tears which flowed down his light brown face.

Cain went silent, slowly lowering his fists..

He looked over to Father Clemantine, he chuckles and smirks with bloodied teeth.

"Fine. But don't follow me anymore Priest" Cain scowled as he walked past Son Aaron, making his way through the wall and into the streets.

Son Aaron watched as Cain walked away, he wanted to say something but didn't.. He leaned down and helped stop the bleeding of Father Clemantine.

"I am sorry father.." he said quietly, taking out some bandages.

"You best be boy! Where have you been!? Have you been speaking with that wretched monster *cough*!?" he hissed and scowled, Son Aaron didn't say anything.

Cain walks through the streets as the rain pours down, he slips into Clemantine's house again and comes back out with a large jug, he points it up to the sky and lets it fill with rain water. He fills it as he finds some scattered clothes lying around.. He finds a black cloak and wraps it around him to his tattoo and face.

As he walks through the torrential rain he feels it drench his clothes, he shivers from the cold.. But smiles, the smell of rain is nice.. He passed by several priests interrogating a young mother about something.. He didn't want to stick around, he pulled the cloak up higher over his face and walked away.

Hours had passed, Cain sat on top of a roof, overlooking Bethel, his tired amber eyes scanning and following any priest.. But he found no trace of this "underground church" that Adam had been talking about, his jug of rainwater sat next to him, now almost full.

Was he tricked? Did Adam lie to make him leave?.. No.. Adam's smarter than that, he knows Cain would return if the apple really wasn't there.. Then where could it be?

He took the gun out from his back pocket and examined it, its glistening metal shining as the rain began to drench it more. His eyes scanning every nook and cranny of the revolver.. He was unsure of its use..

As he examined it he slipped his finger into the trigger guard, he pressed his finger against the cold metal of the trigger and thought to himself, he aimed it like how Adam did..

He saw a small metal bump on the end of the barrel and tried to use that to aim, he pointed it at a nearby statue of God and pulled.

BANG.

The sound shook Cain's mind, he winced and suddenly grabbed his ears as they rang. He dropped the gun onto the roof and tensed his jaw, he opened his eyes and saw the statue had been basically destroyed... the top half of it had crumbled.

"That was fucking loud..." he grunted to himself, he quickly picked it up and looked at it again, he pressed a small button and the revolvers chamber popped out, 5 empty slots and 1 filled with an empty casing..

He didn't have time to figure this out just yet, he picked up his rain jug and began to make his way across the rooftop.. Someone had definitely heard that. He jumped across buildings landing with a wet thud onto the gravel covered roof.

He sighed as he walked ever forward, trying to gain distance from the centre of the sound.. As he steps onto a lower roof he stumbled, cursing the world under his breath.

He then hears a strange snap, at first he assumes he broke something but he felt no pain.. Nothing really.. He looked down, maybe he had stepped onto a weak wooden roof but that was also not the case.

He paused and felt something.. Something moving through the rain, he could feel the slimy and slivering snakes of masochism run up the nearby walls.. And watch him.

So many eyes.. Watching.. Cain spun around but it was too late, his eyes widened as a floating metallic collar connected to a chain snapped shut around his neck, he coughed and his eyes widened before the chain went taught and threw him from the roof.

He cried out as he descended into the street below, he curled up and hit the cobblestone ground with his shoulder first, he could feel a crack and pop as he rolled over to his side with a crash.

The wind rushed from his lungs and he gasped.

Before he could even get his bearings another chain wrapped around him and pulled him to his knees, his head wrenched to face the sky as the chain bound him in that position...

He heard heavy footsteps and a crackling cackle.

"Well, well, well.. You weren't too hard to find" the voice came from a man, he slowly walked into Cain's narrow field of view and Cain paused.. His heart went cold.

The man wore a maroon hood, he had light skin and scars across his face, his hair was an almost silver with blonde highlights.

Vagabond, Prophet of Chains stood before Cain, he put his hand to his head and laughed.

"...." Cain said nothing, he felt the cold steel around his neck and body tighten, he gasped for air and his eyes bulged.

"You've caused quite the commotion, you know that?" Vagabond said, chuckling.

The chains suddenly wrenched Cain into the air so he was dangling by his torso and neck.

He grunts from the pain and pressure.. He looked down below him where his jug of rainwater lay, the gun was in the nearby alleyway far from reach.

Cain's golden and amber eyes glare down at Vagabond.

"Aw don't look at me like that" Vagabond smirks, his sharpened teeth showing. another metal ring snaps onto Cain's calf, his eyes wide as the metal begins to bend and grow spikes which oh so slowly piercing into his skin.

Cain grunts and holds back a scream, his body begins to shake as his mind clouds with pain and emotion.. He feels something give way in his leg and it goes limp.

"And there goes your achilles tendon" Vagabond smirks.

"Simple as" Vagabond waves his arms and more chains fly from seemingly nowhere, they slam into Cain's gut and pierce into him. He grunts and clenches his jaw so hard a tooth fractures.

Something bubbled inside of him.. His eyes shine with rage and pain.. Something very very nasty threatened to burst from him.. The rain poured unnaturally hard, his eyes glance up into the darkened clouds.

He opens his mouth just enough to get rain inside, before he could heal his leg too much a metal ring clamps down onto his jaw, covering his mouth. He growls but it's muffled.

"I'm not taking chances" Vagabond sends another chain into Cain's chest, his screams were muffled.

Metal spikes began to grow from the ring around Cain's neck, slowly threatening to pierce through his skin and into his jugular.

His eyes flash white.. He can't go out like this.. But it's a Prophet.. What else is he supposed to do? He can't win this..

He growls as fear and worry bubbles inside of him, he finally stops holding back.. He goes limp.

"Huh? Dead already?" Vagabond tilts his head, squeezing his neck harder till there's a satisfying snap.

"Yep.. dead I guess" he sighs and walks away whistling.

"Best go tell the boss-" there's a sickening crunch, he pauses..

"Hm?" Vagabond turns a little to see what's going on, Cain's lifeless body is beginning to violently twitch, his bones snapping and breaking against the chains.

"Oh.. this is-" before Vagabond could finish Cain falls out of the chains, slipping past them and landing on his feet.. Vagabond's eyes widened.

Cain's body was murky.. His skin, muscle and bone were all mixing together like some sort of strange slime, his face was featureless goop now. He moves his body in an unnatural way, no longer restricted by bones.

Vagabond growls and suddenly summons dozens of chains which whip and crack at Cain, they strike him and pieces of his body erupt into a colourless glop which flies everywhere.

He stumbles but continues moving forwards, the chains either burst a part of him which grows back or the chains simply go through him..

"You're tricker than I thought!" Vagabond shouts and he flicks his wrist, strange crimson chains burst from the ground and spiral in the air before piercing through Cain's liquid chest.

They slid through him and began to burn him, the chains were hot to the touch.. And yet he simply walks through them, splitting his liquid body in two.

"Ah..this definitely isn't normal" Vagabond chuckles and rips off the maroon cloak, revealing his real outfit. He's wearing tight black leather covered in strange ghostly chains with high boots and an open chest window.

He smirks and whips the ghostly chains around, they smack into Cain's jaw and he actually gets hit. He stumbles into a wall and leaves a chunk of his liquid flesh behind.

"Oh yeah!" he whips the chains again and they strike Cain in the gut and then the face, they didn't pass through him like the other chains did..

Cain stumbles, his emotions flare.. Vagabond whips the chains through the air again, they go to crack against Cain's chest when-

His body reforms and grabs the chain midair, snatching them and crushing them in his hands.. His body reforming its mass as his emotions shift from fear and cowardice to adrenaline fueled anger.

He launches himself across the slippery road. Flying through the air at high speeds he aims an uppercut and reaches Vagabond, his golden eyes shine as he swings his arm high and- misses.

Vagabond slips out the way and strikes Cain in the throat before a chain wraps around him and pulls him away, dragging him across the rough cobblestone road at high speeds, skinning his back.

The chain whips him around and throws him face first into a wall, he cracks into it and falls back.. His head spinning.

"That's a neat trick you got there" Vagabond smiles.

"MIND IF I STEAL IT!?" He shouts as he raises both arms, a new chain forms midair, one made of mud and rock.

Cain raises his hand but before he could block it, it's shoved down his throat, the chain slides down into his stomach and pierces through it..

Cain coughs and tears fill his eyes as chains begin to shoot at him, digging into his flesh and turning before ripping chunks out.. He tries to stand but the chain pulls his stomach out of his own mouth with a rattling clank.

He gasps, blood spraying down his face as he looks at his insides hanging off the end of the chain.

He stumbles, his eyes going blurry..

He feels his body slowly go limp.. He looks up at the rain.. Just before his heart stops beating.. He hears a voice-

"FUCKING FIGHT!" the voice came from nothing and was nothing, it echoed infinitely and yet was never spoken.. Cain's eyes glow a brilliant gold before he catches himself from falling.

His wrists break as his bones spurt out of him like daggers, he begins to rush at Vagabond, his eyes widen.

"You're not dead!?" Vagabond whips a chain but Cain blocks, the force shatters his arm and blood sprays into the air..

Cain didn't stumble, he ducked under another blow and launched to stab Vagabond in the gut with his shattered bone daggers. He almost reaches him before a sudden wave of chains explodes through the air, wrapping around Cain and restraining him, throwing him back.

He tried to struggle but there were too many chains, he could barely move.

"Jeez.. you're a bit tougher than I thought.." Vagabond kicks Cain in the face, breaking his nose and shattering a tooth.

Cain stumbles but suddenly smoke pours from the large pile of chains.. Vagabond tilts his head.

"Smoke?" he sends a sharpened chain into the pile to try and stab Cain through the brain..

He continued standing, the smoke growing darker, turning into a swirling inky black..

Vagabond tried to heat up the chains but they began to melt.. That wasn't supposed to happen, a hand slowly pushes their way into the rain.. It was Cain's.. Its skin black and charred, pieces of it flaking off into floating embers.

The rain hit it and steam shot into the air with a violent hiss.

Vagabond goes to cut the arm off, the sharpened chain whistles through the air before-

A wet explosion rings in his ear as Cain's elbow erupts, his muscles and blood vessels popping creating this force which shoots his fist clenched hand across the street like a rocket.

Vagabond's eyes widen and he just manages to pull it away from him, he chuckles and goes to speak when-

"SHIT!" Vagabond shouts as he realises the arm was just a distraction.. A shape darted across the slippery wet street before a kick landed into his stomach.

He coughed as he was sent flying, chains caught him midair and propelled him back. He tried a flying kick but Cain's burning body dodged it and connected a right hook square in his face.. His hand singing and burning a mark into Vagabond.

He spins through the air and cracks a whip against the back of Cain's head, he stumbles.

Vagabond has chains grab him and pull him away, a growl on his face now as he raises his hands.

"LORDS STRIKE: 1,000,000 CHAINS!" he shouts out, the sky suddenly turns black.. Cain looks up to see 1,000,000 chains floating above him..

His rage filled and thoughtless eyes examined every last one.

"A tough opponent.. But not tough enough!"

Vagabond chops his hand downward.. Signifying the end of Cain's life.

Except nothing happened.

Vagabond makes a face and looks up at the chains, they have vanished.. In fact.. He felt much weaker. He looked around and found a gentle hand on his shoulder.

"Excuse me, Prophet?" Son Aaron asked.

"What the hell- Kid what are you-"

"Is killing really a Christian thing to do?" Son Aaron asked before cracking a punch against Vagabond's jaw.

Vagabond stumbled, spitting blood and Son Aaron stuck his hand between his legs.

"Ow, ow, ow, ow, ouchie" he hisses to himself.

Before Vagabond could do much else Cain suddenly wrapped his arms around him.. His limbs regrow and heal as he lets the rain drop on his tongue, the rage subsides inside of him and he glares down at Vagabond.

"Where is the Underground Church Prophet?" Cain narrows his eyes.

"And what if I don't tell you?"

Cain lets one of his hands be engulfed in rage, singed and turned to a crisp as crimson flame licks Vagabond's face. He cries out as a small patch of his skin bubbles.

"Fine! Fine! I'll tell you.." He hisses, his breath becoming shaky.

Son Aaron taps Vagabond, resetting his nullifying.

He looks at Cain.. they share a long stare..

"Why are you here?" Cain growled.

"Cause you'd be dead if I wasn't..." Son Aaron said calmly, his golden brown eyes seeping with determination.

"..and why would you care about that?" Cain tilted his head.

"... like I said...children of God don't kill.. It's not right.. So I'm going to get to the bottom of this, and make everyone realise they need to change perspectives"

Cain scoffs, chuckling to himself.

"Determined.. But your goal is impossible" Cain hisses.

"Maybe.." Son Aaron said.

"But I'll bet my life that it isn't"

Cain scoffs again, looking away, he tightens his grip on Vagabond's neck.

"Come on you, show us the way"

Vagabond growls and reluctantly shows them the way.

The sound of scraping stone howled down a cold and inky black hall as the gentle blue hue light of the rainy sky leaks through.

Vagabond is slowly pulling away the secret entrance to the underground church.

"Can't you do this any faster?" Cain asked, his body had mostly healed by now from the rainwater, his jug was attached at the hip with the gun back into his pocket.

"You literally took my miracle away! How am I supposed to do this faster!?" he snaps, Cain slaps him hard.

"Hey! No violence.." Son Aaron said, his brows furrowing.

"Sure.." Cain said, dismissing the thought.

Vagabond slowly pulls the cover away, letting them both see a long staircase which leads to a dark hall. Cain's eyes slowly drift back to him.

"Where is the Apple?" he asked, his voice caliced and cold.

"Apple? I don't know what you're-"

Cain interrupts him with a kick, sending Vagabond slamming into the wall, he coughs and slides down to the floor.

"Hey!" Son Aaron glared at Cain as he slowly picked up Vagabond.

"I don't know what Apple you're talkin about.. But if it's important, it'll be in the museum section" Vagabond coughed.

Cain's emotionless face grows colder, all three of them are drenched in the constant harsh rain, it leaks down the stairs and pools up on the floor.

"Show us where" Cain ordered, Vagabond sighed and began to lead them down the stairs.

Son Aaron kept his hand touching Vagabond at all times, they slowly walked down the hall.. The inky darkness wraps around them.. Swallowing them in its infinite being.. Cain shivered lightly, he felt as if he was being watched.

As they walk their footsteps echo down the long hall, the gentle drips from the leaking and cracking stone roof pierces their ears.. It's so quiet.. Almost too quiet.

The only light was the gentle golden glow of Son Aarons hand, it bounces along the wet floor.. Palely baking the area in his golden aura.

Cain remained alert, his cold face and serious demeanour unseen and yet all too well felt by the other two in the hall.

As they walked through the darkened hall thoughts flashed into their heads.. What if this was a trap? What if there were more Prophets? Cain almost died to this one.. Wait.. almost.. What was that voice he heard.. It sounded like it came from the rain itself.

After several minutes of walking the Prophet stops, his eyes widening lightly.

"What's wrong?" Cain asked, his gravelly voice as deep as any piano could go.

"Nothing, I just thought we would have reached the ending by now.." Vagabond mumbled to himself, a swirl of lightly concerned confusion wrapped around him.. Like a beast with no eyes wrapping its long tainted claws around his neck oh so slowly.

They continued to move and Cain noticed it too, the feeling of almost deja vu, even in the dark hall he could recognise small things. The crack on the side of the wall which is only seen by flickers from the water's reflection of Son Aarons light.. They had passed that minutes ago.

Cain raised a brow and looked around, he placed a hand on the jug of rainwater which was still attached to his belt, ready for if anything were to come out of the darkness..

"..I feel it too" Son Aaron said, thinking to himself out loud.

"Yeah.. hey don't tell me you're leading up into a trap Prophet" Cain scowled.

Vagabond shook his head in the dim light.

"No, this is worrying me too.."

Cain knew he was telling the truth.. The doubt was coiling around his limbs now, Vagabond's eyes darted through the shadows.. Overall everything felt so.. Uneasy.

Cain thought to himself before holding out his hand, slowly loosening the valve which had kept his emotions air tight. It hissed as it slowly leaked into his hand.. He could feel it slowly burn his hand inside out.

"What are you doing Cain?" Son Aaron asked in a light panic,

"Hold on..." Cain focused it all to just two of his fingers, he gritted his teeth against the pain and waited until the crimson flame peaked through the cracks.

He suddenly threw his arm back and then whipped it forward, spitting his blood and crimson flame through the air as he shouted.

"WHO'S THERE!"

The flame flies through the hall, lighting up a small portion of it as it travels outward.. Then they noticed something weird.

The light of the crimson flame was coming closer, but from behind them.

Son Aaron and Vagabond turned around but Cain looked ahead as the crimson flame illuminated the hall just enough for 3 figures to be illuminated and..

"BEHIND US!" Cain shouted, jumping head.

The crimson flame had landed on the ground near them, hidden behind a pillar stood someone in a maroon robe. She giggled as she stepped out slowly.

"Aww, you spotted me so soon" she slowly pulled her hood down revealing her light skin and black hair, her eyes shining a petrifying green.

Cain growled and let more of his emotions boil inside of him, patches of his skin turning to ash as they faced her.

Son Aaron goes to speak but Vagabond interrupts him.

"Lilly! Oh you're finally here!" Vagabond smiled.

Lilly, Prophet of Eternity, glared at him with her petrifying green eyes.

"I see you've led enemies into our church.." she said in a hateful, spiteful hiss.

"We're not enemies!" Son Aaron exclaimed, waving his arms.

"Well, he's not" Cain corrected, pointing to Son Aaron.

"I just think there's this big misunderstanding between God, Cain and the church! God doesn't want us to kill!" Son Aaron continued, trying to smile with a bright twinkle in his eye.

"I don't think there is much room for miscommunication.. God has said that he needs Cain dead, immediately" her eyes slowly drift over to meet Cain.

His face was stoic and stone tight, his eyes flickering with a burning rage.. Parts of his skin burn and charr as the embers lift into the air.

"I.. well look, it seems maybe you might have been mistaken somehow?" Son Aaron said, trying to calm the tension down.

"I mean.. I assume it is your great miracle that has us trapped in this hall, maybe you could let us go and we could all go have a nice chat!" Son Aaron finished, clasping his hands together with a smile.

Lilly tilted her head, thinking about it for a moment..

"How about no?" she threw a dagger, it whizzed through the air and dug into Cain's gut, he grunted and doubled over.

"Hey!" Son Aaron exclaimed.

Cain ripped the blade out and quickly drank some rain water before leaping back, gaining some distance.

She giggles to herself, Vagabond looks around.. His miracle slowly returns to him as he sinks into the shadows.

"Don't even bother trying to heal that wound Cain, my eternity dagger will forever remain open" she giggles.

"Please we don't have to finish this with violence!" Son Aaron tried to reach for her but she slipped out of his reach and kicked him in the jaw.

Son Aaron begins to float slowly through the air, his skin rippling in a pattern.

An eternal blow, Son Aaron was now feeling the kick over and over again in an eternal loop.

"I'm only doing my job" she said, a smirk on her lips.

Cain growls as he lets his arms get engulfed in anger, the skin burning and sparking as embers flicker off of them and large molten cracks appear.

He launches at her and she ducks, he tries to swipe at her face and she pulls away countering with a high kick to the face. Cain stumbles and she pulls out another dagger, she kicks him square in the stomach, the sheer blow forces him to double over.

She giggles as her eyes light up, she goes to dig her blade into his spine when a metal chain cracks against her jaw and sends her flying.

She stumbles and falls face first to the wet and rough cobblestone.

"Vagabond!" she yells, the voice echoes inside of his ears in an eternal loop.

Vagabond steps out, his eyes glowering down onto her.

"...I know how you work, you'll just kill me next" chains wrap around Lilly as he speaks.

She tries to break away but he doesn't let her, having the chains slip into every space they can and restrain her tight.

"...Goodbye" he waves his hand and the chains snap her neck with a loud crunch.

The voices vanish from his head and Son Aaron falls limp, tears streaming from his face.. Everything goes slowly dark again as the raging flame flickers out..

Cain manages to get to his feet, clasping the wound which still refuses to heal properly, blood slowly seeping into his shirt and trousers.

"...Why'd you do that?" Cain asked, looking through the dim air into what little of Vagabond's eyes he could find.

"...Like I said, she was going to kill me next.. However this doesn't make us partners" he waves his hand and a chain goes to pierce Cain's chest when-

"Calm.." the chains vanish and Vagabond is stripped of his miracle once more, he scowls.

Cain growls and throws a right hook which connects to his cheek, there's a loud crack and Vagabond stumbles.

"What was that for?" he whines.

"You just tried to fucking kill me" Cain snaps before turning away and continuing to walk away, sipping the rainwater.

Son Aaron slowly gets up, keeping his hand on Vagabond.. He looks over to the limp body of Lilly.. She reminded him of a broken doll that he refused to play with.. Horror filled his eyes and he turned away, holding in his puke.

"Let's-just go.." he mumbled, Vagabond rolled his eyes and they kept walking..

This time it didn't take too long, since the hallway was no longer being infinitely repeated; they soon reached a set of two large but old and withered wooden doors.

Cain pushes on them and they jostle, he tries again and they refuse to budge.

"Fucking locked" he growls, rage boiling in him as-

"It's a pull.." Vagabond says.

"What?"

"It's a pull, not a push"

Cain paused and pulled against the handles and the doors opened with buttery ease.

"Oh.." Cain said, blinking.

"Yeah.." Vagabond walked past him, followed by a quiet Son Aaron.

They now stood in a large circular room with a large statue in the centre of it. The window above them let through a shining bright blue light which baked the air.

Cain looked around, noticing several sets of doors, he walked up to the nearest ones and pulled.. Nothing happened.. He pushed and they slid open.

"Consistency much?" he grumbled inside his own head as he looked inside. It showed nothing more than a long but tall hallway which is caked in blue light which is seeping in from a tinted glass window.

"If you want to go anywhere useful, go through here" Vagabond gestured to the largest wooden door, it had some small hints of gold in its design.

Cain and Son Aaron walked up to it, examining it to see if it was some sort of trap.. The room they were currently in had an eerie silence to it which was unnerving.

Cain glances over to Vagabond, who chuckles and shrugs.

"I would never" he said, shaking his head.

Cain slowly pushed open the large double wooden doors, they led into a wide hall which is decorated in strange banners and suits of armour.

Cain again looks over to Vagabond who sighs and goes first, proving that it's not a trap.

Son Aaron follows him, tapping him every once in a while to keep his miracle subdued. Cain follows behind, sipping some rain water to heal up some of the burn wounds.

They make their way through the cool hall, its blue light baking every corner they look.. Cain tried to peek through the tinted windows but couldn't see anything, he couldn't even locate where the light source was coming from.

They reach the other side and open the doors, it leads into a.. Library? The bookshelves are taller than most houses, they reach high high up into the air, the ceiling itself is incredibly tall..

They look around, the books that are here are all seemingly hand written notes and accounts by prophets..

Cain picked out one book that looked specifically beat down and flipped it open, it was writing in a strange language he couldn't even begin to deduce the meaning of.

"Unless you guys wanna get found and killed in a library of all places I suggest we keep going? You want the apple right?" Vagabond sighed as he made his way to the next door.

Cain nodded and followed him precautiously, keeping the book with him.

They slowly make their way through tunnels and long curving halls, every room or hall was baked in a piercing blue light which seemingly had no origin..

Eventually they made it into a massive cathedral, its roof was so high some of it wasn't even visible.. That blue light continued to bake everything.

The sheer size of this place was enough for Son Aaron to let go of Vagabond, Cain blinked, noticing the large cases of glass.

Each case contained one artefact which looked special or unique in some way.

There was one with a strange cloak made of a dark greyish-blue material, another of a golden cross, a shape Cain hadn't really seen before.

Another was a large and thick black book with the same cross symbol on it.. Weird..

There was an outfit St. Peter wore but with a more reddish tint, another of a twig which slowly glowed a bright white.

Cain continued to walk forward, examining every artefact and every case before he paused..something was here.. Something which held unimaginable power.

"The Apple.." Cain whispered to himself, his starburst eyes widening.

And there it was, just ten or so metres away, a green apple with two bites out of each side.. It irradiated with power, Cain almost felt scared while simply in its presence..

"Now Cain.. before you do anything rash-" Son Aaron began, but Cain began a mad dash towards the apple, even if the aura pushed him away he needed that apple.

He needed it now.

Cain ran through the echoing cathedral, he was within reach of the apple, his hand began to outstretch and-

There was a whistle and the sound of shattering glass filled the air, Cain's eyes widened as he felt the skin on his back slit open.. A blade tearing at his spine and organs as it tore through him.

He fell to the ground with a wet thud, his crimson stains the ground with a splash.. Above him stands a man with beautiful white flowing hair and a pale face.. His piercing blue eyes smile.

"Ah! Saint Peter! Don't-" Son Aaron cried out but Vagabond whipped around, punching Son Aaron square in the nose with a crunch.

The force whipped his head back and sent Son Aaron stumbling.

Vagabond turned and smiled.

"Oh great priest, I have brought to you-" Vagabond began, his words that of-

"-A snake" St. Peter said.. His tone was cold.. Almost inhuman. Two large white wings unfurled from his scarred back.

"Huh?" Vagabond said, his smile falling lightly.

St. Peter points at Vagabond.

"You are a snake" he said again, the tone sent shivers down everyone's spines..

"I brought them here for you oh saint peter!" he tried to explain, his tone that of someone caught in a lie.

"You were caught.. You decided to give up our location rather than die.. You do not deserve God's touch.."

Vagabond opened his mouth and with one silent swing.. Vagabond's decapitated head hit the ground with a thud, his headless body falling to its knees.

St. Peter smiled, the blood soaking into his inhumanly pale skin, Son Aaron looked on in horror, his eyes wide and quivering.

He couldn't believe this.. No.. he wouldn't do that.. No..

Those with resolve so strong will often avoid a contradictory truth.

Cain coughed blood, he slowly tried to crawl towards the puddle of rainwater which had splashed into the cracks and crevices of the floor.. His crimson seeped into a puddle around him, he couldn't use his legs.

St. Peter saw this and smiled to himself as he dug his angelic blade into Cain's hand, piercing through the bone and pinning him down.

Cain screams in agony, blood pouring from his tainted mouth, sweat pouring down his tensed face.

"S-STOP THIS!" Son Aaron exclaimed, trying to stand up.

"...Leave..." Cain managed to cough as he held back the pain.

"Wh-what?" Son Aaron had tears flowing down his face now, he looked at St. Peter.. Then at Cain..

"HE'LL KILL YOU JUST LEAVE!" Cain shouts out, his eyes widening.

St. Peter slowly approaches Son Aaron, a light smile on his blood tainted face. He gently caresses Son Aaron, brushing his soft skin across his..

"What's wrong?.. Don't you wish to kill a demon?" St. Peter said, his voice as soft as velvet and as charming as a bluejay.

Son Aaron stammered, unable to respond.. His eyes kept glancing down to Cain and then to the corpse of Vagabond.. His breathing became more and more unstable.. His hands began to glow a bright golden.. Then his arms, his legs, his neck... his face..

"Stop this.. Stop.. This.. STOP THIS STOP IT STOP IT **STOP IT NOW!**" he screams, his body unleashing a wave of golden energy which washes over the entire cathedral.

St. Peter winces, he feels his wings evaporate as his miracle vanishes.. Cain could feel his body slowly grow cold, his miracle unable to grasp onto him any longer.. The blood loss pulling at him.

He tried to reach out for the water.. But his body goes limp, his head slumping onto the ground.. His dying eyes only able to gaze at the green apple..

"What an interesting Miracle.. To nullify others.. But that doesn't seem like something God would want.. Would it?" St. Peter's blue eyes shine bright as his smile etches ear to ear.

Son Aaron is panicking, his eyes widening as he shouts out.

"GOD WOULDN'T WANT THIS! YOU'RE EITHER LYING OR THE SNAKE IS IMPERSONATING GOD! GOD WOULDN'T WANT DEATH AND TORTURE!" he screams again, his body shaking as the golden energy flows off of him.

"Oh poor child.. If only you knew.." St. Peter's smile stays thin and wide, he slowly pulls out a dagger and flips it in his hand.. Handing it handle first to Son Aaron.

"Kill me" St. Peter said, his soft voice somehow the loudest thing in the room.

"Wh-what?" Son Aaron goes pale as his body goes weak.

"Your friend is dying as we speak.. If you let me live I will fulfil God's will.. And you will not agree to the world we will create.. But you could stop me, right here and now.. You could heal Cain and let him kill God.." St. Peter looked deep into Son Aarons shaky golden brown eyes.

"Do you serve God? Or do you serve Life?" St. Peter said, towering over Son Aaron.

"Do you kill me to protect the sinful life this world leads.. Or do you follow God into the new Eden?"

Son Aaron is shaking badly now.. He looks over to Cain.. his still.. Lifeless body.. He looks back into the eyes of St. Peter's, then up to the roof where the holy blue light shines through.. Baking the cathedral in its ethereal cloak.

"I...I...I CAN'T CHOOSE!" Son Aaron screams, clasping his ears as a ringing fills the air that only he can hear.

"That's unfortunate.." St. Peter said he had flipped the dagger into the air.

"..because I can"

St. Peter catches the dagger as it falls and runs the sharp and jagged blade into Son Aarons gut.

Son Aaron's eyes widen as he's pinned to the pillar behind him, blood slowly leaking from the wound.. His mind was dizzy.. As he begins to lose his balance, blood runs from his mouth down to his chin.. His innocent golden brown eyes waver as he falls.. Limp..

Chapter 17:

I Want To Be An Angel One Day

The year is 280.

"Papa! Papa!"

The sound of a young, joyful child filled the house, an older man raised an eyebrow.

"What is it, you little rascal?" said the older man, standing up and putting the parchment down.

"Look Look!" The kid was in the living room bouncing up and down while staring out the window, his eyes wide with joy and excitement.

The father walked to the window and paused.. Outside a large group of men in black and white marched through the streets, some cheered for them, others boo'd, others simply left them alone.

"It's the holy people!" the kid looked up to his father with such excitement, his eyes sparkled.

The father chuckled nervously.

"Yeah.. yeah.. There they are.." he looked out at them with a colder look, he adjusted his glasses and walked away from the window.

"Why do you like them so much?" the father asked as he made his way back to the parchment.

"Uh, cause they're awesome! Duh! They follow God's rule and protect the world from sin Papa!" he jumped into the air.

The father sat down, he was tall, around 6' wearing a dark grey overcoat and silver trousers.. He had lighter tanned skin and black hair with stubble, he looked around 40 or so.

"Right.. God's rule.."

He looked back down to the parchment, in sloppy handwriting it read:

"Dear Joseph, I am writing to you in a panic. Our camp was destroyed, decimated.. They called our celebrations "ritualistic" and "unholy".. Sam.. she's dead, Joseph. First Abel now this? No doubt they won't admit to it.. please .. get your family out of there. I have heard they're going to try and keep all of us together in just a few small cities, Bethel will be our capital.. You must hurry.."

The father sighed, his face showing signs of stress.. He subconsciously pulled at his hair as he simply stared at the parchment, he stayed like that for a long while..

"Papa! Papa! Can I go out and meet with the church people?" the young boy asked, his eyes sparkling.

The fathers face turned cold and his voice bellowed.

"No! You must not trust them, young man! Do you understand?" His eyes were as cold as a winter's night.

"But Papa! I-I wanna be one of them! I wanna help people and be an angel one day!" he said, his smile wider.

"NO! You must never join that filth, it's disgusting.. You don't want to be an angel! Do you understand?"

The boy paused, unsure as to why.. He wanted to say something in protest but couldn't. He just hung his head and walked away.

The father collapsed back into his chair with a sigh, his hands were shaking as he pulled and massaged his face.. Slowly trying to think of a way out of this.

The boy walked back into the living room and went limp into the sofa, he pouted as he looked out into the streets.. He watched as the men in maroon performed magical miracles far beyond the kids' understanding.. His eyes wide with excitement once more.

The year was 282.

The boy sat down in his chair and began to get ready to eat dinner..

His entire family was at the table, his annoying little brother who cried all the time and his big brother who spent most of his time in his room.

His mother and father were bickering over something, he slowly looked up from his plate of baked potato to listen in on them.

"What the bloody hell do you mean they're building a church here!?" the father hissed, his scratchy stubble turning into a small beard, his eyes wide with anger.

The boy's calm and yet sickly pale mother spoke softly.

"They said they're moving a church here.. They're going to put one up in every village they said.." she gently mumbled.

"That's it! We're fuckin leaving Bethel!" the father growled, his teeth like that of a monster..

The boy's eyes widened, he felt his heart sink.. He gripped the table, his younger brother was annoying as always and making a mess of his plate and his elder brother was sketching something.. They both weren't listening...

"W-we can't move Joseph.. Please.. We mustn't.. The kids are settling in, they have friends, they have-" she tried to calm him down but he lightly banged the table like a violent ape.

"No! We can't let them take our kids and indoctrinate them into some psycho death rally!" his hissing voice sounded like a snake, his eyes were one of a monster.. The boy began to shake lightly..

"Can we think about this first?" the mother calmly spoke.

"Grace!.. My sister is dead because of them-" he looked like a viper about to strike..

The hero had to step up.

"NO! I'm not leaving! Stop saying such nasty things! They bring us water and food!" the boy screamed, he jumped from the chair and rushed out the door.

"No wait come back-" the door slammed behind him before his father could finish.

The boy ran through the cold summer night, his eyes wide with worry and fear.. Tears flowed down his cheeks as he rushed away from home. It felt like he had run a million miles by the time he slowed down, he was panting.. His head felt light and dizzy..

He stumbled and fell, his body suddenly giving up.. He couldn't move anymore, his legs screamed and his mind echoed with his fathers monstrous shouts..

As he felt as if the cold black death was swallowing him.. He heard a gentle voice..

"Are you alright there little boy?" It was a woman's voice, kind and sweet like cinnamon.

She slowly picked him up and brought him around the corner, he opened his eyes and looked around. It was a campfire surrounded by men in armour or maroon robes.

The woman sat down and placed him on her lap, wrapping her scarf around him.

"Where.. Am I?" he rubbed his sleepy eyes and yawned.

"We're a travelling band of holy men" she said calmly, instantly his eyes lit up.

"Holy men!? R-really?"

A man chuckles, he's wearing full armour except for his helmet, revealing his tanned and scarred face.

"You a fan heh?" he spoke with crumpled words

The boy nods, his eyes sparkle in the burning glow of the fire.

"Why were you all alone?" the woman asked, making sure he was getting warm.

"..my family.. Wanted to move away.. Because they don't like the church!" he shouted, a grumpy expression on his face.

They all go silent for a little while before the woman speaks extra softly.

"Oh? Tell us more"

The boy nods, crossing his arms.

"My daddy thinks the church is evil or something! I don't know what got into him but you guys are awesome! But he stopped me from ever meeting you all! He said we should move because you're putting a church here and I don't want to move. I wanna go to church like my friends!" the boy exclaimed.

Without him knowing the "Holy Men" glance at each other.

"What if we talked with your father? Maybe change his mind?" the woman said kindly.

"R-really? You'd do that for me!?" he smiled so wide, that joy sparkling into his eyes again.

The woman nods.

"Of course we would, how about you show us where your house is?"

"Okay!" he said, such innocence..

It was the dead of night, several days had passed since the boy had met with the holy men.

They knocked on the door, the echo only heard to the insomniac father, he walked over and peered through a crack in the door.

He noticed their clothes.. Chills ran down his spine and he backed away, the silent night amplifying the creaks and cracks of his wooden floor.

"Shit" he hissed under his breath, looking around for a weapon..

However he had little to not time left.

A hand appeared from the darkness and grabbed him by the throat, pulling him through the inky black.. He struggled but was eventually spat out onto the ground in front of his house.

He coughed and looked up to see the holy men had him fully surrounded, his wide blue eyes filled with fear.

He went to say something but the woman's boot came crashing down onto his face, forcing him down to the ground.

"Listen very carefully Joseph.. If your family wakes up, they die" she said, her gentle voice sending daggers into Joseph's heart and mind.

"We just wanna have a little talk" said one of the men in armour, slowly picking Joseph up, dragging him away from his house.

Joseph didn't even bother to look up, blood dripped from his nose onto his chin, he simply complied.. Anything but his family..

They throw him against a wall as they reach out of the house's earshot, he grunts as the man in armour pins him there by his throat.

"I heard from a source that you were planning on moving out?" the woman said as she caressed his bruised face.. He looked into her golden eyes.

"S-So what if I am?" he growled, trying to push against the men in armour.

"You'll die. We simply want to bring peace to the land.. To make sure everyone is on the same page" she smiled a sickly smile.

"..You want control.. That's what you want-"

He was smacked, the sound echoed across the empty night sky, the woman's hand had steam slowly rise from it.

"We want peace and equality, now more than ever in these trying times. Haven't you heard of Abels murder?" she said, giggling.

He spat blood and coughed, his chest rose and sank with his heavy breaths.

"Have you heard of Sam?... she was my sister..and you lot fucking killed her.. Is that what this world has come to.. One man makes the mistake of killing and now YOU HAVE THE PRIVILEGE TO DO IT!?" he barks, his eyes wild with determination.

She slaps him again, force applied behind it.. It shook his head and shattered several teeth, he spat the shards at her.

It landed on her lip and she snarled, stabbing her nails into Joseph's mouth, she latched onto several of his front teeth and with one wrench they were torn from his jaw.

He screamed in agony as she brushed the blood off of her.

"You will listen to us, and do as we say, otherwise you won't be alive to see your family's death" she smiled again.

"....bite.. Me.." he managed to slip out between the groans of agony.

She giggled again.

"Oh with pleasure" she said, unhooking her jaw.

What happened next reader was not very nice, so we shall be skipping forward to the dawn.

Grace stood in the kitchen alongside her children, her eyes filled with worry..

The boy looked around and blinked.

"Where's papa! He usually cooks us breakfast by now.." the boy said to himself.

Grace's voice shook lightly.

"I-I don't kn-know.."

Suddenly there was a loud bang on the door, they all spun around to see who it could be. The door slowly opens to reveal the holy men holding up Joseph.. He looked terrible, his clothes were ripped and torn, dried blood covered his mouth and beard, his feet dragged against the floor as they carried him in.

Grace gasped, her face somehow went even paler.

"Oh my god! Joseph!"

"Papa! What happened!?"

The woman slowly walked forward, as clean and elegant as ever, she looked down at the children and then at the mother.

"There's a nasty group of anti-church people, they attacked Joseph here and we managed to stop him.. Unfortunately his injuries were not so easy to heal" she sounded genuine.. Yet Grace's face went impossibly pale..

The boy jumped up and down.

"You saved Papa! Thank you!" he smiled wide, looking over to the woman and not his own father.

The elder brother narrowed his eyes, he said nothing.. The younger sibling pointed to Joseph but said nothing as he had not learned to speak yet.

The Holy Men picked up Joseph and brought him upstairs to his bed, laying him down.

Grace looked towards the ground, not speaking or talking.. Meanwhile the boy jumped up and down, a happy smile on his face that his father was saved by the holy men..

"He must trust them now!" he thought to himself as he hugged each and every one of the holy men.. Oh child..

The year was 287.

The rascal made his way back home, his eyes were bright. In his left hand he carried around a small maroon book called "The Bible", which had begun to be given out to everyone in Bethel.. Over the past few years the small village had turned into the biggest town in the world.

It all centred around a large cathedral like church in the dead centre of town, priests were becoming more popular and a viable option of living well.

Priests are given miracles, free accommodation, free food and can go wherever they want. They also have the incredibly essential job of finding sinners and making them repent.

He smiled so wide, he noticed his friends and quickly jogged to catch up.

"Hey guys!" he waved to them, his pale skin and bright blue eyes shining against the beautiful clear sky.

They waved back.

"Oh hey Cloud!" one of them shouted back, Cloud was one of his few nicknames as he was always daydreaming during Church.

"I told you not to call me thaaattt" he whined then giggled.

"Sorry, how ya doin?" He walked with his friends as they made their way across Bethel.

"I'm doing cool! By the way guys did you know there's a priest exam soon!?" Cloud's shiny blue eyes light up at the thought.

"And you think you'll pass? Come on Cloud, no one your age has even gotten CLOSE to being a Priest"

Cloud pouts.

"I will become a priest in that exam! I'll show you!- oop this is my stop"

He waves to his friends as he peels away from the group, they laugh at the prospect of such a young priest... little did they know he'd been taking special classes from Mother Julia, the head of the local holy men.

He chuckled as he slipped into his house, he placed his bible on the table and expected the sweet smell of pastries to his nose.. But nothing did, the plates had been set but no food was on them..

Cloud paused.. Calling out to his brother..

"Stephen? Roger?" He walked up the stairs slowly.. He noticed the black markings of blood and his heart went cold.

He quickly rushed up to his mothers room and burst in, his eyes filled with panic.

His older brother was asleep on the chair next to the bed, Grace lay in bed.. She looked deathly ill.

"Mother!" he screamed, Stephen jumped awake.

"SHH! She's sleeping!" Stephen tiredly barked at him.

"Wh-what happened..." Cloud- no.. the boy.. He felt like it.. That child, scared and alone, his breathing shaky..

The boy asked.

"..she collapsed.. I don't know what's wrong.. But it has something to do with those holy men.." Stephen said, pulling out a pipe.

"What? Don't say that you still believe in fathers' crazy old tales! You know he isn't.. Right.. After the incident" the boy rubbed his arm.

Stephen blew out a puff of smoke.

"You mean the time the holy men beat and tortured him?"

The boy slammed his hand against the wall.

"Stop! It's a lie! Father is a liar!"

A gentle groan is heard in the next room over.. The boy's eyes widen and he rushes over.

"I didn't mean.."

He looked into the cold and harsh room, his father looked back at him..he had such sunken tired eyes, his body was frail and beaten, his beard was out of control.. He had difficulty communicating.. He'd been bed ridden for days.

The look in his eyes.. One of hurt.. One of sorrow, the boy didn't know this at the time.. But that look was one of knowledge, knowledge which he refused to accept.. Which he claimed as blasphemy..

The boy turned and rushed away, unable to handle these emotions.. He'd be back within the hour.. Everything would turn out fine.. Mother would be better one day.. Father would stop believing such lies.. His brother would join him in church.. Everyone would be happy..

Everyone.. Would.. Be.. happy..

The year was 290.

The house smelled like rat poison.. The flies had swarmed not too long ago.. It was slow.. Painful end.

The boy sat upon the roof, his stomach was empty, his ribs threatening to pierce through his skin.. The church had given him bread but that was all he had..

...first to go was father..

With Grace ill, the children were not up to the task of taking care of their father while also making enough money to feed themselves..

The boy remembered the day he died.. He brought him his favourite soup, he fed his father before he began to cough and thrash, they didn't know what happened till after the doctor came..

He had an allergic reaction to the mix he had put into the soup.. He had killed his own father..

Of course Stephen tried to tell him it wasn't his fault.. It must have been the priests, but the boy snapped at him.. Told him to get an actual life, that his drawings were shit and he had gone crazy.. He left.. And never came back..

The Boy looked out into the gentle candle light filled city.. His sunken eyes filled with moisture..

His smaller brother went next.. He didn't have enough food and fell asleep on his lap one day, and never woke up..

Somehow Grace pushed through till the end, in her ill stammerings she tried to tell the boy to run.. He could still hear her voice..

"Peter.. Run.. please.. Get.. out.. Of..here.. The church.."

Her last words were those of madness..

He slowly stood up.. His friends were right, he'd never become a priest, he was too old now and had taken too much time out of church to help his family..

He almost regretted it..

He looked down at the steep drop below and raised his arms into the sky, he spoke through parched lips.

"Forgive me.. Lord.."

He took a step off the ledge.. And plummeted.. To his death.

To the end of Peter..

And yet as he felt.. He never hit the hard and wet cobblestone.. He never felt the split second flash of white before darkness.. As he opened his eyes he saw something.. The moon.

So high and bright in the sky.

As God spoke to him.

"Peter, your time is not up.. For I have tested you, and you have succeeded, you are my next in line Peter.. You will be the Saint of humanity! Thou shall save the world and bring a NEW Eden! Thou shall be my vessel on earth.. Do you understand?"

Peter's eyes light up with wonder again, he smiles.

"YES! YES I DO GOD! YES I DO!"

"Then let it be known, my light shall pass through you, and only you may speak to me.. My child born not of our flesh!"

There was a thunderclap and a burst of light and a warmth washed over Peter..and he smiled.

It was gonna be alright.. He knew it..

It was all gonna be alright, he passed.. He was going to help the world.. He was going to save.. Everyone.

"Could I be an Angel one day?" he asked quietly to the inky abyss, the only light coming from the shallow moon.

"Of course, if you prove yourself worthy"

And Peter smiled.. peace..

Chapter 18:
One Down

St. Peter's cold blue eyes stare down at the slumped over boy... the kindness in his eyes slowly fading, and something twists in him, he narrows his eyes and pauses.. Moisture wells up but he didn't know why.

He slowly turns around, the golden energy fading from Son Aaron, his wings return to him and he takes a relieved breath, a smile on his face.

He looks down to Cain, his soft hands slowly gliding through the air in an invisible dance as they run along Cain's back.

"Do not worry.. For God forgives your soul" St. Peter steps over Cain and reaches for the apple in the glass case.

"All this pain.. Just for a goal that's impossible.." St. Peter murmured to himself, slowly unlocking the glass case.

He reaches out to grab the apple when-

A cold clammy hand wraps around his wrist, St. Peter's eyes open as he spins his head to come face to face with Cain.

His eyes were motionless and without life, his mouth hung open gently as emotions fueled his dying mind.

"Oh-" St. Peter didn't get to finish as Cain whipped his body around and threw him, sending St. Peter crashing through a wall which explodes out a massive cloud of dust and debris.

Cain's body cracked and shuddered as his bones reformed and his nerves pulled themselves back together.. But something.. Was.. very.. Very.. nasty.

St. Peter's eyes snapped back to examining the figure, this wasn't Cain.. no, something was very wrong.

The person.. No.. the creature which stood inside of Cain's vacant body had eyes that no man should see, its invisible smile could slice the very threads of the world itself... St. Peter's eyes widened as he summoned his two angelic blades and dashed forward, his wings pushing him through the air.

"Oh no you don't!"

The creature grabs the apple and bites down onto it- there's a blinding flash and St. Peter is sent flying, Son Aaron skids across the rough stone floor, leaving behind a trail of crimson..

St. Peter tries to stare through the blinding light.. It slowly subsides as Cain stumbles, his body no longer gravely injured, back to a healthy state.. He grasped the side of the podium, doubling over.

St. Peter narrows his wings, preparing to attack again.. But he noticed it, a shift in perspective..

Cain snarled, that beast.. That creature.. That being of despair, it wasn't controlling Cain.. it was Cain.

Cain launched across the room, jumping from wall to wall, pillar to pillar, his speed was unmatched St. Peter was lucky to even catch a blur. The very ground he uses to jump cracks and breaks into shards from the sheer force.

St. Peter raises his hand and the air begins to shift and change, a freezing cold slowly fills the large cathedral, covering every surface in a light coating of frost.

"I'll make him slip and-" St. Peter had no time to think as the creature appeared behind him, grabbing him by his neck and throwing him upward.

He smashes through the ceiling and lands inside of a small basement under a residential house, he coughs as smoke enters his lungs, suddenly something wraps around his neck and he's sent cascading back down into the vast cathedral.

He's sent crashing into the ground, a massive explosion echoes as St. Peter is slammed into the ground so hard it causes a massive crater..

The figure once known as Cain stood against the backdrop of the holy blue light which illuminated the battleground, St. Peter felt his holy power flow through him like golden blood.

He must take this beast down.. Whatever it take-

Cain aims the revolver.. And-

BANG!

St. Peter falls down backwards, limp.

Cain stands there, his body enveloped in a darker silhouette as his mind is scrambled and burned, his breathing is heavy and thick.. As he breathes clouds of sharp vapour come from his mouth.

His eyes were wide and motionless, everything was too much, he could tell every small detail all at once. An insane amount of information had been drilled into his skull all at once.. He knew of events that he had never seen.. He knew of events that had yet to come to pass.. He knew of lives he never led and those he may..

He even knew the name of the apple.

Adagnitio, the apple of knowledge.

The apple withered away in his hands as he conjured up an emotion, one of rage.. He conjured it into a thick slime in his mouth and he opened the revolver, spitting into one of the cylinders before clicking it back into place.

St. Peter slowly began to climb to his feet, his eyes filled with holy rage, energy began to swell around him. Cain simply aimed the gun.. He knew what it was now.. He knew who he was.. He knew so much.. He knew what a revolver was, he knew what a car was.. Even though the concept seemed quite silly, he even knew his gift.

He simply aimed down the barrel and fired, for he knew how to shoot.

"CAIN YOU MO-" BANG!

The bullet hits St. Peter in the chest and rips through him, pulling with it a chunk of his flesh and insides.. But that was not all, for the bullet was made of anger.

St. Peter screams as suddenly he is ignited from the inside out, his eyes wide as he is engulfed in crimson flame.

Cain slowly and methodically summoned another emotion, this one was fear.

He spat the silver emotion into the cylinder and flicked his wrist, snapping it back into place.

St. Peter cast down holy water which drenched the flames from him, he roared and lashed out- BANG.

He got closer this time, but the bullet of fear went straight through his skull.. St. Peter fell face first and landed limp.

"What a turn of events.." Cain said to himself.. This world was fresh, new.. The entire universe was at his fingertips, it was as if he was watching himself through a screen this whole time.. Only now does he get to play the game.. Game? Screen? He wasn't 100% sure of these words.. But he knew them now..

Even his voice sounded different, the gravelly low was replaced by a coarse velvet.

St. Peter growled as he was brought back to life by God's will, his eyes widened with rage before..

"Brother?" St. Peter froze.. He slowly.. Oh so slowly.. Turned his head.

"S-Stephen...?" St. Peter whispered.. He saw Stephen walk from the shadows, he was an adult now.. Maybe in his mid 30s.

He was a spitting image of his father, his hair was brown though instead of a rustic black, his smile was gone.. Now replaced with a darkened snarl. He wore a brown overcoat and grey shirt, he held up a pistol and aimed it at St. Peter's head.

"N-No! Stephen! What are you-" St. Peter felt a bullet tear through his shoulder, he stumbled.

"You left us to die!" Stephen shouted as he shot St. Peter's knee out, forcing him down.

"I JUST WANTED TO HELP PEOPLE STEPHEN!" he shouted back, his eyes filling with emotion.

"YET YOU ABANDONED YOUR FAMILY!" Stephen shot again, this time the bullet tore through his stomach, forcing him to fall to the ground.

"You.. You didn't.. Trust.. The church.." St. Peter hissed as he tried to stand up.

"The church killed us!" Stephen shouted, kicking St. Peter in the jaw.

"N-No! It didn't! LIAR! LIAR!" another gunshot through the arm.

"YOU CAN'T SIMPLY SHOUT LIAR AT EVERYONE WHO DISAGREES WITH YOU PETER!" Stephen approached, St. Peter crawled away, his bullet wounds slowly healing.

"Please.. They wouldn't hurt.. People.." his eyes were wide with fear.

Stephen grabbed him and threw him.. Suddenly St. Peter sat on his knees inside of a cold dimly lit room.. The sound of dripping was heard, he blinked and looked around.. Unsure of where he was before he saw it.

Even without empathy.. Without care.. He knew this was bad.

Cain, with Son Aaron over his shoulder, stood in front of the mangled, tortured corpse of Caleb... his near black blood slowly dripping into the near full bowl..

Cain's eyes flickered.. St. Peter tried to speak.. The fear from the bullet was wearing off but another fear was coming back.

"...Peter..." Cain(?) spoke, his voice was inhuman, suddenly an aura of pure fear tears off of Cain, filling the room with a suffocating sense of **doom.**

Cain slowly turned his head, his body was no longer human.. Now nothing but a shadow, his edges flickered like the shadow of a flame, his eyes but blazes of pure emotion.. Indescribable by human eyes.

But by a false angels? They were the eyes where you beg for forgiveness... any lesser man would have fallen just by the sight..

For the first time in so long.. Peter felt like that little boy again, fear enveloping him.. He wished to run away, to be taken by the church, so everything would be okay..

But he was in the church.. He had run away.. His family was dead.

And yet, he wasn't okay.

He was never okay.

Cain barely moved, he blitzed across the room in a fraction of a second and stopped as he passed Peter.. His wrist was bent and broken allowing his bones to protrude and act like a dagger.

"Killing you would be a waste.. God simply would bring you back, I'm not strong enough to erase your very existence.. But I am strong enough to take something from you"

Holy golden blood sprays onto the cracked and darkened floor as Cain had cut and then ripped off one of Peter's wings, with a lightning fast kick to the back of the head Peter was sent crashing into the ground..

He didn't even fight back.. He simply let the golden blood flow from his head and lost wing..

Cain, within a moment and a wet putrid sound, fused the wing to his own spine.. The aura of fear was petrifying to all who dared challenge it.

And with a single whisper.. He was gone..

St. Peter took a breath.

And screamed.

He screamed out of rage and fear as his emotions burst from his chest like rabid beasts, the chains snapping and unleashing them unto the world. He clasped his hands and thunder shook the skies as his screams were heard under every house and every street in Bethel..

For St. Peter..

On this day, would forever remember such a whisper, spoken to him by a monster known as Cain.

"You. Have. Failed. Him."

Chapter 19:
A Monster Known as Cain

Cain walked out of the hidden entrance, the rain came down harder than ever before.. The streets began to flood lightly, people panicked as they rushed inside.

Cain's eyes shone a strange shade of gold, he could feel his body slowly being rejuvenated to its peak, he didn't even have to drink it.

A simple touch allowed his injuries to heal, a smile grew on his face. His hands twitched as he watched the world with new eyes, he could perfectly describe the world in front of him, he could almost see the raindrops individually as they fell from the sky.

He recognised every type of stone which the roads were made of, he recognised every smell.. Even the slightest hint in the billowing wind.

He looked over to Son Aaron and quickly placed him down, leaning him against the wall. His eyes suddenly softened to one of worry as he checked up on Son Aaron.

He was pale, his body was limp and his eyes closed. Cain checked his pulse and waited..

Rain poured, its splashes roared into his ears and yet he waited.. His clothes soaked through with water once again.. And yet he waited..

badum.. Badum..

A heart beat. Son Aaron was alive, Cain let out a gentle sigh of relief and looked to his right hand.

He let the rage slowly crawl along his skin, he had so much more control of it now.. It didn't burn him, instead it wrapped around him like an invisible armour, he then let it ignite into crimson flame.

Cain slowly pulled the blade from Son Aaron and then pressed his hand into the wound, the flames quickly began to burn and melt the skin as it completely sealed the wound.

Cain let out another gentle breath and slowly stood up, his eyes shining through the harsh and cold lighting which pierced through the charcoal coloured clouds.

He turned to walk away before pausing, a figure stood in front of him and instantly a wave of presence was felt.

Cain leapt backwards, snapping his wrists to expose broken and sharp bones, his eyes wild like a beast as emotions tore off of him like a violent storm.

A voice spoke.

"Hey! I'm not gonna fight you dumbass, not gonna hurt you either.. Also.. you see me?" his voice was smoother than humanly possible, a tone and reverberance Cain had never been able to hear before.

Cain looked up and his eyes widened.

The figure in front of him stood at 7-8' tall, he had tanned skin and was draped in black cloth, he had four massive black raven-like wings with two smaller white ones hidden in them.

He held four arms and four faces, his very presence seemed to overlap in itself.. An impossibility given form.

"What.. are you?" Cain whispered to himself as he began to examine him from afar.

The creature spoke, his voice echoing.. backwards? It was an indescribable sound, one your imagination could only catch a glimpse of for a mere moment before being gone forever.

"I am Lucifer, Angel of Earth" his four faces looked down upon Cain with glowing white eyes, the same ethereal glow emanated from Lucifer as it did with St. Peter.

"You're an angel? I guess you're here to kill me then.. Come and try me" Cain pulls out his revolver in a blink of an eye, the sheer speed of it lightly cracks against the air.

Lucifer puts up his arms and takes a step back.

"Woah, woah, woah.. No" Lucifer explained. "I'm the motherfucker that's been helping you!"

Cain tilted his head.

"Helping me?"

"Yeah, did you really think you've come this far by your sheer will power?" Lucifer said, crossing his four arms.

Cain looked down at the ground and paused, thinking.. The rain pinning his black hair to his skin again like glue.

"Yes?" he asked cautiously.

"No! I've had to keep you alive because you kept misusing your gift, if it weren't for me you would have died back in the church fight, Vagabond would have killed you and St. Peter would have killed you- I mean it's not even a would have they basically DID kill you! But I used your useless earth form to make sure you were back before GOD got his hands on you!" Lucifer stopped ranting and sighed.

Cain chuckled and put his gun away before spinning on his heel and beginning to walk away.

"Welp, thanks for the help and all but I don't work with others" Cain adjusted his coat as he began walking down the street.

Lucifer paused, his eight eyes blinking with disbelief.

"What.. what's that supposed to mean!? You finally see an Angel, learn that it's the only reason you're still alive and fucking walk away!?" Lucifer shouts, floating through the air towards Cain.

"I don't need you anymore, thanks for the help and all but I have the power of the apple, now I just need to go get the others and I'll be killing your boss" Cain said plainly, not looking back.

"You just expect that you can do this without my help!?" Lucifer shouts, his eyes glowing brighter in disbelief.

"I saved you because I knew you'd be strong enough to help us!" Lucifer appears in front of Cain with a man killing glare.

Too bad Cain was a monster, as he walked past Lucifer, ignoring him.

"I'm not helping shit.. I'm not doing this for selfless glory, I'm going up there to beat God to death with my bare fucking hands" Cain turns the corner and slips into the main road, pocketing his hands.

Lucifer appears alongside Cain.

"And I can help you accomplish that task, God is insane, he's a fucking wacko who needs to be put down" Lucifer snarls.

"Aren't you worried he's gonna hear ya talkin shit?" Cain said, smiling a viscous smile.

"No, because your concept of God is very flawed.. Not only does he not hear and see everything, he can be stopped from peeking into conversations by people of a certain level of strength" Lucifer said, summoning a small ball of blue flame in one of his four hands.

Cain shrugs again.

"Cool I guess, don't care"

"You.. you don't care? I have the most insider information anyone could have! I know more than Adam and you're just gonna say you don't care?" Lucifer said, appalled.

Cain looked across the street, a figure in maroon walks through the pouring rain, dancing and giggling to themselves. They could see it now, a sense of power and motion.. Cain's eyes were sharp and his mind was sharper.

"Yeah. Don't care, I have had enough of trusting people and if you didn't notice I just stole an angels wing"

Cain clicks and a rotting wing of flesh and bone bursts from his back, tearing through his jacket.

Lucifer scoffs.

"He was nowhere near as powerful as a real angel, I mean only NOW can you even possibly see me! You're going to need one or two more apples to even have a chance of facing an Angel!" Lucifer shouts, trying to block Cain's path.

Cain jumps into the air and kicks off a nearby building to launch dozens of metres away, he lands and quickly goes back to normal walking, a glint in his eyes.

"And that's what I'm doing Lucy, I'm getting the next apple" Cain giggles, his body shakes lightly as he begins experimenting with his own abilities.

"You're not going to listen to me are you?" Lucifer lets his many shoulders slump.

Cain didn't even respond, made his way down a thin alley, the rain rushing down to meet them.

"Do you even know who keeps bringing you rain for you to heal!? Me!" Lucifer claps his hands and the sky instantly begins to clear, the rain stops.

Cain looks up and scowls.

"Look, just piss off alright!? I'm not gonna team up with anyone else because I have tried that THREE times and they either end up dead or betraying me!" Cain barks at Lucifer, his entire body being enveloped in an invisible layer of rage.

"I'm not just some random schmuck! I am the Angel of Earth, I know more about your lineage than you do! I can help you with getting more Apples and I can help you understand your gifts and fucking kill that big guy up there!" Lucifer points towards the still dim sky, the blue slowly cracking through.

Cain pauses, almost like he was thinking about it, his eyes scan Lucifer's complex and impossible biology.

"Again, dead or betrayal" Cain turned back around slowly.

"You won't be able to get the next apple without me Cain" Lucifer shouted after him.

Cain ignored it and kept moving.

"I know which one you're going for next! But big twist, an Angel is guarding the Garden!"

Cain stops dead in his tracks and looks down to the large puddles of murky water beneath him, he looks at his own reflection.. At the gentle golden glow that came from his eyes.

"....I'll kill them.." Cain said as he moved forward again.

"You know you can't, you beat St. Peter while juiced up on rage but he's barely a false angel! Real Angels could destroy you!"

Cain grumbled something to himself as he rested on a nearby wall with one outstretched hand, he groaned and looked down at the ground.

"I can show you have to traverse through heaven, I know how to get to God, I know how to kill Angels, I'm your only fucking way forward here"

Cain paused, cutting off sound.. Letting himself think as the world around him became null and void. He places his hand on his head and thinks.. The gentle dripping of rainwater washing off the nearby roofs sending light chills down his spine.

"...I hate you" Cain eventually said, hanging his head.

"I know.. I know" Lucifer slowly glided over towards him.

"May I ask you a question, mortal?" Lucifer tilted his four heads.

"Sure" Cain said, defeated.

"Why didn't you begin this journey sooner?" Lucifer clapped his hands and brought with him more rain.

"...everything was chaos after Abel died.." Cain began to slowly walk as he spoke, Lucifer glided alongside him.

"People needed something to point to and blame... I was distraught at the time, could barely speak...so.. I decided to take it.. For a while"

Cain ran his fingers along the wall next to him, rain water dripping down it.

"It was only supposed to last for a while.. I saw how much the world had unified afterwards.. People were happier, strangely, there was more of a system in place.. It was stricter but not in a necessarily bad way" Cain spoke softly, his golden eyes pulsing with energy.

"Before I knew it, years had passed..." Cain trailed off.

"Years? What a polite way to say decades" Lucifer said, raising four eyebrows.

Cain paused and sighed as he let himself fall against a wall.

"Yeah.. yeah..."

Even if Cain looked to be in his late 20's early 30s, he was actually the ripe old age of 60. I mean he's the grandson of god, you should expect some strange ageing. His father and mother are over 300 years old so you shouldn't be too surprised.

They both hear rushing footsteps and Cain's eyes shine, he quickly turns his body, expecting a Prophet to turn to the corner when-

"Wait!" a weak but hopeful voice shouts, Son Aaron stumbles around the corner and doubles over in pain.

"What are you doing?" Cain growls.

"Go back and rest" he waves Son Aaron away and begins to walk the other direction.

"Please.. Take me with you.. There must be some sort of way we can truly end this without killing God!" he shouts as he uses the wall to help keep him upright.

"Your grand priest stabbed you in the gut and left you for dead! Stop thinking this world can be saved! It's rotten" Cain's eyes were cold, an aura of power radiated from him that even Son Aaron could feel.

"This.. is not.. The end.. We.. can.. Do this.." Son Aaron coughs and falls down, Cain winces as he watches him.

"Just go home Aaron.." Cain whispered.

"No.." Son Aaron hissed, trying to stand up.

Lucifer simply watched this interaction silently.

"Bring me with you..."

Cain shook his head and crossed his arms.

"You're staying in Bethel, where it's safe" he said with a harmonious tone.

"So you're leaving Bethel? You think you can just.. Up and leave.. Someone needs to keep you in check Cain-"

"NO ONE NEEDS TO KEEP ME IN FUCKING ANYTHING" Cain barked, he paused.. Shocked by his own sudden outburst, the rage envelopes his body and spindles into the air sending out waves of power felt all over the city.

Son Aaron winced from the shouts but continued to approach Cain, his golden brown eyes filled with fading hope.

"Please..."

Lucifer finally speaks, his glowing eyes shining through the light mist which slowly began to envelop the city.

"Ditch him, we don't have time for this"

Cain nodded but paused, unable to move his legs from where they were planted, like he couldn't move away..

"..Cain.. don't do this.. Don't become a monster.." Son Aaron begged, his weak grasp on the wall slipping.

Cain said nothing, he just blinked.. His eyes shifting as the entire world began to spin around him, he examined every raindrop which fell to his feet and he truly thought.

"Is killing them all proving their point.. Or is it simply showing God I'm serious?" Cain looked up into the stormy clouds, his eyes shining brightly as he glared at the man above all.

"If you wish to reach the garden by nightfall we must go now" Lucifer said, his voice echoing backwards.

"If you bring me with you Cain I can try to talk to God myself" he said with a false smile on his face, it was clear Son Aaron didn't see the Angel.. Cain stood in a strange position.. In the middle, between getting his goal.. And humanity.

He remembered the days where he begged for understanding.. Where he wished someone cared..

He saw himself in Son Aarons shoes, the worry he felt at the back of his throat and the fear which built up in his stomach which he forced himself to ignore.

If he leaves Son Aaron here, he'd be condemning him to death.. St. Peter would find him and- he shivers at the image..

How Caleb was tortured and slowly drained of his blood..

It sent down cold spikes through his body, he grit his teeth as his rage and anger boiled and bubbled more and more.

"Come on then" Cain said as he began to walk away.

"A-Are you talking to-" Son Aaron began but Cain cut him off.

"Yes, now come on" Cain held out his hand, he didn't look happy about it.. But he couldn't leave him.

Son Aaron takes his hand and Lucifer rolled his eight eyes before placing a hand on Cain's shoulder, there's a whip sound and a crack before they all vanish.. Leaving that alleyway empty.

A figure slips from the shadows, a woman, Opheria, Prophet of Time smiles to herself as she notes something down in her book.

Through the constantly thick mist steps out another figure.. They're wearing a maroon suit which eventually leads to a gas mask type contraption on their face.

Their eyes are hidden behind tinted black glass, they hold a crossbow in their left hand.

"It seems they're going to the garden, we must tell Saint Peter at once" Opheria says, a sharpened smile on her tainted red lips.

The figure in the suit simply nods, not saying a word.

They both slip into shadows, vanishing from sight or mind.

Chapter 20:

Lustitiae Enim

St. Peter sat upon his throne in the cathedral.. Its blue light seemed more like a holy taunting rather than a warm embrace.. His head was lowered as his flowing white hair fell in front of his face.

His one remaining angelic wing gently flexed.. Everything was empty, hollow..

He had done so much, for the church, for himself.. And yet he failed? And yet.. Cain defeated him.. With such each, not only did he defeat him.. He stole something which Peter held dear to his heart..

He took a wing from his angelic body..

"Why.." he weakly mutters to himself, his eyes widening, bloodshot and pale blue.

"WHY! CAIN! GOD! WHY!" he screamed into the hollow and vast cathedral, his very voice shattering the glass around him, erupting the shards outward.

"..I did everything for you..." he hissed through a clenched jaw, he gripped the sides of his throne as it shattered and broke.

"I gave up my life to be your vessel.. And yet you don't trust me enough with true power.." he looked up into the cracking ceiling, a voice responding to him that no one else heard.

"I do not care for your excuses.." he said, his voice cracking.

"I do not care for your standing above me.. KILL ME!" he screams upwards to God.

"DO IT! KILL ME!" he shouts long and hard, the walls around him crack and buckle.

There's a long pause.. And he collapses back into his throat, going limp and laughing.

"Hahaha..hahahaha...hahahahaha..HAHAHAHAHA!"   St. Peter begins to laugh, slowly building up to a wild screaming cackle.

"HAHAHAHAHAHAHAHAHAHA!" he pushes the white hair out of his face and smiles, his ragged and thin body shaking.

"YOU. CAN'T. KILL ME, CAN YOU?" he hisses, his wild blue eyes piercing through the stone.

He then launches to his feet with his arms spread wide as a large smile spreads across his face.

"THEN DO IT! DO IT! IF YOU'RE SO OFFENDED BY MY WISH TO SERVE YOU THEN FUCKING DO IT! BOW TO ME AND ANSWER TO MY COMMANDS!" St. Peter smiles wide, his teeth gritty and bloodied.

"DO IT GOD! KILL ME! LISTEN TO MY WORDS AND KILL ME!" he shouts so loudly the entire cathedral shakes and violently begins to crumble. Large chunks of rocks fall from the ceiling and crash into the ground around him.

He continues to laugh.

"HAHAHAHAHAHAHAHAHAHAHAHAHAHAHAHAHAHA, BECAUSE OF COURSE YOU'D NEVER STOOP TO TAKING ORDERS FROM A MORTAL"

"DO IT GOD! KILL MEEEE PROVE ME TO BE ABOVE YOU IN EVERY WAY! OR IS IT TRUE? THAT GOD HIMSELF REFUSES TO KILL ME? THAT I AM STRONGER THAN GOD!?" Peter smiles so much wider, an inhuman tear appears on his face.. He grins ear to ear as he realises this.

"WHY SILENCE GOD!? OR DO YOU FEAR ME" Peter chuckles to himself.

"You can't kill me because I wish for it.. To abide by my words, to strike me down, not only would you have to start again.. When you don't have time you see.." Peter falls back down to his throne.

"You don't have the time for another me! For someone so devoted.. Because Cain.. is on his way to kill you.. And you're fucking scared"

Peter spits onto the floor in disgust, his glaring eyes meet those of an invisible god.. And yet he does not crumble.

"You have to realise.. You're not in control anymore.." Peter said, an aura of pure confidence surrounding him.

"Simple.. Give me my crown.. Give me my wish I asked you as a child.. As I fell from that roof and you decided to take the choice of death away! FULFIL THAT PROMISE YOU MADE TO ME 10 YEARS AGO!" Peter shouts, his body begins to glow a golden aura.

"DO IT! HYPOCRITE! BOW TO ME AND I WILL STRIKE CAIN DOWN YOU FOOL!"

Three Prophets look on in horror.. As Peter laughs, his body covered in a brilliant angelic hue..

As he stands up.. Standing above God.. his eyes wild with power as a halo appears over his head, its disc sharp and thin..

"Do you have information for me?" Peter said, a grin on his face as a wave of impossible power washes over the room.

Opheria nods, shivering as she kneels.

"W-we know of their location your h-highness-" he interrupts her.

"I AM NOT A HIGHNESS! I.. AM.. HOLY!" He raises his arms as holy flames pirouette through the air and cascade down onto them, burning angelic hymns into the stone with white flame.

"Your holiness!! W-We know where Cain has gone.." she stutters out.

"TELL ME!" his voice booms like a break in the sound barrier.

"The Garden of Eden!" she shouts, her body too scared to let her speak calmly.

Peter slowly nodded, thinking to himself.

"You three, **go**" he waves his hands and strange angelic symbols appear beneath their feet.

"And if you don't carry his head by the time I arrive.. You will be condemned to earth, never to enter the gates of heaven.. For I now decide.." he said, his voice an impossible frequency, his eyes a beautiful blue.. His very hair reminded them of clouds as it flowed down his back, his body although skinny looked stronger than any metal.. Any man..

They try to object, but stay silent..

And so

Opheria, The Hunter & The Sunborn all vanish into particles of white as they travel across the planet in seconds.

The hunt has begun.

And Peter laughs as tears flood his face, blood leaking from his chest.

Chapter 21:
The Three Great Prophets

There was the sound of tearing reality as three figures appeared in the middle of a moss covered road.

Cain, Son Aaron and Lucifer stand there, Cain's eyes sharpen as he examines his surroundings.

Around him are dozens of houses, all of which are broken down and covered in moss, vines and plants, acting more so like large plant pots than houses.

Son Aaron wavers on his feet and falls over, coughing.

"H-How'd you do that.." he groans as he clutches his stomach, his skin sickly pale.

"I didn't do that, that was Lucifer" Cain said plainly as he walked forward, examining the forest which seemed to envelope the town they stood in.

"L-Lucifer?" Son Aaron coughed, but Cain ignored.

Lucifer continued to float behind Cain, his four heads examining the surrounding area as if they knew it like the back of their hand(s).

"What is this place?" Cain asked Lucifer, who raised his brows.

"This is an old town, once called Peace, now.. It is nothing but a remnant of a time before control" Lucifer gestured to a nearby building, it had.. Posters?

Cain walked towards it and ripped the mouldy poster from the wall, trying to read it. Flashes of knowledge which Cain never had slip into his mind and he grunts, closing his eyes.

"..Convenience.." Cain looked up and across through the glass pane, he saw a store that was trashed, wrenches, gears and spanners thrown to the floor without pattern.

"...woah.. Something.." Cain steps back, he grabs his head and drops the poster.

"Cain? Are you okay?" Son Aaron asked as he stood up, he looked around at the strange architecture and materials.

"This.. place.." Cain groaned again, too much information began to swell inside of him, thousands of years of humanity which hadn't even happened yet poured straight from the ether itself into his mind.

Lucifer nodded.

"Yes, Adam built this place, him and Eve.. with their own hands"

Cain groaned and bent over.

"What's that.." Son Aaron said in a whisper as he spotted a strange metallic shell.

Cain's eyes widened as he walked up to it, placing his hand on it as another flash of knowledge pierced his brain like a dagger.

"Ak!" he exclaimed as he tried to grab his head, the world began to spin and he felt dizzy.

Son Aaron grabbed him, helping him keep on his feet, Cain growled.

"Don't touch me!" Cain threw his hands out, hitting Son Aaron in the gut and sending him stumbling.

"Fuck..." Cain turned away, trying to close his eyes to stop the influx of knowledge.

"..A..Car.." he eventually whispered before pulling away from the wall and snapping his eyes open. The vibrant colours of the surrounding world flowing into him.

"Car?" Son Aaron asked shakily as he kept his distance from Cain.

"Yeah.. it transports people places.." Cain slowly began to calm down, he glanced over to Lucifer.

"Why.. Why is this here? Why.." Cain began, trailing off.

"Because the church found no use for it, they cast Adam out, for he was the first man.. He ate the apple, and doomed them all to sin.. Or so they say. They moved past him, told him to basically fuck himself and tried to burn him alive.." Lucifer said gently.

"How.. when.." Cain tried to find the answer in his brain but there was too much to sift through..

"Before you were born.. The reason he even had you and Abel in the first place was to start fresh, to have a life distant from others" Lucifer explained.

"Are you talking to the angel right now, are they right there?" Son Aaron asked, Cain waved them away.

"Yeah... yeah... so.." Cain trailed off again.

"The Apple gives knowledge of all, it gives consciousness, those who eat it know of the present and the future.. Not by exact measurements, but they know a lot" Lucifer said as he floated over to the scrap car.

"If humans had listened to your father they could be among the stars by now.. But of course God doesn't want that, he doesn't want people to be as smart as him.." Lucifer sighs as he picks up a piece of rust from the car and it disintegrates within his hand.

"So they turned those who could hear his words against my father.." Cain said solemnly.

Lucifer nodded.

"...Sorry I'm confused, what's being said?" Son Aaron tried to ask, resting on the hood of the car.

"Nothing, it doesn't matter.. Let's go find Eden" Cain said as he walked out of the little cove where the car lay.

Lucifer slowly followed after him as they made their way through the nature taken city.

"So we just head this way and we find it?" Cain asked, looking up to Lucifer.

Lucifer nods, his eyes shine bright and he pauses.

"Ah.. I see.. They've aligned that way.." he said under his angelic breath.

"Hm?" Cain asked, stopping in his tracks.

They all suddenly feel a different breeze, it spins around the street as small white particles begin to fill the air. Cain narrows his eyes and envelops his body in a thin near invisible layer of calm.

"I know that feeling..." Cain hissed.

Son Aaron blinked, very confused as to what's going on before three figures seemed to form from nothingness behind them. The white particles stick together to dissolve in the figures.

Cain tilts his head and Tsk's.

"Prophets.." he spoke like it was an illness as it slipped from the tongue, his golden eyes shining.

Three Prophets stood there.

One was Opheria, Prophet of Time, she had pink hair and darker skin with painted green lips, her eyes shine. She was wearing the usual Prophet clothing of a maroon cloak, the air around her seemed to speed up, whipping her cloak back and forth.

The next was one only known as The Hunter, Prophet of Hunting, he wore a full body maroon suit with a plague mask like beak and two large glass cylinders they breathed through. Their eyes were hidden behind tinted black glass and they held a crossbow in their left hand.

The last was a tall man with fair light skin and beautiful golden hair, he was taller than most, around 6'6. He wore golden robes and had the smile and eyes of a murderer, wild and vicious.

Zalabar, Prophet of the Sun.

Cain scowled as the clouds slowly encircled them, light rain began to descend.

"Thanks for that Lucy" Cain said as he cracked his knuckles and his neck, a bloodthirsty grin slowly growing on his face.

"I'd prefer if you didn't call me that-"

"Too late, it's your nickname" Cain chuckled to himself, his eyes slowly seeping into a look of enjoyable madness as his emotion of calm flowed off of him like invisible fire.

"I suggest you run Aaron" Cain said gently as he took a step forward, the rain hit his skin and he felt them dash through his body, giving it more and more power.

Opheria spoke, opening her arms wide.

"Oh Cain, this is nothing personal you know? We're just on **special orders**" she giggles.

"Right, could you give me your boss's address? I need to know where to send your corpses" his grin grew.

"G-Guys we don't have to f-fight, please for fucking once can we sit down and-" Son Aaron tried to speak logic and reason into the air and all he got was a crossbow bolt to the forehead.. Or at least he would've.

His eyes widened as near centimetres away it had stopped, Cain had grabbed it, the aura of calm slowing down its momentum to nothing near instantly.

"Let's keep the kid out of this okay?" Cain snarled as he began to make his way towards the three.

"We tried to warn you" said Zalabar, his voice creaky and slippery. He aimed his hands into the sky and suddenly a beam of light pierced through the clouds and landed in his hand, creating a ball of the sun.

Cain blinked, for some reason he knew that wasn't right.. But he didn't know why..

Another crossbow bolt was fired, it aimed right for his eye. The moment it got within a few centimetres it stopped, the aura of calm slowing it down.

Cain chuckled as he pulled out his revolver.

Zalabar roars as he throws the ball of pure sunlight, its blazing heat burning all plants near it. Cain braces for the blow and takes the blast front and centre.

Its heat expands into a massive explosion which burns a bright white for a fraction of a second, the shockwave shakes the damaged buildings and knocks one down.. It crumbled and crashed, sending debris and smoke high into the air.

They looked into the smoke screen to see if Cain had been significantly damaged, the Hunter dashed forward, using sound to try and find him.

They weave back and forth as they try to detect any sign of life..

"Was it that easy?" Zalabar said, chuckling.

"I would hazard a guess, no" Zalabar and Opheria spin around to see Cain behind them with a loaded Revolver.. He fires twice.

There's a loud bang and Zalabar is sent flying and rolls to the ground while Opheria vanishes completely. Cain narrows his eyes before getting a dagger stuck into his throat from behind, a knee slams into his spine with a crunch before a roundhouse knocks into his jaw which sends him stumbling.

Zalabar tries to get up but he's.. Slow. Everytime he tries to move it takes several times more energy to do so. The bullet wound begins to seep blood into his cloak and he scowls.

Cain grunts and tears the dagger from his throat, his blood flying into the air and dripping down to form small puddles of iron smelling liquid. A crossbow bolt sings through the air as The Hunter appears from seemingly nowhere, launching at him with a poison dagger.

Cain swats the crossbow bolt away, his hands enveloping in rage as he quickly grabs The Hunters wrist, twisting it away from him. They quickly kick him in the stomach and Cain coughs, doubling over.

Before he can recover he's sent flying through a wall, slamming into the inside of a building, his body is broken and bones are shattered, blood sprays onto the ground and wall as he grunts.

Lucifer speaks into Cain's ear.

"You must get to the rain to heal"

"Yeah.. I know.." Cain tries to stand but suddenly wires burst from the wall behind him and wrap around him pinning him to it.

He grunts and struggles, trying to burst through them but they're far too tough..

"I wouldn't bother" Opheria giggled, she and Hunter walked in through the door of the building. She smirked to see Cain injured and pinned down.

"Hunters' special 'Trap Wires' get stronger the more something or someone tries to break them. You're stuck" she giggles again and skips towards him.

"I didn't know it would be this easy, did you Hunter?"

Hunter shakes their head, still not saying a word.

"I thought you were supposed to be strong?" she gets right into his face and grins.

Cain chuckles, he begins to laugh, shaking the wires as he does.

"hehe..hahahaha..HAHAHAHAHAHA!" Cain's eyes go wild as the air begins to feel claustrophobic.. Almost suffocating.

Hunter goes to adjust his mask and Opheria narrows her eyes.

Cain keeps giggling as Cain wrenches forward, a sickening snap fills the air as his bones and muscles are shattered and torn, his body slowly turns into a liquid which drips from him as he slips from the restraints..

Like he was pulling himself through a meat grinder and had his body put itself back together, Opheria's eyes widened in horror and she backed up.

His skin stitches itself together and Cain swings a blow faster than the blink of an eye, she vanishes a moment before he hits her.

The Hunter dashes at Cain, pulling out another dagger and Cain laughs, he reaches into his own chest and suddenly blitzes across the room.

As he slid past The Hunter he ripped out his own rib, it shattered and turned to a small sword which he swung through the air.

Cain stood back up as The Hunter stumbled, their guts being split open by the slice.. They clutch their wounds as they collapse against the wall.

Cain's eyes glowed and his body is enveloped in Calm, he feels something hit his back gently before vanishing. Cain's mind began to crank and twirl as it tried to figure out the girl's abilities.

Outside Zalabar had managed to reach his feet, the energy of the sun sliced through the clouds and began to flow around him like a snake. Cain saw this and waited, the world began to click into place..

He felt a sudden punch to the jaw as his aura of calm vanished, The Hunter lashed out, sending a bolt through Cain's neck and then wires which burst from the ground and the walls, piercing through his body.

Pinning him there.

"STAY BACK! FOR I COMPEL THE SUN TO BURN CAIN TO LESS THAN ASH!"

Zalabar had managed to gather enough energy that it was like a blazing snake made of a star which wrapped around him.

"GO FORTH SUN SNAKE!" he yelled out.

Opheria vanished, appearing outside. The Hunter began to dash out from the room even with their injuries they moved quickly.. But not fast enough.

There was a wet splat before something slimy wrapped around Hunter's neck, pulling them back. They looked down to see that they were covered in tendrils and blood vessels which had exploded from Cain's torso... it had wrenched them back.

They were soon enveloped in a Calm aura and just like clockwork.. Opheria vanished and then reappeared with a concerned expression.

He could feel something had tried to tear the blood vessels off of the Hunter, but with the calm aura it had been impossible.

"Time or speed" Cain thought as The Hunter was forced to be his human shield.

He barely gave it another thought as the bright sun snake had enveloped the entire room, with a flash and a tremendous bang Cain was sent flying through the air.

Debris fell from the sky like rain but they simply bounced off as Cain looked up to the rain which soaked into his skin, healing him and increasing the strength of his calm aura.

Hunter lay there beside him, their body covered in burns and their left arm was completely eviscerated. Cain chuckled, he could sense Hunter's heart beat.. But he didn't finish the job, he was having much too fun now to stop.

"YOU BASTARD!" Opheria screamed as she launched towards him, Zalabar coughed and the calming bullet wore off, he jumped at him too.

Cain tried to move but the ground beneath him latched onto him and dug into his flesh like a bear trap. Opheria connected three right hooks within the span of a second, Cain's head whipped back.

Zalabar tried to burn a hole through his stomach but Cain laughed and dug his teeth into Zalabars skull, biting into him.

Opheria striked Cain's neck so hard it snapped.. The bone simply pulled itself back into place and he dodged another punch from Opheria.

He laughed, blood spraying from his mouth but his body healing quickly as the rain descended onto them. They continued to brutally beat into him, punches and burns bubbling his skin and breaking his bones.

With every punch, pull, burn and stab her simply laughs, his body healing itself over and over again.. Son Aaron looks on in fear and disbelief, Lucifer mutters to himself.

"That Apple has done something to him alright.."

Opheria screams as she uppercuts Cain, he spurts blood into the air as teeth fly out from his mouth.. As he looks back down again he's already regrown them, showing a full set.

Zalabar reaches out, trying to burn Cain's face, he dodges, his bones crack and pop as his hand breaks itself, he digs into Zalabar's chest, the shattered bones acting as needles. He screams in pain and throws himself back.

"Fuckin- Just die already!" Opheria shouts.

Cain chuckles.

"Good luck with that" he smiles, his teeth stained red from his and their blood.

Opheria thought for a moment, pulling away out of Cain's reach. He casually slotted his bones back into their place as the rain healed him.. Then she had a nasty idea.

She vanished, time completely freezing for her.

She shook her head.

"If I can't kill you.. I might as well start with those I can" she looked behind her to Son Aaron, his terrifying expression completely frozen.

She slowly makes her way towards him, pulling out a pocket knife.

"Wrong place, Wrong time" she giggled, as she reached out to slit Son Aarons throat something clicked in the air.. Something felt.. Wrong.. Very wrong.

She decided to ignore it, to plunge the knife into-

"No"

She paused.. No.. it wasn't possible, she turned to see Cain looking at her, he couldn't.. Time was frozen he could-

Suddenly a wave of fear tore out from his body, he looked like a flickering shadow, his eyes nothing but pure emotion, an impossible to describe colour and material.. His form was.. Not human.

He truly was a beast..

Now remember reader, when I said that any lesser would fall to such emotion? As Opheria looked into his eyes, the sheer wave of fear smashed into her, she stumbled and gasped.. Time flickered back to normal as her heart began to pound.. Pressure building up in her head..

As she fell down, dead, to a heart attack.

Everyone paused, Balazar's eyes widened and the Hunter made an inhuman sound of panic. Cain turned back to normal and looked at the other two.

He tore his leg from the bear trap, the rain grew it back as he stomped onto the ground, his blood began to pool beneath them, it tangled into strange wires of iron which wrapped around the Hunter and Balazar.

"YOU BASTARD! YOU KILLED HER!" Balazar screams, trying to break free from the iron thick prison.

Cain simply smiled and shrugged.

"What else did you expect to happen?" Cain took out his revolver and loaded it with the rage bullet, he aimed it to Balazar's head and smirked..he pulled the trigger and-

"STOP!" Son Aaron screamed, his eyes wide and his body shaking.. Another wave of golden energy passed through them all, deactivating their miracles.

Cain pulls the trigger and nothing fires from the revolver, Balazar's eyes widen and he stumbles, unable to stand up from the pain of the previous wounds.. He falls to the ground.. Hunter goes limp.

"I..I.." Son Aaron's eyes widen as he realises he may have killed them, tears flow down his face as he begins to shake violently.. Unable to control himself.

"Calm down!" Cain barked, his eyes still wide and mad.

"I...I..I...I c-c-can't" Son Aaron fell to his knees, the golden energy lashing out into the air and around him... he was unstable, his mind state was fracturing bit by bit.

"Kill him" Lucifer said, appearing right next to Cain.

"What!?" he shouts, snapping his head to Lucifer.

"He's too dangerous to the mission, kill him" Lucifer said again.

"I..." Cain looked over to Son Aaron, he could feel his miracle constantly sapped away.. He was having a breakdown, tears flowed down his face as he picked up Opheria, trying to bring her to life..

"You must do it. Now" Lucifer lays one of his hands on Cain's shoulder, he pauses.. He couldn't... could he?..

Lucifer slowly reaches down to Cain's hand and-

He smacked Lucifer's hands away as he walked away, stepping past Son Aaron before stopping..

"This is what happens.." Cain said, not finishing his sentence before moving on, making his way back towards the garden.

Lucifer appears next to Cain, his glowing eyes shining through the descending rain.

"You're making a mistake, he's a danger to the mission. If he follows us and has another freak out like that again you could-"

Cain interrupts him, waving Lucifer away.

"Yeah Yeah, I know what you're gonna say" he snarls, his golden eyes bleeding forth into the fear filled atmosphere around them.

Son Aaron pauses, the tears slowly down as he glances over to Cain as he walks away. He looks back down at his own hands and thinks..

Cain makes his way through the broken and forgotten city, he could feel a slow and powerful pulse of strange power coming from something unseen. He narrows his eyes and adjusts his gun, his miracle slowly returning to him.

"What is even your plan here?" Lucifer asked Cain, his world bending voice given pause.

"Break a few bones, kill a few angels" Cain muttered to himself as he began to tinker with his gun.

"...Right" Lucifer looks back ahead of them as they begin to push through a very wooded area, tree roots bursting from the abandoned brick and thick vines and brambles stretching through the air.

Cain easily slips past all of it, ducking under brambles and stepping over tall roots. The apple of knowledge helped, but spending so much time with Abel was what pushed him to be able to traverse such difficult natural terrain.

Son Aaron followed them at a large distance, unsure of his mental state, his golden energy leaks from like radiation.. Affecting anything within a few metres of him. His eyes were red from crying and his face was solemn, he could feel something was wrong.. Something pricking at the back of his neck.

He left it alone however and continued to follow Cain, tripping over tree roots and walking into sharp brambles and stinging nettles. He scowls to himself and sighs.

Meanwhile back at the destroyed and burnt battleground, Balazar slowly managed to stand up.. Blood seeped into his silky golden cloak as he coughed violently. Hunter simply remained still, their body unmoving, their eyes gently drifting behind the tinted black glass.

"..That...fucker..needs.. Death.." Balazar shouts, tears in his eyes from the overwhelming pain and the loss of his companion.

"He will burn by my hand! BY MY HA-" something shifts in the air around them.. A presence unparalleled steps into view.. A man, tall and thin, his body defined past human likelihood and stepped into grandiose.

His flowing white hair acted as if it slipped through water, never fully settling to gravity, staying afloat in the air. His eyes were a perfect blue.. That of the sky, that of the heavens. For he held one large white wing and wore a sharp halo.

Peter had arrived.

A thin lipped smile present on his face as he walked towards Balazar.

"S-Saint Peter?" he barked out, stumbling.

Peter examined the area, the smouldering rubble.. The still Hunter, the dead prophet on the floor..and the injured, stumbling Balazar.

"Do you not remember what I spoke of?" Peter asked, his voice as light as a feather and as inhuman as God.

"I-I remember but sire you-" Balazar was cut off with a deadly slash.

Peter moved far faster than the eye could see, his hand distorted into strengthened pillars, his nails contorting into daggers sharper than any iron blade.

Balazar saw the world spinning as his head was thrown from his body.. A clean cut severing his skull from his neck.

Balazar's headless body fell to its knees in a praying formation, Peter chuckled as he caught the decapitated head, playing with it.. Throwing it up and down like a ball.

"I should have known.. Sending others to do your work will never end well" Peter's tone echoed out with an aura of fear.

The Hunter tried to silently crawl away, making sure not to make a single sound so they wouldn't be noticed. However..

A single gust of wind blows past them as they feel the thin, tendril like fingers of Peter wrap around their head.

"You gave me so much hope" Peter said gently before wrenching his two hands, an awful cracking sound was made as Hunter's head was spun till it faced the wrong direction.. Gentle black blood leaking from them.

"But I should know hope doesn't mean anything by now.. Isn't that right, father of lies?" Peter said with a sharpened smile as he looked up to the sky, staring into God's very soul.. If he had one.

Peter stood up and slowly walked forward, his blue eyes sharper than any sword. His presence drenched the surrounding area in dread and despair.. Hatred even. For Peter hated.. Not just Cain.. not just God.. but everything, he had been lied to.

And he was going to make it everyone's problem.

Chapter 22:
The Garden

Cain stepped through the thickened woods and slipped into the large open space in front of him. The grass was soft and a brightly coloured green, the sky was clearing and turning to a sharp blue and the air smelled like.. Home.. almost.

Cain stood at the edge of the lush path which led into the strange dome like structure which stood before them, its walls were made of an angelic metal which rings with a sense of power and aura. Its glass is made of a material long forgotten, even when Cain tried to focus the knowledge he had gained from the apple he failed to come up with its name or composition.. Truly a mystery.

Inside they could see a massive and lush forest with birds of sizes normally impossible and beasts roaming free and wild, rushing water pouring down small cliffs and strange green orbs which floated to and fro in the air.

"So that's the garden huh?" Cain asked, taking a step towards it.

Lucifer nodded and looked around, his four heads spinning slowly.

"Yes.. however I could have sworn there was top security.." Lucifer said with a hesitant breath.

Cain shrugged as he made his way forward, his revolver in one hand.

"Nothing a little bullet can't fix" Cain chuckled to himself as he loaded the revolver's cylinders.

"Actually a lot of things little bullets can't fix.. I was told this place is guarded by two cherubs.. Even though they're at the bottom of the angelic pyramid they are incredibly powerful to entities like you" Lucifer said as they neared the entrance to the Garden.

"What do you mean entities like me?"

"Mortal born" Lucifer said plainly.

They had reached the entrance to the Garden, no form of security was in sight and Cain narrowed his eyes.

"Something's weird about this..." he said to himself, a gentle tone of worry flickering through his words.

"I understand the sentiment.." Lucifer agreed, they both began to slip through the large metallic doors.

Cain and Lucifer pushed against the massive gates, they swing wide open and reveal the beautiful bustling Garden. They start walking forward when-

Something flickered.. The entire Garden vanished, an illusion.

Lucifer's eyes widened and Cain gritted his teeth but it was too late, the doors slammed shut with a loud bang and locked themselves tight.

"Shit!" Cain hissed, Lucifer's eyes glowed as they scanned the area they now stood in.

The garden was gone.. Replaced with nothing but ash and death, the air was polluted with the stench of rot and disease.. The cold grip of a long dead area latches onto Cain and Lucifer..

They could sense the aged ash and the sense of lingering fear and hatred from those beasts that once lived here.

"What.. the.." Cain looked around, his golden eyes widened with surprised interest.

The few trees which remained were blackened and burnt to their very core, leaking ash and charcoal onto the rotting grass below. Cain coughed, spores of things unknown slowly filling his lungs, his eyes were quickly pulled to the most colourful thing in the room.. That of a faded grey apple, its form was retained and yet its colour was off.

"I do not have a good feeling about this" Lucifer said as he tried to find the nearest entities but Cain wasn't listening, he was already in a full sprint towards the apple.

His heavy footsteps kicked up layers and layers of dust and ash, flinging it into the thick and warm air, he reached out to the apple just before-

There was a loud crack and a thud as a massive chunk of the ground shook, Cain was sent flying as his arm was cut clean from his body.

Cain cried out and slammed hard into the side of the dome before landing face first in the settled rot, a blade strike had dug into the ground where he once stood, sending soot high into the dome.. Covering it in another layer.

Lucifer whipped around and noticed two angels flying towards him, he blocked both of their strikes but was sent flying through a nearby tree with a loud crash and thud.

The two angles stood as guardians to the gate, each holding a sword which was engulfed in white holy flames.. They were humanoid, much more so than Lucifer, their eyes were hollow however and simply seeped into nothingness.. Black..

Their bodies were off too, their arms were too long and their legs were thicker than the rest of their body, their torso was strangely shaped and their heads resembled that of a woman and man.

"Cherubs.." Lucifer scowled as he raised once again into the air, his four black wings spreading wide.

Cain groaned as he slowly stood, his flesh wrapped around his wound to stop the bleeding. His arm had been sliced clean off, sent somewhere within the mounds of dust and dirt across the "Garden".

Lucifer tries to summon rain but it bounces off the glass of the Garden, so healing was not an option..

Cain slowly stood up to his feet, pulling out his revolver. The cherubs spoke, their voices in unison.

"ALL ARE FREE TO ENTER THE GARDEN, HOWEVER, NONE MAY LEAVE. YOU HAVE LET YOUR HUBRIS GUIDE YOU TO AN ETERNAL JOY YOU NO LONGER DESERVE. YOU WILL ROT HERE, DEATH COMES TO ALL"

"Well fuck me then.." Cain grumbled as he spat a small fraction of rage into the cylinder of the revolver. He aimed it and fired it towards the cherubs.

There was the sound of clashing metal and the bullet was chopped in twain.. Falling into pieces to the rot below. The strike was so fast Cain couldn't even see it...

"Oh.. definitely fuck me then.." he whispered to himself.

Lucifer looked over to Cain.

"These are cherubs.. They're angels, do not doubt their abilities.. You are not strong enough yet to even think about taking them!"

The ground began to slowly shake and rumble, Cain furrowed his brow and a hand burst from the coarse rot below him, it was a skeletal hand.. One of someone who had come here and never made it out.. The corpse slowly pulled itself from the ground.

Lucifer looked around as all kinds of entities began to do the same, this place was a mass graveyard for all those poor souls who thought they could return to the Garden.

"Oh fuck.." Cain jumped back, he loaded up the Revolver full of bullets and prepared himself.. He began to get surrounded.

Lucifer shouted, a mighty blast of angelic energy tore through a massive group of them, turning them into less than dust.

But then something else began to pull itself from the rubble...

At first it was just the slippery thought of the snake.. Then it was the arm of a giant, then its bone wings burst from the ground as a fallen angel arose from the ash itself.. Lucifer's eyes widened.

"Oh.. Oh no.." Lucifer summoned a holy blade and prepared his stance as the skeletal giant slowly poured the dirt from its decaying corpse, its eye sockets gently engulfing the area around them in a black.. An anti light.

"CAIN! This is more serious than I thought!" Lucifer shouts, worry stricken across all four of his heads as he tries to prepare himself.

Cain dodges one of the skeletons as they try to bite him, he spins around and cracks against its jaw with his boot, turning into a pile of rubble.

Cain dodges another creature.. It looked almost like a humanoid wolf skeleton, it launched at him, trying to cut him in half but he dodged.

Spinning around he kicks the beast in the ribs with a crack, his entire body is engulfed in an aura of rage as he sends the creature skidding alongside the Garden like a skipping stone.

"Yeah.. seems like it!" Cain jumps into the air and fires the bullets of rage into the skeletons which reach for him. Each bullet erupts into violent crimson explosions which blow the corpses to pieces.

A rotting wing bursts from Cain's back and flaps, bringing Cain higher into the air. He turns to Lucifer who is staring down this decayed Angel.. The air is tense with rotting malice.

"What if I just eat the fuckin apple!?" Cain shouts, his eyes glancing at the shape of the ashen grey apple still lodged in the blackened tree in the middle of the large dome.

The cherubs speak once more.

"ALL WHO TRY TO TASTE THE APPLE WILL BE WROUGHT WITH ROT AND DECAY, YOU WILL BE CONSUMED BY PESTILENCE!"

Cain rolled his eyes as he managed to keep himself airborne and out of reach of the jumping corpses.

"Of course it wouldn't be that easy.."

Suddenly something swooped through the air, its skeleton that of a legendary beast. Cain's eyes widened as he managed to narrowly duck its claws.. The knowledge filled his mind as he whispered its name.

"Dragon of Dragons.."

The beast whipped around, its skeletal tail slashing across Cain's chest and he cried out as he began to fall from earth. He lashes out, blood vessels bursting from his wrist and wrapping around the beast as it entangles its wings.

It screeches into the air and dives into the ground, erupting the rot into the air and dragging Cain into the earth with a crash. The force shakes his body and his mind goes blank for a moment, the white hot pain of his bones breaking stuns him.

Lucifer dodged an attack so fast it was barely seen, the rotting angel tried to lash out and claw Lucifer's eyes out. Its attacks were monstrous and without thought, they tried to rip his skin off but he dodges narrowly retaliating with a kick to the chest which sends the beast back.

He slashes his sword through the air, catching the rotting angel by the shoulder and damaging their arm. They step back and screech.. Dark magic leaks into the air and Lucifer's eyes widen as he summons a shield.

The blast of magic shakes the dome as tendrils burst from the air and strike the shield, they wrap around it and dig into Lucifer's skin, he strikes back with a sword jab which the undead angel dodges, connecting a slash to Lucifer's jaw, sending him stumbling.

Cain grunts and jumps back to his feet, corpses surround him and all try to pile onto him, they dig their claws into his skin and try to bite and rip chunks off of him.

He screams as his eyes fill with a powerful blaze of anger and there is a wet crack, Cain's body splits itself open as his blood shoots from under his skin and hardens as it travels through the air piercing the beasts behind him on spires which drive through their skills and hold them up into the air.

Cain groans as sweat pours down his face, the skeletal dragon turns to him and roars, Cain shoots at it, erupting chunks from it. It rises into the air and takes a deep breath, inky black absorbing into its mouth as it prepares to attack.

Cain grunts and looks over to the apple.

"It's too dangerous!" Lucifer shouts as he counters a flashing strike.

"...Fuck danger.." Cain's blood retracts back into him and he leaps away, the ground beneath his feet erupting into dust as the dragon sends a pillar of shadows to where he once was, erasing all the corpses it touches.

Cain lands and tries to fly again but something wraps around his wing and he's pulled back down to earth with a crash. He looks up with rage filled eyes and scowls..

The mostly rotting corpse of a man in a brown overcoat pulls on the chains which have been thrown around him. Cain takes a deep breath and feels his emotions slowly build up inside of him, rage flickering like flames as fear clouds like mist.

"Sorry about this Stephen!" Cain grabs the chain and suddenly a massive wave of heat rips through it turning it white with heat, the corpse is forced to let go of it.

Cain whips the chain around, spinning it through the air as it begins to smash into the corpses' skulls around him.. As they approached they had a heavy metal and burning hot chain smash into them, turning their skulls to nothing more than fragments.

He throws it back at the corpse, pinning the chain through its chest and keeping it down to the ground as the chain burns into it, melting into its decayed flesh.

The skeleton dragon roars and dives towards Cain, he lets his body be enveloped into an aura of calm and the dragon slows down the moment it approaches.

He grips the dragon's skull and pulls it, flipping it through the air and slamming it into the ground hard, sending dust high into the air as rot fills Cain's lungs..

He stumbles and coughs, his body spent and tired, the rot slowly sapping away at his energy and life force, he wobbles on his feet. Cain coughs again as he stumbles through the ash and dust, it catches on his feet and he collapses.

Lucifer punches a hole through the rotting angel's chest, it screeches and plunges its hand into his back. He screams in agony and falls limp as black magic begins to absorb into his flesh.. Burning away at his very being..

"..Lucy..fuck.. LUCY!" Cain shouts out.

Lucifer slowly looks over to Cain and shakes his head, the decaying angel rips one of Lucifer's eyes out and he roars in agony as he's brought to the floor.

He sends out angelic blasts of energy which the decaying angel simply tanks as it beats into Lucifer, tearing away at his flesh.

"..God...fucking.. Dammit.." Cain slowly drags himself towards the blackened tree.. He looks up to the grey apple, a massive wave of rot washes over Cain and he feels his muscles begin to weaken as it eats away at his mass.

He gasps, feeling his stomach begin to consume itself as his brain starts to lack its resources.. He slowly reached for it.. More corpses simply pulled themselves from the ground, digging into his back and legs.

"..Fuck.. everything.." Cain grabs the apple, his skin begins to dry and age, turning to a black mess.. His arm loses its mass as it shrinks.

He plunges his face into the apple and bites down into its flesh.. It tasted like rot incarnate, its skin melted into dry bark and its flesh stank of aged death.. And yet as he continued to chew into it.. Something began to shift and change.

"Wrong.. Apple.." Cain managed to think as his body began to give up on itself... he plunged his remaining hand into the bark of the burnt tree and ripped out a perfectly ripe red apple.

For there is always hope for life even in death.. *"Or some pretentious shit"* Cain thought.

"Fuck you and your stupid morals" Cain bit into the red apple and-

Potentia, the Apple of Power.

A white blast completely fills the arena, the dome glints brightly and amplifies the light into a small beam which tears through the sky.

Son Aaron looks from behind a tree, his eyes wide and his skin slightly pale as he clutches his stomach...

On top of the rooftops sits a figure with a large angelic wing and a sharpened halo.. A smile slips onto his face.

As the bright white light slowly fades and flickers Cain is seen standing.. His body heals as steam slowly pours off of him, his hair is a little longer than before, covering his eyes now as he begins to slowly walk towards the cherubs.. No smile on his face.. No determination.. Simply walking.

Lucifer growls and pushes the decaying angel back before swivelling to look at Cain approaching the cherubs, his eyes widened.

"CAIN! DON'T!" Lucifer shouts as the decaying angel stabs Lucifer with the tip of his bone wings.

Cain opens his mouth to speak before the sound of a singing blade fills the air. Cain paused.

He then realised he had been cut in near half, he coughed a massive amount of blood and stumbled backwards. A burning cut had sliced straight through his chest, cracking his ribs and destroying his lungs and heart.

Lucifer goes to rush towards him but Cain puts his hand up to signify for him to stop.. Cain stands there for a moment, struggling to breathe.. Blood pouring from his fatal wound..

And then he continued to walk forward.

It took a few more steps before another strike came. It cut into his leg and shattered his femur bone before he collapsed to his knees.

"Cain! What are you doing!?" Lucifer cried out.

Cain chuckled, smiling through blood soaked teeth, his eyes were wild.. Suddenly a wave of.. Not just fear.. But **power** ripples through the air.

Cain took another step, the blade strike came from the male this time, piercing through his stomach and exploding his guts out his back. He laughed with no lungs as he reeled from the blow and took another step forward, unrelenting.

His eyes were wild, more beast than man.. His smile remained ever still.. He took another step.. The woman this time, slashing across his face, destroying his jaw and throat.

Cain reeled from the blow and fell down limp, Lucifer's eyes widened.

"Dammit.." Lucifer hissed..

Cain then raised an arm.. He was still moving, dragging himself along the burning grass, his one remaining golden eye shines brighter than any star.. And yet dimmer than any sun.

The two figures turned to each other in confusion and disbelief before they both attacked at once..

Turning Cain into nothing but mush.

"Fuck!" Lucifer dodged another strike from the decaying angel... however.. slowly Cain's blood and guts began to shake and slide across the ground.

The cherubs looked in shock as Cain's entire body began to reform, his bones and blood vessels pulling each other into place. His skin wraps around his vacant flesh and his eyes grow back from brain matter.. An aura of pure fear reeks off of him..

Lucifer pauses.. His remaining eyes glow.. Cain began to laugh as his lungs popped full of air and his eyes were that of a wild.. Feral.. No.. not beast.. Something more than that.

Not angel or man.. Not beast or snake.. Cain was something different. However no one knew what they could possibly call him.. But he sure was a descendant of God himself.

"Hahaha..HAHAHAHA..HAHAHAHAHAHAHA! FUCKING KILL ME! DO IT! TRY I-" another slash, this time it cut Cain clean in half, he was sent flying through the air and suddenly his intestines and tendons fired from his bottom and top half, interlocking and pulling him back together with a wet splat.

His skin stitches itself into one and he smiles wide.

The male cherub points their blade towards Cain and he's ignited in holy flame, burning and bubbling his flesh and bone as he's slowly turned to ash.

And yet he laughs.. His body igniting into his own flame, one of hatred and rage, his eyes become completely blank as he reels his head back in laughter.

"HAHAHAHAHAHA! IS THAT ALL YOU GOT-" another slash, this time taking out a whole chunk of his chest, his eyes wide as his smile widens, his body begins to flicker.

Lucifer watches as Cain gets back up and is then beaten down again.. And again.. And again.. Lucifer watches Cain get butchered.. Over and over..

However something became apparent.. Cain wasn't staying down.

In fact, with every strike his body reforms faster and faster, his eyes a blank rage as he simply walks forward. No matter the speed of the blow Cain simply reforms, no matter the heat of the holy flame he ever marches onward.. His body held together through rage and bloodlust.. His figure soon contorting into a shadow, a flickering silhouette.. The cherubs each took one step back.

Cain kept smiling, he clicked his shoulder into place and stood still.

"HIT ME!" Cain screamed his body slowly flickering in and out of existence..

The male cherub tries to cut Cain's head clean off, moving at impossible speeds, the blow was sure to connect only an angel could block-

The blade the cherub holds is knocked from his hand, his eyes widen.

Cain smirks as he batted it away, the blade fractured from just his hand alone.. His eyes grew more and more mad as the aura of sheer power became slowly overloading.. The ground beneath him began to contort and break apart just by Cain's very existence.

"Don't tell me that's all you got" Cain smiled that of a crescent moon.

The female cherub tried lashing out.. There was a wet splash as her arm was ripped from its socket by a blade. She screamed in agony as her arm fell to the ground.. Cain had barely moved.

"HOW IS THIS POSSIBLE FOUL BEAST!? YOU ATE FROM THE ROTTEN APPLE! YOU'RE CONDEMNED TO DEATH! TO ILLNESS AND SICKNESS!"

Cain kept smiling.

"Oh I don't do that illness shit.. You may not know, or you may have forgotten.. I'm not an ordinary motherfucker.."

Cain leaped through the air at horrendous speeds, appearing behind the male Cherub.

"I'm God's grandchild"

Cain struck the cherub at the back of the head, the force blew the angel into the ground with a loud crash as he went limp, the female cherub tried to smack Cain away but he pulled out his own rib.. Using it as a sword he flies along her arm, cutting deep into her before ripping it out of her elbow and slashes across her throat.

She gasps and stumbles, crashing into the side of the dome.. Sliding down to the ground, limp.

Lucifer managed to get the upper hand on the decaying angel and used a holy blast to take off its skull as it dug its talons into his chest.

The decaying angel fell limp and crashed into the ground below.. He turned to look at Cain, as he stood in between two dead angels.. His body flickering, his very essence leaking into the world around him like radiation.. Burning and eroding.

Lucifer speaks gently, healing himself.

"...Fights over.. You can calm down now"

Cain said nothing, he walked out from the dome, picking up the rotting apple again and throwing it behind his back. He pushed against the metallic doors and with an ear shattering bang they're torn to shrapnel and sent flying across the green lush grass outside.

Son Aarons eyes widen as he feels a sudden wave of fear shoot up his spine.. Like spiders slipped under his skin and began to crawl around, he almost screamed from the emotion but managed to keep quiet, laying against the tree.

Cain slowly walked into the lush garden of green grass, his breathing was slow and heavy.. His power flickered off him like an igniting barrel of explosives, the sheer aura raging from him was enough to completely wilt the flowers under his feet.

He was not human.

Not anymore, his hands twitched and pulled against themselves as he held back even more energy from being unleashed.. The world had changed again.. Everything was different, he could feel and see the very life force around him.

Every living being all at once being dragged around through the air, as he looked up at the sky.. He no longer saw the calm blue, no.. he saw stairs.. Stairs bigger than the stars, stairs bigger than the galaxy.. The earth..

The earth was simply a single step towards God hood

And only now did Cain feel the pure fear of grandiose.. The fear of the unknown and the large.. His power was off the charts, inhuman and yet he looked upon those stairs and realised the gap in power.

Lucifer followed him, Cain looked at him with his eyes and he nearly screamed.. Lucifer was different, for he had a thousand eyes and ten faces surrounded by the eclipsing moon, his every essence bled into the air around them as strings of heaven played on the harp of life.

"...Κάιν?" Lucifer spoke in a language Cain couldn't understand.. He stook a step back, his emotions flaring causing the earth beneath him to ignite in crimson inferno.. The sheer heat began to melt the dirt around him.

Son Aaron cried out as the heat blasted at him, turning the tree he sat under to ash, he felt his skin begin to berate and burn as red patches began to form. He cried out through the pain and the heat.

"CAIN!" he shouts, panicking as his skin sears.

Cain turns to see Son Aaron and opens his mouth, all he sees is an entity.. Not human.. A life.. He could stare into Son Aaron.. He could see his very soul, his essence.. What makes his existence a measurable distance.

He saw more than any human was meant to see.. And he screamed..

Lucifer lashes out, a strike to the back of his neck with a golden hand and Cain's eyes go blank.. His power shuts off like a switch and he falls unconscious.

The burning crimson flame of hatred vanished without a trace, the heat subsided for cool chill air.. Son Aaron winces as the tears flowing down his face sting his burns.

And all the while a man.. No.. a false angel.. Watched from a distance, a smile on his face and a glimmer of hope in his eyes.

"We'll have a good fight, you and I" Peter said to himself, and he waited..

Lucifer picked up the unconscious Cain and began to float away with him, Son Aaron ran out from the burnt trees and cried out.

"Wait! Angel! I know I can't see you but I know you're there! Can I come with?.. Cain needs something to ground him! Please!" Son Aaron shouts, trying to plead with Lucifer.

Lucifer pauses, his inhuman form shifting and clicking as his body separates and reforms almost like a rhythm of breathing, he thinks before his thistles shake.. In human terms, he shook his head.

Son Aaron didn't get an answer, he simply saw Cain being slowly carried through the air.

Son Aaron paused.. He didn't give up though, he simply slipped into the woods, vanishing from sight as Cain was brought past the treeline.

Soon there was peace.. No sound..

A beautiful golden bird flies through the air, its song shines beautifully through the pale clear sky.. It flew past the burning trees when-

Snatch.

The bird was caught in the pale iron tight grip of a man with long flowing white hair and pale perfect blue eyes. He brought the bird to his mouth slowly and bit down upon its neck, spraying its blood into his maw as the bird's struggle ended.

Peter finished the bird and threw the bones away, spitting them out, he made his way towards the Garden of Eden. as he entered he could smell the stench of death and disease.. In the middle of it, next to a fallen black tree, lay a grey apple with a rotten bite taken from it.

Peter walked up to it with a smile on his face as the violins of heaven began to play an orchestra of birth, Peter gently placed his hand on the rotten apple and spoke a word.

"Rise"

Suddenly the entire dome and enclosure began to shake violently as the rot and dust picked up against itself and thrashed as the apple began to bubble and boil turning into a vile liquid of illness and cancer.

It seeped into the blackened tar of the earth as suddenly a form began to grow from the power of it, from the remnants of eden a figure bursts from the ground with angelic divinity filling their body and bones with might and will of God.

Peter smiled his thin lipped smile, his calm and thin demeanour open as the being writhed.. Born from angels and rot.

Born..

"Pestilence" Peter hissed through his teeth as he smiled.. The figure cracking and slipping discs into place as its body formed in front of him.

The creature's head, a horse's skull, fuses to its spine as its flesh is brought from the blackened earth, turning into melted skin and rotting tissue.. A nearby corpse was dragged along the floor as a base, absorbing certain components into the being..

And there stands Pestilence.. A being made of illness and rot, wearing a blackened overcoat and carrying a chain covered in rust and blackened blood.

Peter smiled wide.

"You're going to be very useful, dear creation of mine"

Pestilence nods as a mosquito crawls into his empty eye socket.

Chapter 23:
Requiem of Loss

The sky was bleak on this summer's morning.

Houses built on the sides of mountains, a man stands in the front doorway, his darkened skin shining beautifully in the pale light of the full sun.

Another man stands of course, hidden with his refuge, his home, as he begins to pack his bags.

For where would he go?

"North. North until I can't go north anymore, then, I'll go West, I'll go West till I can't go West anymore.. Then, Cain, I'll do it all over again.. 100 times over, until I know this world in and out.. Only then can I die a happy man"

But of course reader, we know how this ends. We know the origin for pain and misery.. We know it all.. Or at least, I do.

Do you know the smell of rain dear reader? How it permeates the air like it belongs? Like it sticks to the very air you breathe.

Hope does the same, something you can't get rid of.. But Despair does that better.

It's the flickering dilemma in a way.

The brighter the light, the less shadows. Yet the shadows are much darker.. Only in pure light can the darkest shadows be born.

And only when compared to darkness, can light be seen.

Cain was 33, going about his usual business when he felt something change in the air, he paused and peaked out of his house.. Looking around.

He saw the cloak, its white cloth dragging against the lip of the doorway as it slowly slipped from sight. Cain's eyes light up and he smiles.. His grandfather must be visiting Abel, he should go say hi.

Cain steps from his house and walks down the hill, a smile on his face as he approaches his brother's home.

His feet crunched into the healthy grass, the hopeful wind blew across the beautiful and shining landscape. He reached the doorway and paused as he heard Abel bark something, his eyes widened in light shock and he didn't enter.. Simply listening.

"No!" Abel barked as he opened a drawer.

God spoke, his voice thick and clear.

"Abel, you are my grandchild, for I love you so very much. But this is a mistake, you mustn't leave this place"

"Why? Why am I not allowed to leave and have my own life? Why am I not allowed to choose what I get to do?" Abel hissed, clearly pissed.

"You're disrespecting me and my wishes!" God shouted back.

"You're not in control of me! I'm not your puppet that you get to order around, maybe Cain is but I. Am. NOT!" Abel shouts, Cain narrows his eyes and peaks his head in.. barely able to see the two figures arguing.

"You must not raise your voice against me!"

"Why not? Did I finally strike a nerve? Did I get under the controlling old man's skin!? I don't owe you anything! You tried to keep us locked in a cage like fuckin sheep but we broke out and now you want us back on a damn leash!" Abel shouts, the angriest Cain had ever heard him.

"You will find what you are saying will lead to terrible consequences" God spoke slowly.

"I'm not scared of you anymore! You are a bad fucking person! You let children die of illness and you let people go without food!

I'm glad that I'm going to fucking escape you" Abel finished packing his bags..

An aura of fear filled the air..

"Yes.. escape.."

"Hey what are you doing? Hey, stop that!"

There was a sudden wet thud and Abel went silent.. Cain's eyes widened as blood sprayed upon the floor.. Another wet and violent smash as Abel's limp body hit the ground.. Another blow to the skull which split it open and sprayed even onto Cain.

The world began to shrink.. The sound of ringing bells filled Cain's head, his eyes dilated as he tried to find a reasonable explanation.. Anything but this.. Anything but this.. Anything but this.. Anything but this.. Please no.. no...

Cain looked up to see God standing before him.

He stood tall, with light skin and a long white beard with thinning hair, covered in crimson liquid which dripped from his cloak.

"....please.. Help.." it's all he could think to say as he stared into the hollow eyes of God.

God waved his hand as the blood transferred to Cain, he kicked him in the gut, hard. Cain was sent flying back across the pale green grass and crashed into the ground, his head began to spin as God shouted.

"YOU HAVE CAST THY BROTHER DOWN ONTO THE GROUND WITH WET AND SULLEN BLOOD! FOR YOUR HUBRIS WAS YOUR OWN SOUL AND MIND. ROTTEN!" God shouted as the sound blasted through the air.. Heard from all the nearby villages.

"YOU, CAIN, HAVE KILLED THY BROTHER FOR NOTHING MORE THAN STICKS AND STONES TO IMPRESS ME! AND WITH YOUR BROTHERS INNOCENT

BLOOD ON YOU.. I HEREBY CURSE YOU WITH A MARK!"

Cain didn't hear a word he said.. Everything was just white noise to him.. He looked down to his brother's blood and then up to his parents who looked at him with shock and fear..

Cain felt a blazing pain as a tattoo of a dagger with the handle of a snake seared into his skin, he arched his back and screamed into infinitium.

Cain didn't hear the next part.. All he felt was the vibrations of speech..

He couldn't even see his father dashing towards him, gun in hand.

However.. Adam's eyes never one laid on Cain with violence, but on God himself.

Adam pulled the gun and aimed it at God's head.

"You fucker! DON'T YOU LIE ABOUT MY SON! THEY'LL KILL HIM!" Eve tackle hugged Adam, holding him back. Adam thrashed as Eve pulled him away.

"YOU BASTARD! WHAT HAVE YOU DONE!?" Adam continued to scream and shout, he kicked and lashed out but Eve continued to keep him under control, dragging him away.

"Fine, CAIN! I GIVE YOU A MARK WHERE ANY MAN WHO KILLS YOU WILL FEEL JUSTICE SEVENFOLD" God waved his hand as his own name was burned into Cain's skull and skin, he continued to scream and thrash.

Adam continued to shout heresy and violent threats as Eve continued to pull him out of sight, tears flooding down her face.

"I'LL FUCKING KILL YOU FATHER!" Adam shouted out before Eve threw him behind the front door, locking it.

Cain slowly but surely came to.. His eyes filled with flowing tears, pain filling every ounce of his body as his own world view broke and crumbled..

He felt someone grab his collar and slap him, the pain was minimal.. He didn't care much.

Eve screamed at him.

"HOW COULD YOU DO THIS TO YOUR BROTHER!?" she screeched, tears streaming down her face.

"...I didn't-" Eve slapped Cain.

"DON'T LIE TO ME!"

And so Cain said nothing, he just stared into empty space.

"LEAVE! LEAVE AND NEVER COME BACK!" Eve pushed Cain away.. He slowly rolled to his feet, climbing back up..

He didn't even look back, he just stumbled away.. His eyes empty and hollow.. His body filled with such an emotion.. Something he could never control..

The indescribable sense of your world being shattered.. Of loss.. Of confusion and false conviction...

As Cain slipped from sight, stumbling through the woods covered in his brother's blood.. Eve looked at the ground.

"I see we're on the same page" God said smiling, placing a hand on Eve's shoulder, she pushed him off.

"DON'T TOUCH ME!" Eve glared at him with rage in her eyes.

"I know what you did.. Just.. leave us out of this.. Please.." Eve rubbed her eyes and walked away.

God simply chuckled.

"Very well.."

He turned and walked away, vanishing before her very eyes into a bloom of white butterflies.

"....." Eve ran back home, the ground beneath her coiling into jagged shapes.

Cain eventually found it.. The ravine.. He stood on its mossy edge staring down at the darkness, memories rushing through him as he simply slipped from the edge.

He let himself fall down, crashing into the side and spinning through the air before cracking down onto the rocks below, slipping into the shadows.. His skull snaps against a large rock, his blood spraying out everywhere as he goes still.. His eyes motionless and lifeless.

Silence.. Finally..

Until it began to rain,..

Lucifer pressed their heads together as he began to take control of Cain's body, flipping it over and opening his mouth.. The dew drops landing on his dead and cold tongue which shoots life through his body, his eyes regain life as air fills his lungs..

His skull heals and his brain reforms as his heart begins pumping blood again and cells return to their normal state of working, Lucifer slips out from Cain and simply sits there.. Watching him as he realises what had happened.. As he broke down into tears and curled up, screaming and wailing..

And yet no one ever came to help him..

"....." Lucifer stared at Cain with his glowing eyes and shining black wings.. And he knew.. He had something in him, something no human or angel had.

"Drink up" Lucifer said, knowing Cain wouldn't hear him.

"We have a long journey ahead of us.." Lucifer bowed his head.

Chapter 24:
Requiem of Hope

Peter sat in a well lit room, he sat within a bathtub that was mostly full. Six older nuns surrounded him as they slowly scrubbed his body with their hands and soap.

Peter said nothing, he just looked forward with a blank stare..

It had been 4 years since God tested his faith on that roof.

Peter thought about what he had been told as the Nuns slowly dried him off and clothed him.. Placing on his smooth velvet red robe and brown trousers and an offwhite blue shirt.. They styled his blonde hair and dabbed him in light makeup.

He continued to say nothing as they led him through the winding halls of the Church.. He heard the distant cheering and clapping as someone announced the sinners they had caught and forced to repent..

He was placed in a room off to the side, sitting down in the small cupboard-like area with a single candle and a bible next to him.. He slowly picked it up and waited.. There was a shift in the box next to him as a man walked in and sat down.

"..is that you Peter?" said the voice.. Unfamiliar yet sure.

"Call me Father" Peter said gently as his eyes drifted along the passages of the book which he had already read thousands of times.

"Right... I'm here to confess my sins" he spoke slowly and gently.

"Then begin my child" Peter said, a small smile on his face.

"..Right.. I abandoned someone long ago when I knew I shouldn't have.. Now they're being turned into something they're not supposed to be.."

Peter still recognised nothing, he spoke with clear intention.

"Then you should apologise to those you abandoned and say grace to god for giving you the chance to repent" Peter said, still smiling.

"...Right... Sorry, Peter.."

Peter shook his head.

"I am not the one you must apologise to" Peter said, his eyes unmoving from the bible.

"....Right... well.. Thanks.. A lot...I.. I have a plan to save the person I abandoned.. From this world which is turning them into something they're not.."

"I wish you the best, and remember to follow the path of the lord!" Peter said happily.

The figure in the other room paused before slowly standing up.

"Goodbye Peter..." he walked away, slipping from the church and making his way out of town.

But Peter remained without knowledge, without realisation.

The day went past as normal, Peter spoke to those who needed help with their sins and eventually he left the small and enclosed space.. A smile on his face.

He began to make his way back to his quarters when he walked into someone, his eyes widened and lit up as he saw the holy men around him.. With one woman in the middle, smiling gently towards him.

"M-Mother Julia!" Peter said, his smile widening.

"Hello there Peter, I have come with great news" she places her hand on his shoulder and smiles.

"It is time" her voice was soft and caressed his ears like velvet.

"W-wait.. R-really?" Peter said, his voice stammering from the sudden rush of adrenaline.

Mother Julia nodded as she placed her hand on his back and slowly led him through the church.

Some of the Holy Men undid a latch to an unseen trap door which led them downward.. Peter's eyes widened as she led him through the winding dark corridors and eventually into the massive cathedral.. It was baked in a warm orange glow.

"W-Woah! H-how..." he began.

"The church is often given great gifts by god!" Mother Julia said, her smile was just as soft and beautiful as the day they met on that cold summer night.

"One of those gifts.. Is you" she looked down to Peter, he paused, his eyes shining with excitement.

"M-Me!?" he bounced up and down.

"Yes, you" she continued to smile at him.

"You've proven such devotion to this life of God, you're the most special person we've ever seen.. No one has been able to save the sinners like you" she said in her sweet tone.

He gleamed, his smile wide and his chest puffed out with pride.

"That's why we've decided.." she gestures to the throne.

"For you to become the first great priest"

His eyes widen as his jaw drops.

"I..I..but.."

"Go on, sit on the seat.. God has a gift for you" she said as she lightly shoved him forward..

For a moment Peter paused, but the shove snapped him back into place and he quickly rushed to the throne and carefully sat down.. His heart was racing and joy overflowed in him.

"This.. is.. Amazing.." he thought to himself, he just couldn't stop smiling.

As he sat upon his throne he could hear the voice of God as a holy light beamed down from the window above him and engulfed him in light and love.

"Peter! You will become my first Saint! You are worthy of the highest honour, to become my vessel to bring hope and joy into the world!"

"R-really Lord?" Peter had tears of joy in his eyes as he slowly began to float upward.

"Yes! From now on you will be known as Saint Peter the first! You will be able to harness a fraction of my grand power!"

Peter was shaking in excitement.

"Y-Yes God! Lord!"

"But first you must know your goal, shall you not? To bring everyone to such a perfect world"

Peter nodded as suddenly his mind went blank...

He saw a world where everything was peaceful.. There was no illness.. No rot.. There was no war.. No murder.. The world was flourishing with plants and animals which lived in harmony.

Lions and Gazelles drank water besides each other.

And two figures walked alongside them, not a cloth on their skin as they held their hands. They were a gender Peter could not discern.. Man or woman.. But he knew they were joyous.. And everything was brilliant.

As Peter was lowered onto his seats he opened his wonder filled eyes and asked.

"What do I have to do for you God!?" he asked excitedly.

"You must bring about a new Eden, and for that we must make sure this population repents so they may all rise to Heaven with me upon the Rapture"

"Rapture?" Peter tilted his head.

"Don't worry about that, all you have to do-"

The memory fades..

St. Peter sits on top of the church spire, his large angelic wing and rotating halo shine in the darkened day as rain pours from the sky.

"All I gotta do is listen to you huh?" St. Peter chuckled and shook his head as he stood.

"You're lucky that I continue to follow your orders old man" St. Peter looks down at the streets below.. At the crowds of priests and the few scattered prophets.. How everyone in the town stands there, looking up at him..

He speaks with a booming tone, his sharpened blue eyes a window into the soul of a man regretful by nature.

"PRIESTS AND PROPHETS OF BETHEL!" He raises his arms as angelic light washes over the town.

"CAIN HAS OBTAINED TWO APPLES FROM GOD! DEFYING HIM!" the crowds boo at Cain's name.

"HE IS PLANNING ON KILLING OUR GOD!! BUT I KNOW WHERE HE IS BEING TAKEN, AND I KNOW WHAT WE CAN DO!" the crowd goes into a shocked silence and waits...

"WE GO TO WAR TONIGHT" St. Peter smiled as the priests began to cheer and whistle as the prophets laughed and licked their lips.. Some looked at each other with worry and some tried to sneak away.

But he'd deal with them anyway.

"PREPARE YOUR ARMS AND MIRACLES, FOR WE WILL BE FIGHTING TO PROTECT OUR SAFETY, OUR WORLD, OUR GOD IN THE HEAVENS!" The crowd continued to cheer and shout.

St. Peter relaxed back onto the spire, lowering his head.

"Oh Mother Julia.. If only you could see me now, you'd know how terrible of a choice you made" St. Peter let his smirk grow larger as the entire priest population of Bethel prepared for war.

Chapter 25:
End of the Road

Cain slowly awoke, his eyelids peeling back to reveal his shining golden starburst eyes.. The infinite black of his pupil glimmered like a galaxy hidden behind a facade.

Cain awoke as he usually did, to loud sounds.

His mind was reeling as the fresh memory of his brother's death was reimprinted on his mind.. The knowledge from the apple made his dreams less like dreams and more like being transported into the memories.. Reliving them.. Unable to change their outcome, almost a torture.

As he looked around he realised he was laying in a smaller bed.. The walls around him were exposed wood, the window was dirty and grimy and the bed he lay in was creaky and swayed lightly.

He slowly slipped out of bed, adjusting his clothes.. He looked down at his hands, realising his clothes had.. Changed? Given a silver overcoat and a fresh black long sleeve with black trousers and fresh tight fitting shoes.

He heard the crashing sound again of pots and pans clanging together, an older voice mumbles to themselves. Cain stands up and makes his way out of the room, brushing his hair back away from his face, he went down the creaking stairs and stepped into an open space..

It was like the whole house was just one big room, the kitchen, bedroom and living room all in their own little corners. He spotted an old man who was trying to heat up some water on a small furnace.

The elder man was slightly hunched over, he had a tangly white beard with a thick flowing head of pale grey hair and a big red nose. His skinny frame shook lightly with every step, he carried a walking stick with him as he made his way out of the kitchen.

"Oh hello there Cain, you're finally awake.." he said, his raspy voice catching the air.

Cain paused, slightly confused.

"Yes.. I.. Am.." he looked around, he could still feel it.. The immense power that coursed through Cain, he could sense the old man's life force.. His soul flickered like a dying flame.

Cain's eyes widened and he took a step towards the old man.

"Hey are you alright?" he asked with worry in his tone.. Although something felt.. Off with Cain.

A thought passes through his mind.

"I don't really care"

The old man chuckles and sits in a large red chair, nodding.

"Seems like he aint too far gone" he says to himself as he looks up at Cain.

"I'm fine kid, I'm just getting old.. My life force is dyin' out" he coughs into his hand.

Cain furrowed his brow.

"How did you know-"

"I'm an old friend of your fathers" the old man said, interrupting Cain.

"...Right.." Cain pulls back, standing up straight.. The world around him flowed differently, the very concept of existing was in a different context..

He felt like the ground beneath him wasn't real.. Like the world around them was nothing but a painting, a facade built to comfort the small children they called humans.

"You've eaten two apples by now, correct?" the old man asked, resting into the soft chair.

"I.. three, but one of them had gone bad.." Cain said as he continued to try and examine the surroundings he stood in.

"And yet you're not too far gone.. That's good" the old man chuckled to himself.

"What do you mean too far gone?" Cain asked, he began to sit down on nothingness.. He realised there was no chair beneath him before- a chair appeared and he sat on it, a little startled.

He could have sworn that wasn't there before.

"I'm sure your father has told you that these apples have.. Effects on your brain"

Cain nodded, the chair began to warp and adjust to his comfort.

"The more you have, the less human you become Cain.. you lose that part of yourself that's human, and.. To put it lightly, you go insane"

Cain paused, thinking to himself.. The air was too loud.. *"What?"* the air was too loud, he couldn't hear himself think.. *"How can I fucking hear air.."*.

"You thinking about how you can hear air now?" the old man chuckled.

Cain swallowed and nodded, a small shiver was sent down his spine.. He didn't like this feeling.. This detachment from humanity, this dissociation from himself and this world. He felt like an alien, he knew so much about the past, present and future.. Yet none of it made sense..

There was too much information, he couldn't sort through it properly... all there was were a few simple flashes of something every now and then.

"I know of your goal, and I respect it" the man said, chuckling.

"...You...Do?" Cain narrowed his eyes.

"Come with me boy.." the old man slowly stands up, wobbling himself over to the front door. Cain stands up and follows him.

They step out into a large green plain, shrubbery and trees grow in symmetry as paths are carved into the ground itself. Leading from one house to the other, it was a full fledged community.

Cain closed his eyes and sent out what felt like a wave of slight energy.. He waited and got small little mental pings of human life force, he discovered this place had well over 300 residents.

"This is the last real place on earth not owned or controlled by the church.. We don't rely on money.. We don't rely on control or fear.. We live in nature and learn about the ins and the outs of the world.." the old man began to walk alongside Cain, showing him around.

"...." this reminded Cain of Abel, he tightened his fist.. His emotions began to rise up and it radiated off of him causing the old man to cough and almost fall over.

Cain snapped out of it and caught him.

"I'm so sorry" Cain helped the elderly man get back to his feet.

"Eh, nevermind it.. It's to be expected around you.. And I know what you're thinking.. Our journey, our wish is similar to your brothers is it not?" he said, a gentle smile on his aged face.

Cain nodded slowly, he looked around at how people went around day to day.. He could simply feel how much joy and satisfaction they felt living in this place.. The difference is night and day.

Back in Bethel it was dreary, people were having fun but they weren't fulfilled.. Not like they are here..

"That's because it's based off of his ideologies.." the man said, smiling.

"Wait really?" Cain turned to look at him.

"In Abel's life.. He was able to talk to a lot of people about his dream, he'd never stop.. He visited every village known to man and told them about how amazing the world was.. He'd teach us things the church would never even try to" the old man smiled gently, loss in his eyes..

Yet.. Cain could feel it, what he would have seen as something negative before.. He could sense it deeper, he had much more control over his miracle.

The loss was surrounded by hope..

"After Abel's passing.. Some people decided to follow that dream, and so this place was born, Journey. The place for us to get away from it all, to explore the things we couldn't otherwise" the old man pointed over to some of the civilians.

One of them was doing a one man play for some local kids, they seemed to enjoy it, their laughter filling the air.

Another was playing the harp, another was practising card tricks, another was studying plants.

"...So his legacy.." Cain drifted off.

"His legacy created the last sanctuary.. Now, I am not opposed to the church.. Or at least the concept, but they became twisted and corrupted.. God created life.. But he did not wish for us to be alive.. He wished for Adam and Eve.. and that is all, but they betrayed God to create more people to enjoy this life.. And I'm so thankful for them" the old man placed a hand on his heart and smiled.

Cain shakes his head, tears welling up in his eyes.. He couldn't control his emotions as an aura of sadness leaked from him.. The old man didn't seem too affected.

"It's a wonderful world when you look at it through your own eyes.. But they stopped doing that, and they tried to look through the eyes of God instead.. They projected their free will, their lives to him.. Mostly for comfort, but of course where there are people giving up their free will.. There will always be those who wish to profit from it"

Cain nodded, agreeing with the old man.

"Cain.. you could try and live here with us.. Ignore God, I know what he did to your brother.. But it's not your fault.. It doesn't have to be your fight.." he placed a hand on Cain's shoulder.

"..wait.. You don't think I killed him?" Cain said gently, his voice shaking lightly.

He shakes his head.

"None of us do.. You'd never do such a thing.. But if we ever tried to help you, we'd be wiped from the face of the earth.."

Cain swallowed, he felt his legs get shaky as his body and mind filled with complex and connecting emotions.. The joy of having a chance at a new and better life.. But.. no.. he had to.. Right?

"..I have to kill God.. I can't let him carry on.." Cain eventually said, determination filling his eyes.

"..but why Cain?"

"Because he killed my brother!" he barks.

The old man nods.

"And so you will give up your life to avenge him.. But what would Abel want? Would he want you to drive yourself to insanity-"

"I'm not going insane!" Cain barks, his eyes filling with madness.

The old man pauses and nods.

"Would he want you to go insane and kill God.. would he want that?"

Cain paused.. Thinking...his hands begin to shake as his breathing becomes heavier.

"I...I..."

Another voice speaks, this one is familiar.

"Of course he'd want you to harm him Cain" Lucifer said as he appeared in front of him.

"He's going to hurt people.." Lucifer continued.

The old man shouted.

"Hey! Back off ye angel!" the man poked Lucifer with his walking stick and he sighed, floating backwards.

"...you can.. See him?" Cain asked, his breathing still unsure and shaky.

"Yeah, it's a curse I tell ya" he sighs and shakes his head.

"...." Cain lets himself think.. His mind being flooded with thoughts and concepts not of his own, he grabs his head.

"Hey.. it's okay Cain.." the old man pats Cain on the back, he flinches but allows him..

"I have a way to get rid of the apples from your system.. If you so choose.. If you wish to stay here, with us.. To help make your brothers dream a reality..."

Cain looked at him with confusion, tears flowing down his face.

"Wh-what?"

"Follow me" the elderly man said as he made his way back into the house.

He leads Cain down some stairs into a basement that was slightly hidden, he makes his way into the darkened room before lighting a candle with a breath.. Cain followed behind, still unsure about this.. Anxiety began to build up in Cain and his eyes darted from corner to corner...

What if this was a trap.. What if the old man was peter?

"Kill him"

"No..."

"Kill him now, it's the only way we can be safe, he's trying to get rid of our miracles you idiot"

"Stop it.. Stop it.. Stop it.. Stop it.."

The elderly man stops and opens a wooden door.. And Cain's eyes widened.

Four apples stand on a small podium lit by the small cracks in the tunnel lighting it up with a gentle gold.

"While most people focused on finding different plants and the like.. I focused on locating and storing every apple I could find..."

The elder man coughed into his hand again, Cain looked at them..

There was an apple with.. No texture, it was white and smooth like something incomplete.

Delere, The Apple of Nothingness.

Upon consumption, this apple will erase all previous effects.

He looked to the one next to it.. It was bright purple which swirled with orange and small white dots across it.

Vita, The Apple of Eternal Life.

Upon consumption, this apple will give your corporeal form infinite regenerative properties. Your body can never die.

He looked to the next one.. It was the opposite, a yellow and green apple with black marks digging into it.

Mors, The Apple of Death.

Upon consumption, even an immortal will be erased, for it targets the soul not the body.

And then the last apple..

It slowly spun in the air, it was a dark eerie blue with strange lines running across it.. It looked almost like it wasn't a 3D object, more like a doorway into another room.. Another world which was infinite and vast.

Om, The Apple of Omnipotence.

Upon consumption, you become completely Omnipotent, you become infinite and can ascend ever higher.

"...How.." Cain shook his head and asked a different question.

"Why haven't you eaten any of them.."

The old man chuckles.

"Life is nothing without flaws.. If I were infinitely powerful and immortal.. I wouldn't know what to do with myself.. I'd slowly go insane.. That's for sure.. And I don't think that's a very good life" he said, looking over to Cain.

Lucifer appeared again, his inhuman form speaks.

"That's it Cain. Take the apples, that's all we need, that's all we got left! We can leave! We can kill go-"

Cain raised his hand.

"....." he stayed silent however.. He was thinking..

"You can live out your life here.. Safe from everyone.. How your brother would have wanted.. But I won't stop you from taking them.. Your life, your journey" the old man turns away and begins to hobble back into the basement.

"Just know.. Taking even one more apple may prove fatal... not for you.. But for those who stay by your side.. You will never be the same again.."

And with that, the elderly man walks away..

Cain paused... completely silent... not a sound leaving him... not an inch moved... not a single blink.

Above Cain back in the house the older man looks at the doorway as a young boy walks in, his eyes filled with hope and bandages wrapped around him.

Son Aaron spoke, his voice hoarse but still chipper.

"Thank you for letting us both stay here Father Randall" Son Aaron bows to him and Randall shakes his head.

"Don't call me Father, I'm not apart of the church" he chuckled.

"Oh yeah! Sorry.. Hehe.." Son Aaron looked down at the ground with some hesitancy on his face.

"..Sit down, something is wrong" Randall rasped as he sat back down in his comfy old chair.

Son Aaron collapsed into a wooden chair with a groan.

"How could you tell Fa- Randall.." he asked, raising a brow.

"I mean, it's written all over your face" Randall said.

You see dear reader, it was written on his face, literally in ink. He however.. Did not know this, and maybe never would.

"Yeah.. hehe, I know.." he in fact did not know.

"Tell me what happened son.." Randall said, leaning forward.

"I feel.. Torn.. my duty is to my church.. But.. I don't know.. Something about Cain makes me follow him, I thought maybe I simply wished to stop him from attaining his goal of hurting God but even now I do not know.. I follow him for him not for another purpose..."

Son Aaron looked down at his hands, a gentle golden glow leaks off of them. Randal seems to pull away from Son Aaron at the sight.

"Well.. I can tell your journey here was... indeed stressful, Cain is going through a lot.. From the loss of his brother to the conviction of the world around him. The Church controls Aaron, it latches onto someone and doesn't let go like a parasite"

"But it's not a parasite!" Son Aaron exclaimed, pouting.

"I understand your dedication to such a place.. I understand it can bring a lot of good and maybe in another world, another life, it is indeed good.. But for now it is not.. Did you not see your Saint kill his own men with your own eyes?" Randal asked gently.

Son Aaron went quiet.. Then went pale.. Then began to sweat.. Then sighed.

"Yes but.. I think he's being tricked by the snake of Eden! That nasty thing must be in Saint Peter's head! I must reach God and inform him of this at once! The snake shall die!" Son Aaron exclaimed, red in the face.

Lucifer gently floated behind him and crossed his thousand arms.

"Well that's rude"

Randall threw a shoe at Lucifer.

"Ow" Lucifer floated away to check up on the outside world.

Son Aaron blinked, from his perspective Randall just threw a shoe and it hit something invisible.

"Well.. to meet God you must travel with Cain, you see he is on a different mental level than you.. He can see angels, touch angels, sense the life force of others and soon he may either have none of that or more of that..."

Son Aaron began to think to himself.

"Uuuuh, Old Man!" Lucifer shouts, Randal raises a brow.

"What is it you blithering 4th dimensional blister..." Randal slowly stepped outside and instantly he knew something was wrong.. The sky was turning black as the sun was hidden behind a cloud of ash.

His eyes widened and the residents of the town looked up to the horizon to see an inferno sweep across the forests, burning and crumbling them to the ground with white holy flames.. And over the horizon.. Comes not just one silhouette.. Not just 10..

But over 600 figures, most of which were on horseback.. As the fire blazed high into the sky and the smoke coated the town in artificial night.. Two figures rode up on horses to the front of the line..

One was a man with perfect light skin and long flowing white hair with eyes as sharp as daggers and as bright as the clear sky.. He wore no shirt, which revealed his skin yet built physique.

Next to him on a horse as black as midnight sits a man with a horse skull for a head and rotting flesh for the rest of his body coated in a black overcoat with a decaying chain wrapped around him.

The false angel's smile grows as the people of the town realise.. As Randall realises.. As Son Aaron realises..

That Cain.. down below..

Might not have a choice anymore.

Chapter 26:

Sin is Privilege

The priests quickly stepped off of their horses and got into position, St. Peter slipped off of his horse and made his way down the hill.. Each step let out a shaky echo which filled the air.

Randall stood his ground, his tired and aged face contorted into a harsh glare as he planted his feet into the ground.. unmoving.

St. Peter stepped up to Randall with a thin lipped smile on his face, his eyes sparkled with a sick enjoyment. He summoned a white and gold angelic blade in his hand as his wing flapped against the air and his halo spun.

Son Aaron blinked, he went pale and took a step back, Randall continued to hold his ground.

"It would be wise to surrender Cain over to us" he said, his dagger-like eyes piercing into Randall's soul.

"I'm not scared of your kind" Randall chuckled to himself, bracing himself.

St. Peter chuckled.

"Then you'll die braver than most"

St. Peter raised his hand into the air and shouted, his soft and perfect voice rang through the air like a gunshot. Son Aaron winced and held his ears as Randall winced.

"FIRE!"

Behind him on the hill a priest threw a fireball through the air which another priest caught, wrapping it in a strange gravitational aura before shooting it to a nearby house. It crashes into the front door before exploding, sending the building flying into small little pieces of debris and then suddenly the pieces are dragged back together and engulfed in an orb of pure fire.. Incinerating anything hit by the blast.

"NO!" Son Aaron shouts before someone grabs his shoulder, pulling him out the way as another attack is sent.

A small needle is thrown through the air before a priest increases its size, having a massive bus size needle pierce through another house, injuring many.

The people of Journey rushed to the front line with weapons in hand and growled as they bared their teeth. Randall continued staring ahead at Peter, their eyes interlocked as a wave of angelic rage was sent washing over the surrounding area.

People of Journey begin to charge into battle, combating the priests and prophets, slicing them down and getting struck down with bolts of lightning and grass as sharp as swords..

"PETER!" Son Aaron asked, his entire body shaking from the horrors around him as the priests began to approach.

Peter looked over towards him with delight in his eyes.

"WE DON'T HAVE TO DO THIS! PLEASE!" Son Aaron screamed, his eyes filling with tears as his breathing became ragged.

"Shhh, it's gonna be okay child, you won't see it anymore" Peter smiled as he brandished his sword.

In a blink of the eye he launched towards Son Aaron, aiming to pierce him through the heart before-

CLANG.

His sword was redirected by something as his eyes widened and he pulled back, the elderly man stood in front of him now.. Steam slowly seeped off of him.

"You didn't think I was just any old man right?" Randall chuckled to himself as his eyes shone a gentle apple green.

Another fireball cannon shot straight towards his house and Randall snapped his palm against the air, the attack stopped as it hit an invisible golden wall before being thrown back into the troops, erupting into flame and ash.

Peter nods to himself.

"Oh yes.. This **will** be fun" Peter summons his second angelic blade and begins his blitzing assault.

His attacks send sparks flying as they heat up the air around them from the speed, Randall manages to block many of the strikes and dodge over others. He counters Peter with a strike to the chest with his walking stick which is then deflected as they continue their battle.

Down below in the basement Cain sits in darkness.. His eyes gently glowing..

Four apples sit in front of him.. Their power combines into this torrent of confusion.

Son Aaron shouts out as more and more of the surrounding forest is lit in flames, his eyes widen as he watches another resident of Journey fall.. His eyes blank and dead as his body was torn apart.

He curls up into a ball, shaking badly and unable to breath properly, he rocks back and forth as he whispers to himself.

"I wanna go home.. I wanna go home.. I wanna go home.."

A familiar voice calls out to Son Aaron.

"Kid!"

He looks up to see Father Clementine make his way towards Son Aaron with a smile on his face.

"Father!" Son Aaron's eyes light up as he reaches out.. But just before Father Clementine reaches him he holds out his hand.. Creating an orb of black.

Son Aaron goes pale.. He shakes his head and pins his back to the wall of the house as tears stream down his face.

"N-N-No! Don't do this father!!" Son Aaron sniffled and cried out, his shaky hand unreliable as he put one in front of his face.

"Do not call me Father you worm.. You BETRAYED THE CHURCH!" Celemtine chuckled as he raised his orb above his head, ready to throw it through Son Aaron's body, it crackled with energy.

As the orb left his hand something appeared.. It was almost too fast to possibly see, it was a dark shape which held two eyes of pure white energy.

It slapped the orb in the air, catching it with its bare hand and throwing it back harder, sending out a shockwave which tore open the ground beneath them.

Father Clementine furrowed his brow as he felt himself begin to fall backwards, he glanced down to see a perfect orb shape cut straight out of his chest.. Erasing his heart and parts of his lungs and stomach.

"Oh.." he fell down, his eyes going limp as his body went limp..

Father Clementine was dead, the orb continued to sail through the air and caught a Prophet's head, erasing its contents and having their body fall limp to the floor.

Aaron looked up with shaky eyes and tear filled eyes.. A gentle golden pulse echoes from him as he looks at the figure in front of him.

Cain stands there, his eyes completely blank as lightning arcs from his eyes, his overcoat floated gently like it was suspended in water.. An impossible power emanated from him.

He looked upon the hundreds of miracle filled soldiers charging them and simply smiled.

Another fireball was sent flying towards them and Cain backhanded it, sending it flying back at the soldiers. Before it hit them his eyes lit up in a blazing white and the ability duplicated, pelting the enemy backlines with dozens of insanely powerful eruptions which killed dozens.

One of the prophets made it to the front lines, they threw grass which was sharp enough to cut the skin of an angel.. Too bad Cain wasn't an angel.

He stepped through them, the blades of grass bounced off his skin as his eyes began to glow, he reached out and the prophet could feel his body begin to tense up and retract.

He screamed out for help.. But none came as his body imploded, bones cracking and scraping against each other as Cain turned the Prophet into a small ball.

Cain turned and saw the elderly man and the false angel fighting on the battlefield. Randall moved quickly but he wasn't going to be able to keep up for much longer, every other blow landed.

St. Peter landed a strong kick to the ribs and Randall coughed blood as he was sent flying across the grass, Cain's eyes narrowed as he began his march towards Peter, energy began to build up in his hand as created a sword from nothing.

But something wrapped around his neck, it burned and singed, he tried to tear at it but it didn't stop. He was thrown backward, sent flying across the battlefield before landing in a ditch.

Cain instantly shot back up to his feet and looked around, in front of him stood a figure in a black overcoat with the skull of a horse for its head. Cain cracked his neck.

"You've made a mistake" Cain growled as he approached the figure.

"I must say the same for you" Pestilence spoke, his voice echoing through the sky like he was the heavens himself.

Cain picks up his sword and slashes it, engulfing it in pure rage, Pestilence dodges and snaps his palm against the air, sending a blast of rot to erode the blade.

Cain's eyes widen and the blade reforms, he slashes downwards, narrowly catching Pestilence's coat.

Pestilence lashes out with the chain, raking it across Cain's face, he cried out as it began to eat away at his body and power, like an infestation of maggots consuming his very essence and life force.

Pestilence strikes Cain faster than lightning, sending him flying back. Cain crashes into the ground and lays on his back, he tries to sit up but Pestilence cracks his boot against Cain's chest and pins him down.

Cain lashes out, his arm explodes from its socket at blitzing speeds, Pestilence barely manages to dodge as Cain's arm flies through the smoke and out of sight.

"It seems you weren't that strong after all" Pestilence chuckled.

Cain didn't look too worried, in fact, he smiled.

"Sure thing"

The gunshot was silent but the bullet wasn't.

It CRACKED into Pestilence's back and he screamed in agony as it began to dig its emotional claws into his very essence, stripping away at him.

Cain quickly kicked Pestilence in the chest and sent them flying across the sky like a ragdoll. Cain snapped back to his feet as his arm fell from the sky and reconnected to his shoulder, it held the revolver in his hand.

"Greed Bullets, have fun with that weirdo" Cain leaped back up to the main battlefield.. Most of the homes had been broken or were on fire, his eyes widened as Aaron screamed, the golden pulse of energy washing over the surrounding area.

Randall coughed, the golden warp covered his hand and it shrank, wrinkled and weak.. Peter's eyes widened and he had his plan, he flew behind Randall and kicked him into the golden aura of Aaron.

He cried out and tried to catch himself but was too weak, he rolled into the aura and his miracles were latched from him, his body became frail and weak as he stumbled to his knees.

St. Peter slowly walked towards him, his silhouette encased in the surrounding carnage and fire as he raised the angelic blade above his head.. Randall chuckled.

"...hehe.. Dying by an Angels hand.. What irony" Randall kept smiling as there was a wet slicing sound.

Randalls headless body fell limp as blood sprayed from him, his head landed nearby with a thud. St. Peter licked the blood from the blade and giggled to himself.

Cain threw several priests through a building, breaking their bodies and killing them as they were engulfed in crimson flame, Cain looked over to Randall's corpse and paused.. The fighting continued, men and women were slaughtered and any who came close to Aaron had their miracles stripped from them..

Cain locked eyes with Peter, the aura around them both erupted outwards, warping the very reality which held them down.. The ground under Cain's foot eroded and turned to gold before shattering.

The air around Peter began to rush around him with a pinkish hue, his blue eyes filled with bloodlust..

Cain looked at Peter and let his own wing burst from his back, it was black and rotting, bones showing through the fading black feathers.. His eyes arced with a massive amount of energy as he prepared himself.

Peter chuckled, as carnage sung around them like a pathetic symphony he fell into a pose, his angelic blades humming.

"I'll be taking my wing back now" Peter said with a smile.

Cain growled, clenching his jaw and cracking his knuckles.

"Over my dead body" Cain hissed.

St. Peter giggled.

"Yes, that is the idea"

Cain lashed out, summoning his own blade as their weapons clashed, the sheer force of the counter sent nearby houses collapsing down to their foundations.

St. Peter zips behind Cain and aims a wide slash towards Cain's neck. Cain's eyes widen as a massive aura of calm condenses into him forming into incredible armour which deflects the blow.

He spins around with a high kick which St. Peter narrowly blocks, the backlash sending him high into the air, his wing beginning to flap as he flies around the sky at insane speeds.

Cain growled and vanished, appearing in front of St. Peter, their eyes widened as they clashed yet again. Cain brought down his blackened blade onto St. Peter's angelic white, they slid their blades across each other, each of them landing a small blow.

St. Peter scratches Cain's cheek and Cain cuts into St. Peter's arm. There was a flicker and they both vanished, travelling through the sky at insane speeds, most surrounding humans couldn't even follow their movement.

Seemingly random shockwaves and explosions lashed out from the smoke filled sky as the two titans among men continued to fight..

Cain landed a blow on St. Peter, punching him in the gut, forcing him to cough.

St. Peter landed a blow on Cain, his foot crunching into Cain's jaw and sending them spinning.

They evaded eachothers attacks again, St. Peter swung for Cain's neck and he vanished appearing behind St. Peter and trying to plunge a shattered rib into his spine which St. Peter dodged narrowly, retaliating with a kick which he dodged.

Aaron lay upon the blood soaked grass, unable to move as his mind was being overloaded.. His golden aura had leaked into the earth itself.. The surrounding Priests were beginning to lose the fight as they stepped on tainted grass and had their powers stripped away from them..

Back up in the skies St. Peter looked around for Cain.

"Come out, Come out, wherever you a-" suddenly something else hit St. Peter across the jaw, sending him cascading down and smashing through Randall's home.

Lucifer sighed as his fist began to sizzle and burn.

Cain appeared on the ground and waved his hand, his eyes a sparkling white.

"1000 CANNONS!"

Suddenly 1,000 cannons appeared midair, they seemed to be made around the 14th century and they all fired in unison, lighting up the sky with ground shaking thunder.

They completely destroyed the house, sending debris and dust into the sky with a large blast... Cain narrowed his eyes as he saw past the smokescreen.

St. Peter laughed as he stood there, his body covered in very mild scratches and burns, dancing with the angelic blade.

"quam infortunatus" St. Peter said in his snake-like tongue.

He launched at Cain and swung for his head, he ducked and spun around, landing a harsh roundhouse to St. Peter's ribs. He grunts as he's sent skidding into another house, he quickly dashes out of it faster than even Lucifer could see, Cain hissed as he narrowly dodges.. Three large cuts appear on his arm.

"LET'S GET SERIOUS!" St. Peter scowled as he kicked the ground, an angelic blast of energy sent Cain high into the air before St. Peter pointed his blade.

"HOLY STRIKE, HOLY STRIKE, HOLY STRIKE!" St. Peter smiled wide as three massive blasts of heavenly energy came from the sky to strike Cain, slamming him into the ground with such force the dirt around him crumbled and fried as it was sent dashed across the battleground.

It shakes the very earth, Lucifer lashes out, trying to take St. Peter by surprise but he vanishes.. Lucifer widens his eye as he feels his abdomen get split open and his body sent flying into the flames.

"Weaklings.. All of you" St. Peter snarled, he jumped over to Cain.

He slams into Cain, pressing his boot into his chest, snapping his ribs and pinning him into the crater. He raises his blade.

"I will be taking my wing back now!"

Cain lashes out a moment before the blade sung into his wings flesh, he makes a fist and points it at St. Peter.. There was a pause where nothing happened before-

CRUNCH.

A loud crunching sound echoed like a gunshot as one of Cain's knuckles fired from his flesh like a bullet, it ran through St. Peter's collarbone and he screamed as he tore his flesh apart and snapped his bone.. It sent him flying back, he flipped and managed to land on his feet.

Cain slowly stood up, laughing to himself as a massive amount of opal coloured energy surrounded him, his eyes a shining spiral of every colour known to man mixed into the spectrum unseen by most.

"You're right Peter.. Let's.. Get.. serious.." Cain summoned his gun again and placed 12 bullets in the 6 cylinders, his smile widening as reality began to bend and break away.

St. Peter shot forward, moving as fast as he could, dragging his blade along the air causing the very surroundings to combust into an explosion.. He went to run the blade through Cain's chest when-

Cain's chest opened like a mouth, his ribs acted as teeth as they bit down onto the blade and crushed it. They shattered the blade and St. Peter's eyes widened as suddenly time seemed to slow as several Cain's appeared, all lashing out an attack on St. Peter at once..

Punches, stabs and kicks all met St. Peter's face as he was sent cascading through the air like a doll. Cain appeared above him and clicked, St. Peter could feel his soul being latched onto by Cain's hand as he was thrown through the ground.

The sheer force of the throw dug St. Peter hundreds of metres into the coarse dirt and stone until he landed in a small opening.

He coughed and tried to stand only for the ground beneath him to open up.. Cain reached through it like a portal, wrapping his hands around St. Peter as he engulfs him in an inhuman blaze of crimson rage.. Hot enough to melt the earth's core, strong enough to outpower the sun.

And St. Peter screamed, angelic energy began to warp around him as he shouted.. The ground erupted into a shockwave which was felt all the way in Bethel..

The sheer force turned the nearby stone to ash as his dagger-like fingers latched into Cain's skin and ripped, his tendons and bones shattering against immense energy.

His hand was torn from his arm as St. Peter stomped his arm back into the opening as the cave collapsed in on himself.

Cain pulled his arm out of the portal and looked at his missing hand.. With a blast of energy a new hand formed from rage and anger as flame flickered from it constantly, its deep red colouration glowing in the ash filled air.

The ground around him began to break apart.. The last few standing houses fell..

Cain aimed the gun back down to the ground and fired, they broke apart the ground and shifted the sky and smoke as they pierced through the back of the false angel with imperfect malice.

There was silence.. If not for just a moment..

Lucifer held onto his stomach as he floated back down to earth, standing next to Cain.. his eyes shifted slightly as he felt a small fleck of fear run down his spine..

Cain's very presence was impending.. It felt suffocating.. The power of the apples had multiplied tenfold..no.. a thousand fold.. He had not just consumed the last two apples.. He was now omniscient..

This was no longer a joke..

Cain... was strong enough to kill God..

One of the few survivors stumbled up to him, a young boy with bright red hair and wide eyes of joy.. He placed a hand on Cain's shoulder as he became dizzy.

"D-did we win?" he was from Journey.. An innocent boy.. And yet Cain paid no mind to him.. Or at least.. That's what we would have wished.

"Don't touch me.."

The boy erupted, his body inflated before popping like a balloon, his skull sent fragments flying across the battlefield as his skeleton was spread like seeds.

Cain remained staring at the ground, unmoving.. Unfeeling..

Something moved under rubble.. A little voice called for help as Aaron tried to reach out.. The house had collapsed onto him, he was stuck under too much debris.. He could barely breathe.. He couldn't move.. He desperately tried to call for help..

"Help... me... please....someone..." Aaron said, trying to reach out.. For anything.. Anyone..

Cain noticed this and his eyes drifted across the burned and broken land to grab Aaron by the hair.

"Ow.. Cain.. what have you done.."

Cain said nothing as he wrenched Aaron from the wreck, the sheer force broke his spine and tore his flesh.. Aaron screamed in agony but suddenly he stopped.. He felt calm and cold, Cain's raw energy flowed into him and healed him.

Cain began to drag Aaron away by his head.. He continued to weakly protest.. He tried to touch Cain.. but even his golden aura did nothing against him.

Cain looked ever forward as he walked through the burning corpses of Priests and innocents alike. Not making a single look of despair or shock..

Cain was gone..

The beast had won..

Cain, Aaron and Lucifer left this place.. As the last remnants of Abel.. burned to the ground.

Hours after they had left, a hand burst from the dirt.. The ash.. It pulled itself out and back onto land.

St. Peter chuckled to himself.. His golden blood flowed from him like a river.. He laughed for he had everything he needed..

St. Peter looked at the two apples which sat in front of him.. One of which was blank.. The other which was a spiralling mix of colours withholding the inky black..

He dropped one of the apples to the ground and the bodies of everyone and everything around him began to twist and turn.. Their flesh bubbled and blood slipped through the ash and dirt..

They began to come together, fusing into one beast around an apple, its very being forced together as bones fused and blood mixed.

The very essence of the war itself pulled from the battlefield.. As an older man's skull was placed on top of the abomination. Its skin bulged and hardened like armour as the skull was attached by the visible muscle fibres which held it in place.. No skin latched onto the skull however.. Its hollow empty eyes rung the symphony of screams.

"War, my second horseman"

Pestilence walked through the fire behind them, finally making it back to the battlefield...

"...And now I know of the next..." Peter said to himself as he began to laugh, he collapsed to his knees and laughed into the sky.

"I know of the next..." he said again, this time his tone echoed as he let himself rest.. His wounds not healing as they usually would, his eyes a fiery mess of rage and anguish.. As he accepted the fate of this world..

How it would end soon enough..

This story

Is coming to an end.

Chapter 27:

First Heaven: Somnia

Aaron slowly opened his eyes.. His mind was thick with mental fog.. He could barely process the information around him. He was laying in a bed and stared up at the ceiling... but nothing was quite right.. The ceiling didn't seem correct and the bed felt wrong.. He slowly slipped to his feet and yawned..

He looked down at his body, it was covered in scars and burn marks.. He remembered the horrible war.. The death.. His eyes went wide and his skin pale.. He sat in complete silence, his heart beat fast and noiseless tears flowed down his face and hit the wooden floor below him...

He could hear the door slowly open but he dared not look.. He just closed his eyes and wished for death to befall him.. To end this pain which reached throughout his body, it wasn't physical.. But mental..

A pain that couldn't be fixed with bandages and prayers.. A pain that would echo on for what seemed like forever.

"Kill me now.." Aaron said to whatever figure had entered the room.

"..I wish I could" spoke a voice Aaron had never heard.. He slowly looked up and jumped in panic.

Before him stood a figure around 7' tall with tanned skin and four heads with four large black wings and two small white ones..

"...What.."

"I'm an angel.. Lucifer, angel of earth.. I've been the one helping Cain" he said plainly.

"Cain..."

Aaron thought back to it.. The horrible sight, how Cain killed Clementine right in front of him.. How he fought St. Peter with no care for others, he didn't defend Journey.. He let such nice people get slaughtered..

Rage boiled inside of him and he grit his teeth hard as he grabbed at his trousers, gripping as hard as he could while holding back his screams of pain and rage.

"...I understand how you feel... he's outside if you wanna see him.." Lucifer said gently.

Aaron paused and fell limp, his rage couldn't catch hold in his body.. A sense of hope washed over him, a sickly hope.. A hope he didn't want.

Cain was a monster.. No doubt about it..

"..Why would I want to see him?" Aaron said, sniffling as more tears flowed down his scarred and pained face.

Lucifer shrugged and sighed.

"I don't know what you humans ever want..."

Aaron looked at the angel.. A real angel in his presence, but he couldn't bring himself to smile or dance.. He just asked.

"Why... Can I see you now?" Aaron asked gently, trying to sit up again.

Lucifer shrugged again with his four shoulders.

"..I think Cain gave you some sort of boost in power.. I mean, he can do that now.." Lucifer looked at a nearby wall like it was a window, looking out at something..

"..."

Aaron thought about it for a while, his body continually fluctuating between limp and adrenaline.. His mind was unable to comprehend what had happened..

"Take me to him.." Aaron finally said, a gentle wisp of hate in his saddened and beaten tone.

Lucifer nodded and floated out of the room, Aaron slowly followed. As he made his way through the house he couldn't stop thinking about how wrong this all felt.. Everything was out of place and he had no clue where he had been taken, this sure didn't feel like a town in Bethel or Journey..

He was led out of the front door and instantly Aaron's eyes widened, the ground was white.. No, it was.. Clouds? Cloud for as far as the eye could see, the sky above them was a shining blue and strange figures, places and creatures danced all around them.

None of them fit together, some of them had different anatomy, some small some not.. Different homes or places he recognised seemingly taken out of Bethel and slapped here with no rhyme or reason.. However as he looked left he did notice a ledge..

Cain sat upon it, his silver overcoat blowing in the non existent wind.. Aaron slowly made his way across, not trusting his every step. The ground sank as you walked, giving away to your weight.. Although he didn't find it any harder to walk.

He continued to approach Cain before speaking, still a few metres away..

"Cain?" Aaron said, his voice hoarse and his eyes welling with tears and fear once more..

Cain didn't even look back at Aaron.. He just kept staring forward.

Aaron approached the edge and peered down..

The entire earth was seen below him, the immense height sent a wave of vertigo through him he'd never faced before and his legs buckled as he fell to the soft and comfy ground with a thud.

Cain still didn't look over to him.

"...Answer me Cain.." Aaron said as he slowly got back up to his knees.

"...Cain.."

Cain didn't respond.

"CAIN! YOU HAVE TO AT LEAST ANSWER ME!" Aaron lashed out at Cain, trying to hit him across the cheek but his hand automatically stopped before he was flung back.. Landing again on the soft ground.

Aaron just lay there and began to sob, he couldn't take it.. His body shook and tears spilled into the clouds..

"...We're in heaven.." Cain eventually said, his voice void of emotions.

"H-heaven?" Aaron said, wiping his tears away as he sat up.. Adrenaline flowing through his body and making him shaky.

"The first layer.. Somnia.. The layer of mind and dreams.." he said again, his voice gentle.. Smooth.. Like multiple people spoke at once.

"...Oh.." Aaron looked around, it made more sense now.. The house.. The creatures.. The people..

All of them were projections of dreams people on earth were having.

"...why didn't you kill me.. Or leave me behind.." Aaron asked, looking over to Cain.

Cain didn't answer for a while as he stared down at earth.. At layer 0.

"..because I want to prove you wrong" he said gently.

"...."

"God will not forgive me or you.. God is a nasty person.. He is not someone you can simply talk to" Cain said to himself, pocketing his hands.

"...." Aaron remained quiet, his mind rushing with thoughts and memories he hated, he just wanted to tear off his face.. The pain was too much.

"...There is nothing for us here, come, we must rise to the next level.." Cain said, standing up... his eyes remained that colourless white as he walked past Aaron..

Aaron refused to stand.. He just wanted to wither away and die-

"No ageing occurs in this place... you won't be able to die like that, now come on" Cain said, responding to Aaron's thoughts and feelings..

..Aaron slowly stood up and followed him, dragging his feet as he did..

He passed by dreams of people he knew and loved..or.. He used to...Aaron took a shaky breath and let the tears drip from his face as he followed the god known as Cain.

Chapter 28:

Second Heaven: Limbo

Cain walked alone.. Or at least that's what it felt like. The clouds were now more akin to storm clouds than nice fluffy white clouds.. The ground was a harsher grey and people simply wandered in this place.

For this place was where those who died before knowing of God or those who had been manipulated out of God's love went. Forced to forever walk in an infinite sea of grey.. No homes.. No days or nights..

If they were lucky they'd find holes back down to earth, but they wouldn't find much hope down there.. No reincarnation.. Now they just wandered earth, without much thought or care. Ghosts, unseen, unheard, unloved.

Cain hated that he knew this.. He hated it deeply within himself that he knew every name of every person who had been sent to Limbo. His white eyes hid behind them a focused yet hurting glare forward..

The old man was right.. His mind was warped, the world was his own.. He could turn the rules of the universe upside down if he wanted to.. And he kind of did.

His mental state was off, he continued wishing the worst upon the best, lashing out at others and tearing their arms off.

Cain continually had the thought of pinning Aaron down and ripping his skin from his flesh...

That wouldn't be very good... and yet he still had this urge to do it.. To blow up this universe and turn it to void, to make his own, make his better..

None of the people on Limbo cared enough to try and stop Cain, Aaron and Lucifer from their goal.. They didn't care if they were erased or not.. And so Cain put that to the test.

He walked by a nearby soul and tapped them on the shoulder, the soul looked into his eyes a moment and they widened.. No words spoken or screams..

They simply looked into Cain's eyes as their very existence was wiped away, erased.. Aaron would have objected if he remembered.. To erase a soul is to rip it from the timeline, to turn it into nothingness.

It never existed.. And never will exist... the only way to kill St. Peter.. Except it would be harder on him, his divine prevention is about strong enough to prevent Cain from doing that with ease.. But it's still possible..

Cain continued to walk through the eerie grey land, his eyes fogged over as he could hear the wails of those who wished to be in a better place.. Or erased..

Cain could see far beyond the infinity ahead of them.. He could see intricacies which would never be seen by another human.

His eyes examined as the world was being created in front of him.. For that was how time worked, in truth.

Luck, Destiny and Free Will occurred all at once..

Imagine time like a rope, a really really long rope, that rope will have a set of knots.

Those knots are points in time which can be unchanged, afterall, how can you untie a knot on an infinite rope?

However, where these knots are placed can be changed or decided by random chance and the rope in between the knots? They can be manipulated to your heart's content.

You could live your life in a billion different ways, with a billion different events, some things however would remain constant. Whether you go left or right, existence will allow you to bend the rope as much as the knot allows.. For you will always meet a knot, a point which is always going to occur no matter how much you try and change it.

Now.. imagine your life being just a single thread of that rope.. Something which can go its own way but is connected to the greater rope and will hit those same knots although in different ways. You could wrap around the rope left to right and the knot right to left.

You could go in the centre of the rope or on the outside, there are an infinite amount of these threads.. Because this rope is you across multiple universes, timelines, however you wish to say it.

Cain knew this.. Because isn't that how writing a book is?

You know the ending, you know the plot points you have to meet, but the actual words can change and differ, does it not?

It is luck if the writer is interrupted mid sentence and forgets where they were going.

It's free will for the writer to write their words in their order.

And yet the story will always end, one way or another. A knot that can never be avoided.. No matter how hard you try.

So, if time is so much like writing, who's to say we're not being written? Who's to say we, you and me reader, are not in a story or our own. I mean, characters don't simply stop existing when they're not on the page.

I have yet to mention Aaron in a while

And yet he's been walking all this time, he has been acting as free will, because I have not been writing his actions but you can assume his actions..and his actions could even differ from your concepts.

Isn't that the definition of free will? To choose what to do or not? I don't know what Aaron or Lucifer is doing until I begin to write the page.

So when I stop writing, or when you stop reading.. Do they vanish? Are they erased from the ether that is our consciousness? Or maybe they continue to exist in some form or other, doing things we cannot control, things that I the writer cannot control for I'm not writing them.

So doesn't that mean they're alive?

Even if it means they're just in our heads? Because they sleep, they eat, they breathe

Our time acts as their time

Because i'm writing

And I don't have to follow rules

I dont. Have. to.. Put, corre,ct punc-ctioation or spelllinnnggg

When you create a story, are we not the gods of a living, breathing place? A place we cannot see with our eyes?

And if you think I'm reaching, remember that people don't believe australia is real. So.. you know.. I might not be the most crazy person out there that thinks just because it's not in front of us doesn't mean it's not real.

Cain clears his throat.

Oh yes, the book.

I apologise.

Let us leave this dreary and strange place.. The ending is nearing.. I wonder how the readers feel... I've done my best... but I know my pacing is probably flawed.. Oh well..

Chapter 29:

Third Heaven: Terra Servorum

Cain, Aaron and Lucifer step through the gentle clouds, their bodies felt weightless for but a moment as the dark grey of Limbo vanished.. Now replaced by a gentle orange glow of a sunset bouncing through the clouds.

The sky hummed a gentle yet uncertain reddish hue to it.. It seemed like they had stepped into a massive city, buildings reached high into the infinite sky, streets were built of well polished stone and brick and yet the clouds pierce through it all.. Rising and falling like the city wasn't even there.

There were dozens of figures standing at the entrance to this place, they looked back at the three figures.. Their forms flickered like uncertain shadows cast by a dying candle.

There was a certain sense of foreboding in this place.. The air felt too warm for comfort, tense and with a seeping sense of dread.

Aaron swallowed, gripping his shirt as his heart beat loudly..

"Wh-why are they looking at us like th-that..." Aaron asked gently, his eyes wavering.

"This is the level people go when they accept the Lord before death.. Those who led lives of 'sin' only to ask for forgiveness.. They are given a spot in heaven, but more so as the workers" Cain said, pointing to his left.

Aaron glanced over, there was a large group of people farming the cloud they stood on and moving it towards a large factory.. Black clouds leaking from its chimneys.

"...." Aaron looked back at those souls which continued to watch them, Cain began to walk through the streets, his silver coat flapping in the non existent wind.

Aaron nervously followed him, Lucifer simply floated alongside the two.. Knowing these souls could do nothing to him.

"...Hey Cain?" Aaron looked around, his heart beat faster and faster as his breathing became unstable.. His voice shook.

"Yes?" Cain continued to walk, his hands pocketed.

"...Can we.. Die.. in heaven?" he asked tentatively.

Cain nodded as they walked, their footsteps cracking against the black stone ground. The clouds rose and fell like calming waves.

"We're not natural residents of this realm.. So dying here would lead to not such nice things" Cain said casually, his golden, star-like eyes began to scan the souls which slowly poured from the nearby buildings..

"O-O-Oh..." Aaron began shaking badly, fear and adrenaline pumping through his body.. His breathing was rattling his chest as his eyes widened..

He could almost hear the sounds of priests marching.. Or those who fell screaming in pain as they choked on their own-

"Hey. Stop thinking about that, you're too loud" Cain growled, rubbing his temples.

"H-huh?" Aaron shook his head.

"He can hear thoughts.. He's omniscient.. And-"

"GAH! CAN YOU SHUT UP!" Cain shouts towards a nearby soul, a massive blast of energy rips through the air and a massive crater is formed where the soul once was.

Aaron blinks as the very existence of the soul was torn from this mortal coil.

"What.. happened?" Aaron blinked, his mind reeling from the effects.

"Nothing" Cain said as he kept moving.

"...yeah.. That.." Lucifer said to himself, watching Cain with a close eye(s).

Cain and the rest slowly made their way through this layer of heaven.. Cain's mind began to crinkle and crackle.. His eyes sparkling and fading back to a pure white. He stops in his tracks.

Aaron paused, that sound sending another wave of fear through him, his bones locked up and he freezes... he barely manages to speak.

"Wh-wha-what's u-up.."

Cain raised a single finger.. His eyes slowly glide down to a nearby street.. A creature stood there, no.. floated there.

Its existence was mind bending to even the strongest of men, its body was that of a massive eye, a thousand wings surrounded it as hundreds of rings spun around it, also covered in eyes.

God had a weird obsession with eyes Cain realised.

He waits there, staring at this angel..

Lucifer paused as he turned the corner and saw it.

"Lucifer-How-Could-You" it spoke like a machine, its words spat out of it at the same speed with the same pause between them, no matter what.

"Hello there Gabriel.." Lucifer hissed under his 100 mouths.

Cain simply stood there.. His eyes as blank as a canvas, the aura surrounding him was immense, reality bent to his will.

"I-See-You-Didn't-Destroy-The-Apples-Lucifer" Gabriel said as its eyes all blinked in unison.

Lucifer summoned a large blade in one of his many hands.

"You know God is wrong for what he has done.. And what he plans to do"

"..What does he plan to do?" Aaron said, still frozen in fear.. His head turned to Cain and Lucifer..

"He's planning on eradicating all life on earth to start again in a new Eden" Cain said plainly.

"Wh-WHAT!? No, this must be a misunderstanding s-surely!" Aaron laughed to himself, his mind slowly cracking.

Cain slowly turned his head to Aaron, his entire being soon engulfed in indescribable energy which crackled and flowed off of him into the sky.

"I am omnipotent now Aaron, and yet I am still on my path.. Does that say nothing to you?" His voice seems to pierce Aarons mind like an arrow...

"I..I..."

"I-Apologise-Lucifer-but-now-you-die" Gabriel summons two large orbs of light which begin to glow and pulse as energy fills the air.

The nearby souls suddenly jump at them, trying to claw and dig their hands into them. Cain simply backhands them, erasing them with a mere touch.. Aaron however goes limp, letting them scratch and dig into him.. He braces his jaw but the pain is non existent.. Instead it's.. Cold.. so cold..

Lucifer flies high above the souls and meets Gabriel.

"This will end poorly for you" he points his blade at Gabriel.

"You-will-fail-Lucifer-forging-a-false-god-will-only-lead-to-failure"

"Let's test the theory shall we?"

Lucifer swung his sword, it sings through the air and lashes out with a golden flicker of light which Gabrial deflects with the orb.

Cain blitzes across the entire city, the ground erupts into puffs of clouds as he breaks it apart with the sheer speed he's moving.

Cain pulls out the revolver and fires a bullet of greed, Gabriel blocks it with a golden orb. The bullet is absorbed into its light before suddenly the light begins to try and attack Gabrial, absorbing his energy and life force.

Lucifer slams into Gabriel and pulls him down to the earth, the rings tear off and begin to lash out and strike Lucifer, pushing him back with angelic might.

Cain launches into the air and snaps his wrist, his tendons and blood vessels burst from his body and wrap around Gabriel and his rings, he tries to break free but the material is reinforced with an almighty glow.

He spins around midair and throws Gabrial over his shoulder before slamming him down into the ground like a hammer at a playfair, Gabrial slams into the heavens and the entire layer shakes violently.

Lucifer stabs his blade through Gabriel's eye and he screams, it pops Cain's eardrums and yet they instantly heal with a flurry of opal coloured energy. Gabriel sings into the heavens, sending beams of holy fury down upon them.

Lucifer deflects a blow with his blade while Cain uses his rotting wing to blink from one place to the next, moving too fast for the beams to hit him before holding out his hand.

There was a massive shockwave that rippled reality before suddenly the very clouds beneath Gabriel turned black and red, lashing out at him and absorbing his very life force.

He cries out and tries to escape but suddenly the ground bursts with blood vessels and nervous systems, wrapping around Gabriel like living chains, pinning him to the essence sucking cloud beneath him.

"You-Can-Not-Defeat-Me-"

Cain clicks his fingers and Gabriel explodes into sparkles and dust.

Lucifer lowers his blade and Cain slowly floats back down to the cloud soaked ground, his eyes continue to spark with energy.

"Well, that was easy" Cain said to himself as he continued his walk back up the levels of heaven.

As he passes by the group of souls trying to kill Aaron he flicks the air, turning them all into mush and erasing them with a shockwave. Aaron blinks and slowly sits up, with a sigh he stands up and follows Cain.. he feels cold.. He didn't know why.

Lucifer goes back to following them both, Cain had energy arc off of him, burning the ground where he stands.

"...Cain, why don't you just bring us to the top?" Aaron gently asked.

"Because I need God to get the message, I'm going to walk through heaven to get to the bastard.. I'll kill anything or anyone who gets in my way" Cain growled.

"...." Aaron stayed quiet, a gentle sigh slipping from his lips.

Lucifer narrowed his eyes.. The sense of impending doom didn't seem to let up.. Was Cain.. scaring him?

Chapter 30:
Fourth Heaven: Caelum

They stepped through the light red fog and entered a place which smelled like your favourite smell, the wind was your favourite temperature, the sky was a brilliant blue with white clouds with hints of gold.

Aaron blinked.. His eyes were tired and his body sagged gently, adrenaline seemed to refuse to leave his body...he sighed.

"Where are we now?" he asked gently, his voice shaking.

"Fourth Heaven, Caelum.. This is the place most people go when they die" Cain explained as he walked forward.

"...Oh..." Aaron followed him, looking around them there were small microcosms of blissful places.. Some were mountains, some were lakes, some were simply houses taken from Bethel and placed here..

"...So that means...anyone we once knew is.. Here?" Aaron's eyes quivered.. Joy and irreparable fear filled him.

Cain sighed and pocketed his hands as his overcoat whipped in the wind.

"Sure.. you could say that.." Cain growled to himself.

"...Can.. I.. See someone?" Aaron asked gently, trying to smile.

Cain glanced at him and growled gently before looking away and taking a sharp dagger like breath.

"Yep, go on kiddo.. Meet me back here within the hour though"

"Thank you!" Aaron rushed off through heaven, going to look for someone.. Anyone..

Cain simply stood there, not moving an inch. Lucifer raised a brow.

"Don't you wish to go find those you lost? You know your brother cou-"

"He's not here"

"...."

"God wouldn't give him the mercy... he erased his soul.." Cain hissed to himself.. Reality bending and wrapping in on itself around him from his sheer emotions which lash out.

"...Oh.." Lucifer continued to gently float.

"Yeah, God dumped his only bargaining chip against me.. Now there's no escape.." Cain looked down at his hands.

"What are you gonna do to him exactly?"

Cain chuckled and smirked.

"I'm going to beat him to death with my bare hands, nothing flashy.. Nothing special.. He's just going to beg until his jaw doesn't work.. Then cry till his body shuts down.. Then I will be finished.." Cain smiled at the thought of God's warm blood running down his hands.

"...Then what?" Lucifer asked cautiously.

"...I don't know Lucy... I don't know.." Cain pocketed his hands again.

Aaron was running through the cloudy landscape before finally catching sight of two people he had not seen in a long while..

"Mom! Dad!" Aaron leaped at them and tackle hugged them both to the ground.

They yelped before their eyes lit up and they hugged him back.. Then they paused and pulled away, worry and fear stricken in their eyes.

"Did you die!?" his father asked, panicked.

"How are you here?" His mother screeched lightly.

His father was tall and thin, he had fair tanned skin and black hair with green eyes.

His mother was darker skinned with light brown hair and golden brown eyes.

"i-I'm not dead.. I came here with Cain, we're going to speak to God" he said, tears flowing down his face.

"Cain? You mean the murderer?" his father said, a frown on his face.

"N-no! Well.. maybe.. But things have gotten really crazy.. Down there on earth and stuff.. So we're gonna have to talk with God about it all" Aaron gently chuckles.

His mother placed a hand on his cheek.

"We missed you, our little A..." she said gently, tears welling in her eyes.

"I m-missed you too!" He hugs them tight.

An hour had passed.. They had a nice and gentle conversation about life and about the world around them.. But soon the hour came to an end.

"I'll be back with you two soon with great news! I promise!" Aaron said as he walked away, waving.

I would love to have the rest of the book be their one hour conversation reader, to have this book end on a happy note with joy and reconciliation.

But that's not exactly the case.

Aaron made his way back to Cain with a smile but still shaking.

"...hey Cain.. I'm b-back.." he waved.

"Right. Are you ready to move on?" Cain looked over to him, his golden amber eyes looking deep into Aaron's soul.

Aaron paused.. Then nodded.

"...I'm ready.." he prepared himself, swallowing his fear as the realisation they would soon meet God himself sank in.

So they continued walking through the living graveyard.

Chapter 31:
Fifth Heaven: Nam Supra

Aaron didn't remember much of this level of Heaven.. He had no clue why.. He just remembered.. Emptiness..

This was the layer, the heaven, where the priests ended up.. Those devout to the church till the very end.

Cain walked through with his eyes engulfed in energy.. Black flame dragged through the heaven as it corrupted and erased every soul they came across.. Cain massacred them..

I do not wish to describe this much longer dear reader.. For a pit is forming in my stomach.

I do not wish to inform you of how he dug his hands into people's chests and erupted their ribcage.. Or how he ripped them in two.. Or how he dug his claws into one of their spines before tearing it out..

Afterall.. Cain is supposed to be the hero.

He's supposed to save everyone.

So why would he be ripping and tearing the priests apart, eradicating them from this world.. From this lifetime..

When he threw them across the land, turning them into a skid mark.. Did he care if he was the hero?.. Maybe not..

Let us move on.. Quickly.

Chapter 32:
Sixth Heaven: Beatitudo
Destiny

The sky sparkled with golden grandeur, Cain and Aaron slipped through the blue tinted haze and looked around this new level of heaven.. The ground slowly ebbs and flows like an unsure pond lapping against the edge of a nice pasture.

The air itself smelled and felt like bliss, it filled Aaron and Cain with this sense of belonging and love.. Aaron paused, unsure as to what to do, Cain simply continued walking forward.

His eyes crackle and sparkle power simply washes over the surrounding area with a breathtaking push. Aaron stumbled and Lucifer narrowed his eyes.

"...I see.." Lucifer said to himself quietly.

"..What's going on?" Aaron asked, his hands beginning to shine a golden aura.

"...The bastard is here.." Cain scowled.

In front of them stood a set of stairs leading towards a massive and golden gate. A figure began to descend from the infinite sky.. Their angelic wings flapped slowly as they were lowered to their feet in front of the gate.

The thin yet built figure of St. Peter stood before them, his flowing white hair gently whipped in impossible wind similar to Cain's jacket. His eyes were a piercing blue while Cain had a shattering gold.

"Oh hello there Cain" St. Peter said, a thin lipped smile on his face, his eyes shining.

"...Peter.." Cain summoned his pistol and began to load a set of bullets into them.

"Tell me Peter, what do you truly think will happen if you create the new eden" Cain said to himself as he put a match in his mouth and rolled up his sleeves.

"I know what you're trying to do.. And it wont work" he snarls.

Aaron takes a step back, swallowing.

"You dedicated your entire life to being this great priest, God's vessel, but you know he's going to throw you away the moment he gets the chance" Cain said, his eyes glinting.

"...You're right, I don't trust God with my life anymore.. But I still have one vendetta to finish" he summoned his angelic blade and let out a gentle breath.

"Why don't we team up, kill God ourselves, he's screwed you over just as much as he did to me" Cain said, slowly making his way forward.

"And then what? You take control?" Peter chuckled as he slowly descended the stairs.

"Nah, either we rule together or we don't rule at all" Cain smiles, the match still in his mouth.

"Right.. Like I'm supposed to trust you.. You'd betray me in a second" Peter's eyes narrowed.

Cain shrugged and chuckled.

"Ya got me-"

Cain appears behind St. Peter and connects a punch to his spine, a satisfying crack is heard as he's sent flying through the air and crashing into the clouds.

St. Peter launches from the clouds with a laugh and holds up his blade.

"HOLY STRIKE OF FURY!" he slashes his blade, a sudden wave of energy fills the sky and Cain glares at it as it spirals towards him.

He holds out his hand and catches the devastating blast before throwing it behind him. It smacks into the gates and explodes, covering them in burns and scratches, he shrugs.

"Resistant"

"So this is how you want to go.. Very well then.. This will be our FINAL FIGHT YOU HEATHEN!" St. Peter raised his blade into the sky and summoned a flurry of holy magic before four beings surrounded Cain.. all on horseback.

His eyes widen and he spins around.. What was this? He was infinitely powerful and knowledgeable and yet he felt like.. He was taken by surprise.

A rotting chain wraps around his neck and singes into his unbreakable skin, his eyes widen as he waves his hand.. Trying to order the very universe to erase the four creatures.. Yet the universe said no.

Cain coughed as he was sent slamming down into the ground with an almighty crash.. A violent shockwave was sent through the ground, Aaron fell onto his back and Lucifer stayed hidden.. His eyes glaring out towards those who surrounded Cain now..

They were above him, staring down at him as he lay on the floor, his body feeling weaker as the chain sapped his power and strength.. St. Peter lands in the centre of them all with his arms wide and his eyes filled with great holy magic.

"Say hello to my four horsemen of the apocalypse" Peter's snarl burned into Cain's eyes as he growled.

"Pestilence, born from God's rotten apple" the horseman looked down at Cain, his empty horse eye sockets infinitely dark..

"War, born from the deaths you gave to me so generously, using the body of Randall as a host" Cain's eyes widened as he looked over to the second horseman.. He rode upon a red horse and held a floating human skull with eternal burning flames in his eyes, he wore the corpses of dead that have deformed into armour carrying a great sword made from flesh and bone.

"..Dammit.." Cain struggled as he tried to stand up, his body slowly rotting from the inside out, he tried to instantly heal himself.. And the universe rejected him.

"Fear, born from the late Mother Julia, my mentor and saviour.. Also the reason we're even here in the first place" she rode upon a white horse, her skin was that of someone recently deceased.. Pale and stiff, a blindfold wrapped around her eyes and carrying a lantern.

"AND FINALLY! THE GRAND GUEST! DEATH! USING THE BODY OF ABEL HIMSELF!"

Cain froze, his eyes glancing across the other horsemen to one who rode a pale, skeletal horse.. He had faded red hair and a gaunt figure, his empty eyes constantly poured tears as he wore sleek and nimble armour.. Carrying a scythe over his back.

Cain managed to make it to his feet, his eyes shining bright. Pestilence pulls taught on the chains but he pulls back and refuses to budge, even though his body was rotting.. His emotions flared and burned through it, forcing him to stand up.. Rage and fear filled his mind and he began to laugh.

"Hahaha..hahahahaha..hahahahahahahaha!"

St. Peter's face fell and he snapped his fingers.

"Kill him"

The horsemen of the apocalypse charge, Pestilence tears Cain off his feet and into the air with the chain, War aims his great sword to cut Cain's head off... and he lets them..

There was a violent swing and blood sprayed through the air as Cain's head was detached from his neck and sent spiralling through the air.. For a moment everything went quiet..

Lucifer's wings furled.. Aaron's eyes widened and golden energy covered his body when-

Tendons and blood vessels burst from Cain's disembodied head and it reattached to his corpse, he used this to his advantage and tugged on his skull.

Using his blood vessels like elastic he sends his own head flying through air like a projectile, it strikes Pestilence with force and a loud BANG.

The headless body pulled out the revolver and fired into War's chest, sending them off the horse. Fear raised her lantern and sent out a wave of holy flame which burned the headless body to less than ash.

Cain chuckled as a whole new body sprouted from his flying head, his spine burst from his muscle before the rest of his bones, tendons, muscle and blood formed around him as he spins. He finishes the flourishing spin with a full new body with his clothes back, he kicked Pestilence in the face and bounced between the horsemen.

He landed on Fears head and kicked off, sending her sliding off her horse, he launched himself at Death and their eyes met.. Cain looked into the eyes of his brother and paused.. This pause was just enough for Death to swing his scythe and cut Cain in half.

He grunts from the pain but his body reforms, using the large wound as a mouth as his bones bent inward to form teeth.

He lands on Death's head and bites down on it before kicking against the air, breaking his leg but spinning him around.

He uses himself as a catapult to throw Death from his horse and across the heavens. Cain lands and his body heals, he turns around and Death's horse strikes him in the jaw with a kick, it shatters his jaw bone and he stumbles.. Another chain of rot wrapping around his arm.

Pestilence launches at him, hitting him across the jaw with a cracking left hook, Cain stumbles as War approaches them, aiming to slash Cain's arm off.

His eyes light up and he spins around, the blade misses his arm and strikes the rotting chain, Cain leaps up into the air and using his wing flies over War trapping him within the chain..

War screams as he felt his very flesh bubble and weaken at its structure, Cain flew down the staircase.. Dragging War along with him and Pestilence coming along.. Still attached to the chain.

Cain stops flying suddenly and twists, throwing War through the air and lifting Pestilence off the ground. Cain turns around and strikes Pestilence in the chest with a lashing kick-

The lantern spins through the air and slams into Cain's jaw, forcing him to spiral and crash into the ground wrapped in rotting chain.

He's soon engulfed in holy flame and Cain screams, he struggles against the chains and slowly begins to stand up as his own bones break and shatter against the harsh metal binding.

Even while he was being turned to a crisp, his muscles weakening.. He continued to stand.. And he screamed.

"COME ON THEN! IS THAT ALL YOU GOT!?" Cain laughed hysterically.. Lucifer and Aaron watched from the sidelines in borderline fear.. He continued to walk through rot and inferno like it was nothing simply because he was too fucking angry to die.

War lashes out, sending a blade through his neck.. Cain laughs as his throat is slit open and his blood sprays out, it hardens midair and acts like arrows, shooting small daggers of solid blood through the horsemen.

Cain roars as he begins to snap the chain and push against it, his body healing as fast as it's getting burnt. Death reappears and strikes him in the back, the blow begins to erode his body into nothing but dust.. Bit by bit he begins to fade.

Cain laughed as he doubled over, his melted eyes regrowing in the harsh holy flame.. The chains tighten around him as War recovers from the blow Cain dealt to them with his blood.

Cain turns back to look at Abel's possessed corpse.. He chuckles.. "Oh dear brother..." Cain shook his head.

He became almost liquid and dashed through the chains before catching War by the jaw with a kick, sending them high into the air before slamming them back down with his tendons.

Fear tried to burn him again but he deflected her lantern and kicked her in the chest. Death launched at him again but he ducked under it and flipped Death over his head.

Pestilence through the chain at Cain but an armour of calm deflects it before he launches into the air.. He brings his fist down as it's enveloped in crimson rage, he strikes Pestilence and sends them crashing into the cloud.

War slashes at him, cutting off one of his arms and aiming for his head.. He leaps high into the air above War and loads a bullet of fear, sending it into his back, his arm heals.. War stumbles, his eyes become overloaded with a strange white energy as he freezes.

He twists as he lands, loading his gun with a greed bullet, firing it into Fears lantern. She tried to cast a holy flame but it reversed, beginning to burn her arm to ash. She screamed and dropped it.

Death came for his head but he managed to dodge.. He could feel himself start to turn more and more to ash, the attack Death had landed before was catching up to him as he ran circles around them.

His eyes then flash a bright red as he slams his shoulder into the following Death, sending them blasting back off their feet and into the air. He dodges Wars slash at his neck and ducked his right hook before cracking the side of the gun across Wars skull, sending them stumbling.

The rotting chain wrapped around Cain and ripped him back, he flew towards Pestilence and slammed into them, he reached into his skull like head and ignited his hand into a small eruption of rage and crimson flame which burnt their insides and began to crack the skull-

Before he could do more Death slashed his arm, sending him skidding back along the golden clouds..

Cain looked down at his rapidly dissipating body and sighed.. His breathing was ragged and he let himself fall to his knees..

"..Fuck.."

Aaron's eyes widened and he wanted to cry out but Lucifer quickly put his hand over his mouth so he wouldn't be heard..

Cain's body turned into nothing but dust..

St. Peter, who sat on the top of the stairs smiled to himself, his eyes shone so bright as he began to clap.

"You did it! Wow, actually successful!" Peter laughed and slowly stood up, he turned to the gate and waved.

"Open it up" the gate indeed opened for Peter, he went to walk through when-

Dust began to pick up in the air, simulating a storm.. It circled them all, the horsemen looked up in shock before the dust shoots downwards like a spear-

Piercing Pestilence's skull, they tried to writhe and fight back, but their bone began to crack and break as their body began to fall apart.

Before anyone could do anything Cain rips his way from Pestilence's skull, shattering it as his body is reformed inside of Pestilence, he punches and pushes his way out as the horseman falls down limp.. His clothes appear back on Cain as his eyes flash a shining white.

"Did you honestly forget who I am?" Cain scowled, Fear sent forth a pillar of holy flame and Cain backhanded it, sending it back with five times the force and strength, she screamed as it eviscerated her.

War lashed out at him and he shattered his forearm to stick the jagged bone through War's skull before tipping them up and slamming them down into the ground.

"Tsk, Tsk, no tact" Cain shook his head.

Death stood in front of him.. His gaunt familiar face staring into Cain's soul..

"...I'm sorry brother.." Cain said, shaking his head.

"You must die" Death spoke, trying to replicate Abel's voice..

Cain shook his head.. There was a flicker and Cain stood back up, pocketing his hands.

Death slowly fell apart, put to sleep as quickly as possible.. Cain's glaring eyes meet none other than St. Peter's.

"Dammit.. Close the ga-"

Aaron dashed past St. Peter, he tapped him to erase his miracle for a mere moment as he slipped through the golden gate and rushed into the final heaven.. To speak to god..

"Oh well.. Not my funeral.." Saint Peter turned back to face Cain... their eyes met with rage filled intent..

"So.. you take my wing.. You kill my creations.. And you still expect to win?"

Cain shook his head and smiled.

"I don't expect to.. I know I will"

"Power corrupts Cain.." St. Peter shook his head as he looked down at Cain..

"Oh I know.. But I have nothing left to corrupt" Cain shrugged as he began to walk up the stairs, St. Peter shook lightly as he summoned the angelic blade.

"You're a sinner!" St. Peter shouted.

"So are you.." Cain grumbled as he made it up another step.

"I have committed no sin! I have simply done what had to be done in the name of God" St. Peter snarled.

"Oh yeah? Wanna bet on it? If I can make you sin.. You give me a free hit?" Cain smirked.

"..Try it.." St. Peter was shaking, his breathing was out of control.

Cain pulled out a cigarette and gestured to St. Peter.

"You got a light?" Cain asked, his eyes shining golden.

"No I do-" St. Peter froze, his entire body wrapped in a strange force, he couldn't breathe.

"Oof.. lying, a great sin" Cain reached behind St. Peter's ear and pulled out the match he had laid there beforehand, he ignited it and lit up his cigarette.

He took a harsh puff before blowing the smoke into his face with a smile.

"Now I get a free hit... and before we try and insult each other's feelings do know.. You were almost a good guy"

Cain vanished and appeared behind St. Peter. Peter's eyes widened as he felt golden blood trickle down his back...

As Cain stole yet another one of his wings.

Placing it on his back with a nasty crack and snap, he made a satisfied sound.

"Wow, two wings do feel good" Cain said, chuckling.

"BASTARD!!" Peter lashed out at Cain, trying to scratch him.

Cain simply dodges and backhands him, sending him flying back into the gate.

Peter slowly gets back up to his feet and groans, he summons his blade and tries to stab into Cain's gut but-

His stomach rips itself apart, forming nothing but a gaping hole, Peter's eyes widen as the hole condenses down onto the blade.. His bones and muscles snapping into place, shattering the blade in the process..

"NO! NO NO NO! THIS IS MY FUCKING BIRTHRIGHT!" Peter tried to punch Cain but he dodged and pulled out the revolver, firing a calm bullet into his foot.

Peter scowls and his entire body begins to move slowly, Cain cracks a right hook against him, sending him flying back.

"Your birthright was to choose a path.. The church took that right away"

Cain stepped on Peter's face, digging his body into the cloud so he couldn't get up.

Peter struggled to dig his claws through Cain's boots..

"You had a choice.. Peter.. To be with your family.." he adds pressure to it, crushing Peter's face slowly but surely. "..or to sell them out.. For them to die by your hand" Cain said, his tone deeper than any thunderstorm.

"Stop.. no.." Peter slowly became weaker and weaker, trying to desperately grip at Cain.

Cain pulls his foot off Peter before kicking him so hard it sends him bouncing into the air.

Cain whips around, his forearm shatters and he stabs Peter in the side with the bone, the punch sends him fluttering through the air.

Cain whips his arms wide as his wrists explode, tendons and blood vessels whip out and grab him, acting like elastic and pulling Peter back.

Cain's chest rips open and a fist made of Cain's own heart punches Peter in the jaw.. The force shakes his head and sends him rolling to the floor with a wet thud and crash.. His breathing was sporadic..

Cain picks Peter up before throwing him onto his knee, snapping his pine.

Peter rolls to the floor, he picks him up by his white flowing hair.. Golden blood runs down his face as he looks forward..

"Look.. look at your family" Cain points to a place where- oh..

"Oh look..they're not here.. Because God erased them.. Peter.. He didn't just kill your family.. He erased them" Peter shakes his head, tears in his eyes..

"Liar... lies.. Lie... liar..." Peter weeps to himself.

Cain shakes his head as he adjusts his position, wrapping his hands around Peter's skull..

"...I didn't want this life..." Peter gently whispered as he felt his skull lightly crack.

"I know.. No one here wanted this life.." Cain applied pressure, his nails digging into Peter's flesh.. He winced but lay limp.

"...I want to help you.. I want to take him down.." Peter whimpers like an injured puppy..

"I know you do, Peter" Cain dug his nails deep into Peter's skin before slowly peeling his hands back.. Ripping and tearing his skin from his body slowly and painfully..

Peter screamed.. A terrible scream.. Only silenced by the blood which filled his throat.. Cain continued to peel it back.

"Shhh.. it's okay.. You'll see them again soon.." Cain whispered to Peter as he continued to slowly and agonisingly kill him.

"I have no reason to lie to dead men.." Cain dropped Peter to the floor as he slowly choked to death on his own blood.

Lucifer watched this in the distance in utter disbelief..

"Pure of heart..Peter.. You just weren't good enough" Cain shook his head and kneeled down by Peter's body, he loaded a seed into his gun.

The smell of rain.. That's all that was in Cain's mind.

Chapter 33:
The End of the End

Aaron looked up to God...he sat on a throne, he was as tall as a mountain, his beard as large as a river, his eyes a gentle green.

"..And.. s-so.. G-God.. You know.. Maybe you should.. Um.. you wouldn't.." Aaron had been trying to speak to God.. his body shaking badly, his eyes shaking..

"I see..."

God stood up, his form shrinking so he was just a human's size, he patted Aaron on the shoulder.. His eyes staring back through his soul..

"Thank you for bringing this to my attention..."

Aaron nods a lot, unable to process he was talking to God.

"Unfortunately... I do not need people who question my judgement in my faith"

Aaron furrowed his brow..

"But, God I-"

There was an ear cracking snap.. As Aaron fell to the ground, his eyes lifeless, his body limp as a doll..

There was a wet slap as Cain dropped the decapitated head of Peter onto the marble floor... the area was pure white cloud with massive marble pillars and floors..

The crimson was stark against the angelic white.

Cain looked over to the limp body of Aaron.. He felt something boil in him.. He felt something twinge in his skull.. In his mind...

"...You killed him..."

God remained smiling gently, like a kind old man..

"Yes. Do you much care?"

"No..." Cain said gently.

"It's so bad for you to make your way here and for your plan to crumble in front of you"

Lucifer appeared behind God, raising his blade to strike and-

God spun around and striked Lucifer in the face, sending him spiralling from heaven.

"LUCIFER! I CAST YOU OUT!" God laughed as Lucifer screamed, his very essence being torn from heaven.. He looked to Cain.. holding out his hand to be saved...

And Cain didn't move.. Letting Lucifer fall from the heavens.

"And there it goes.. Your plan.. You've come all this way and you've failed" God said, still smiling.

Cain shook his head.

"You don't realise... I meant it when I said I'd beat you to death with my bare hands.."

Cain began to walk towards God.. God chuckled and summoned an army of angels- Cain blinked and they vanished, erased from existence.. God paused, furrowing his brow..

He tried to strike Cain with holy strikes.. Cain didn't stop walking, the energy ripped through him and he healed faster than it hurt him.

"Is that all you got?"

"I.."

"Your pride, what a flaw you sinful whore" Cain slapped God, the sheer sound and shock made time almost stop..

God lashed out, trying to punch through Cain's chest..he just moved out the way and snapped his arm in two. God screamed in agony and stumbled back...

Cain continually approached.

"You made this world.. And yet you can't even fight.. Pathetic"

Cain cracked his fist against God's head, sending them crashing to the ground.. He stepped on God's chest and looked him in the eyes.

He then looked back over to Aaron..

"You're a murderer, a pathetic old man who grooms children to do his bidding..." Cain held out his hand and placed it on God's forehead.

God screamed in absolute agony as his skin began to melt and sear.. As Cain pulled away a single mark lay upon God's head.

"ABEL"

"That was for my brother" Cain said, he grabbed the side of his neck and pulled at his skin.. The tattoo burned into his flesh began to warp..

Into a dagger with a snake for a handle, he stabbed it through God's hand, pinning him to the floor.

"That was for Peter..."

Cain punched God across the jaw with a cracking sound, he lay into him striking him across the face with violent lashes.

God coughed and shouted in agony.. For anything.. For anyone to save him.. He coughed blood as Cain began to punch his teeth out, every punch had a violent crunch fill the air.. Soon a puddle of red had covered the floor as Cain raised his fist in the air and let it fall with an almighty crack.

"You. killed. Those. Whoever would have helped you" Cain continued to brutalise him, beating him violently, his nose poured crimson and his face was missing most of his teeth as blood seeped down his chin.

"CAIN WAIT! I CAN HELP YOU! I CAN BRING ABEL BACK! I CAN BRING EVERYONE BACK! I HAVE THAT-" Cain didn't hear a single word..

"You framed me for my own brothers murder!" Cain lashed out, snapping God's jaw..

"PLEASE LET ME-" Cain didn't listen.. Not a sound entered his ears..

"YOU MADE PEOPLE BELIEVE IN YOU!" Cain smashes his nose till it was nothing but fleshy soup.

"YOU USED THEM! THEY TRUSTED YOU AND YOU WERE GOING TO KILL THEM!" Cain reached deep into God's throat and pulled..

With a horrendous snap and pop.. Cain tore off God's jaw, the blood covering them now as it created a sea of red which bleached the very clouds into crimson..

"YOU KILLED YOUR GRANDCHILD!" Cain tore out his eyes violently, blood spraying across the ground.

"YOU! VILE! OLD! MAN!" Cain stopped as he smashed through God's skull.. His hands began to shake..

Cain shook as his breathing became unstable.. He looked down at his blood soaked hands.. At how the ground was covered in God's never ending crimson..

He slowly stood up..

He stepped over Aaron's limp body and made his way out of this.. Place...

Cain made it to the steps and paused.. Collapsing down onto them.. Sitting.. His eyes dilated..

He looked out onto the heavens... how God's blood slowly seeped into the clouds.. Turning everything crimson...

He simply sat there.. Looking down at his blood covered hands..

And he began to sob.. Tears flowing down from his face.. He sobs.. For those who lost.. For those who loved...

Below him.. People stepped from their houses as they looked up to the storm clouds.. As they began to rain a deep crimson.. As God's blood began to rain onto the people below..

On the side of a mountain.. A man with tanned skin looks out the window at the crimson sky...

"....He did it..." Adam said to himself.. Eve slowly wrapped her arms around him..

They rest their heads against each other.. Tears silently falling down their faces..

Silence..

So silent..

As Cain stayed on the stairs of heaven.. His head lowered..

And with that, reader.. The book is over.

For Cain has won.

Don't miss out!

Visit the website below and you can sign up to receive emails whenever Devon L. Mulvihill publishes a new book. There's no charge and no obligation.

https://books2read.com/r/B-A-SSGV-NFUCC

BOOKS 2 READ

Connecting independent readers to independent writers.

Did you love *I Didn't Kill Abel*? Then you should read *Geir Goldenheart: The Rise of Heldanoor*[1] by Devon Mulvihill!

[2]

In a world far different than you remember a new Kingdom by the name of Disreeguard had been discovered in the infinite desert of ash and sand. Follow alongside Geir Goldenheart, the too trusting girl who wants to save people as this new kingdom is being fought over by opposing factions.

Geir wants to help shape this desolate and destroyed kingdom so that the most people can be helped, however her plans are thrown into conflict and confusion as her world continually is flipped on its head.

The mystery of how such an isolated kingdom came and went without a single record floats in the ash covered air, but will Geir be

---

1. https://books2read.com/u/bW5W21

2. https://books2read.com/u/bW5W21

able to solve anything? Or will her attempts at bringing forth a new capital of hope be dashed and erased like those who used to live upon these cursed grounds?

When face to face with deadly enemies and internal conflict.. will she stay strong in her beliefs or fall victim to manipulation?

Is the hope for Nevermore gone before it even has time to shine? Or will a new age be born from blood and sand?

About the Publisher

Ayo. It be me. a totally not serious author who wishes to write for fun and have fun writing.

I want to tell some fun, sad, fantastic and glorious stories but I'm still getting used to this.

the world is wacky and crazy right now and I just want to bring entertainment to you all, the medium of writing has been seen as so stingy as of late, everything has to be serious.

and all I gotta say is chill, sit down, relax. I'm not gonna spend 2,000 bucks to hire editors and artists and marketing stuff

no, that's not what writing should be about, writing should be about pure and absolute expression!